WITHDRAWN

Book Three

Published by © J.C. Cliff LLC, 2014

Blyssfully Undone

Copyright © 2014 by J.C. Cliff

All rights reserved

https://www.facebook.com/BLYSS.TRILOGY

Http://JCCLIFF.COM

Edited by Kayla Robichaux, Hot Tree Editing

http://www.facebook.com/kaylathebibliophile

http://www.kaylathebibliophile.blogspot.com

Cover Design © Sommer Stein

with Perfect Pear Creative Covers

https://www.facebook.com/PPCCovers

Cover Photography by: Eric David Battershell

https://www.facebook.com/ericbattershellphotography?fref=ts

http://www.ericbattershellphotography.com/index2.php

Cover Model: Zeke Samples

https://www.facebook.com/ZekeSamplesFanPage?fref=ts

http://www.SurrealBodySolutions.com/

Celtic Knot Medallion Necklace

Silver Insanity

http://www.silver-insanity.com

DEDICATION

~ To Kayla Robichaux ~

I don't think I will ever be able to convey my personal gratitude to the one person who is able to bring a fine polish to my stories.

Kayla Robichaux has edited an untold amount of books that have gone on to become best sellers. I firmly believe it is because of her special touch that I, too, became an Amazon Best Seller. She should be in an Editors Hall of Fame somewhere. She deserves recognition for her abilities and intellect.

At the end of *Blyssfully Undone*, as a special treat to you, she has allowed me to share with you the first chapter of her first book, *Wished For You*.

If you don't know Kayla, you should take the time to do so. She has been around quite a long time and when the internet was brand new, she was the first to create a Bibliophile. Kayla's Bibliophile, a special place she nurtured and grew to bring readers of romance together in one place. To know Kayla is to know a great person. There is nothing but unconditional love in her soul and she always gives it with a warm-hearted smile. When I read *Wished For You*, I read it with a silly grin on my face, because I could picture Kayla doing all of those free spirited, and silly antics.

She has such a zest and love for life and she always has a way to make you feel special. I am more than blessed to not only have her in my life, but am able to call her a true friend for life. I hold will always hold her in the highest of regards.

CHAPTER 1

~Jules~

I'm frozen and helpless while being pinned underneath Travis' heavy bodyweight. All of this has unfolded so quickly. I don't know what to think as he lies on top of me with an intruder at his back. I'm astounded over the fact Travis did indeed risk it all for me, and is still risking it all by shielding me with his body from the imminent and immediate danger in the room.

It dawns on me he must have been under some serious stress over the past few weeks. He's been shouldering the responsibility and impending ramifications all by himself for breaking me out of the facility. Not only did he get me out of there, but he also nursed me back to health and took care of me...damn good care of me.

He knew this day was coming, and even took steps to prepare me for this very moment, and I understand now why he was being so dogmatic about repetition and practicing until I could load a gun blindfolded, needing me to be able to defend myself. All of his training will be in vain if I lack the courage now to help him fight. The way he's fought for me all this time, and wanting to protect me, he was right to bring me here. I can see it now. If I would've gone to the police not knowing who I was, I would've been broadcasting my whereabouts right to Nick and his men.

My veins pulsate in my neck as my adrenaline continues to spike off the charts. There is no way in hell I'm going to be able to calm myself down. My blood pumps through each vein like a set of bass drums as I try in vain to force my heartbeat to slow. Travis firmly squeezes my wrists, which are hidden underneath the pillow, garnering my attention and pulling my mind back into the here and now.

He narrows his eyes on mine. I know that look. He's silently telling me to pull my shit together. I steal a deep, silent breath and slowly let it out. Our fate, most likely, will rest in my hands. I close my eyes tightly and imperceptibly nod, agreeing to whatever it is he's going to signal me to do for us to survive. Everything makes perfect sense now, from learning his special sign language, to how to handle a gun, to knowing about the bunker and what to do from there.

Travis wordlessly gains my attention again by tapping his forefinger on my wrist. I open my eyes to see him shift his eyes to the side, indicating I need to be ready to use the weapon I hold in my hand. I barely give him a wink using my right eye, letting him know I understand.

Even though I get the meaning of his signals, actually having the guts to follow through with the action he expects me to do is a whole different matter. I realize it's going to be much more difficult to kill someone when I can see their chest rise and fall with each living breath. A profound, physiological process takes place in my brain, and I swallow hard against the lump in my throat at the thought of taking a life. It's going to be all up to me to help him acquire the upper-hand, and I'm not sure if I'm capable of achieving such a feat. I mean, these men are accomplished criminals, and I'm just an innocent, inexperienced nobody caught in the crossfire.

The man behind him startles me as he pierces the air with strong promises of Travis' demise. "Jackson, one wrong move from you, and you'll meet your maker today, understand?"

I watch as the muscles in Travis' jaw flex, and he grits out his reply between clenched teeth, "Understood."

"Very good. I hope you've enjoyed your little fuck-fest, because your honeymoon is over," the man says in a threatening tone, and then his voice changes from hostile to a deliberately mocking tone. "You've gotten sentimental in your old age, Jackson. Your love-speech just made me go all gooey inside."

Travis' green eyes morph before me, turning cold and hard as he narrows them in anger. I know he wishes he had an even playing field, because with the death glare Travis is emanating right now, I have no doubt the man wouldn't last five seconds.

"Now, Travis, listen closely...as I wouldn't want any unfortunate accidents to happen. I also don't think the young lady would appreciate getting soiled from any of your splattered blood getting on her, all because you decided to make a wrong move thinking you can take me. You understand that?"

"I got it," Travis gruffly states, and then he lightly squeezes my wrists, and I don't think it means anything other than an *I care about you, and I hope we get through this alive* type of squeeze.

"Good, I want your hands up in the air. Then, I want you to slowly slink off the bed nice and easy. If you so much as move a micrometer in the wrong direction, you know what happens." Travis tenses and reiterates his signals to me again by flicking his eyes to the concealed gun in my hand. My heart hammers hard against the walls of my chest as I try to control tremors that are beginning to develop in my extremities.

Travis slowly removes his grip from my wrists, and at a snail's pace, he leans back, placing both his hands up in the air. His weight slowly begins to lift off my body while he keeps his hands held high, indicating he's unarmed. His steely gaze continues to penetrate through mine the entire time as he slowly stands to his full height. He looks so vulnerable at this moment, something I'm not used to seeing from this dominating, strong-willed, and always in control kind of man.

"Young lady, the same rules apply to you," the man threatens, his voice unsettling me. I look at him out of the corner of my eye, petrified to even breathe. "My orders are to take you alive, ma'am, but accidents can happen, can't they?"

Holy shit. The reality of the situation slams into my chest, the very fear stealing air from my lungs. What Travis has been trying to instill in me all along is now ringing true. I will have to kill in order for us both to survive. I imagine this man didn't come alone either. They would have to be more than stupid to believe only one person would be enough to capture Travis. I wonder where the other men are and if they're surrounding the house.

The intruder slices through the thick tension in the room, breaking into my distraught thoughts as he speaks to Travis with pure menace lining his deep voice. "Keep your hands in the air." His gruff voice twists in my gut, and my adrenaline spikes. *My God, I don't want Travis to die.*

I know Nick will have him at the guillotine the second he's captured, but only after he makes him suffer first; I'm sure of it. It seems as if all Travis has ever tried to do is keep me out of harm's way since the very beginning. He's risked his own life to get me out from under Nick, and now he's paying the price. I may be out-of-my-mind angry with Travis right now, but he doesn't deserve to die.

I slowly turn my head to the side just in time to witness the man roughly grab Travis by one wrist. He twists it, bringing it around Travis' back to put him in an arm lock. This man is big and burly, full of muscle, but he's not as big as Travis. Travis holds the look of Black Death in his eyes. It's a look of his promised wrath I've never seen before, but always imagined it could exist on his handsome face.

The aura his entire body is exuding right now screams *warrior*, promising his rival a wicked, painful death if given the opportunity to gain the upper hand, and I imagine he would've already taken this guy if he didn't have me to consider.

I watch as the man begins to place a handcuff on Travis' wrist, and something twists in my gut. Anger begins to brew and bubble in the pit of my stomach. This asshole has no right, nor does Nick have the right to lay claim to my life, my future, or anyone else's for that matter. Sporadic emotions of vengeance, hate, and fear play in my head, unleashing a fury

I've never felt before. I can literally feel the venom seeping out of my pores.

Travis shoots me a glare out of the corner of his eye, which says I'm letting our time to take action tick away. The intensity of his eyes consume me as they blaze for me to pull out of my shock and make a move.

Travis asks over his shoulder while keeping his scrutinizing gaze on mine, "How did you find us?"

"Now that's the million-dollar question right there, isn't it, Travis?" the man sardonically replies. "I imagine you would like to know that bit of intel, wouldn't you?"

I steal a deep breath while they banter. I know I will have the element of surprise, because who would think in a million years a young female would be wielding a gun from underneath a pillow. *It's now or never, Jules.*

My fingers wrap around the gun's grip a little tighter, thankful for Travis' foresight in preparing me for this very moment. Knowing the safety is already off, it's one less thing I have to think about.

Travis' voice echoes through me as I've practiced this very routine ad nauseam. *You shoot to kill the enemy, Jules, not maim them, or they'll come back for you.*

As adrenaline rushes through my blood vessels, all I can hear is my heartbeat pounding in my ears, but I refuse to allow my body to freeze in fear and let Travis down. I quit thinking about what I have to do and just do it. Push comes to shove, and I quit rationalizing with my thoughts as my instincts take over. My reflexes intuitively respond without another conscious thought.

I draw the gun out from underneath the pillow at warp speed, and a bizarre feeling washes over me as everything seems to move in slow motion. I watch, feeling detached in an out-of-body experience as my left hand meets the other to help stabilize the gun.

I cock my head to the side as my right eye lines up with the sight on the Sig. I don't fuck around. I aim for the man's head, and before I know it, three successive shots have rung out, shooting off rounds just the way Travis taught me.

I don't even remember feeling the recoil from the handgun as it fired, nor do I hear the shots ring out, but my ears sure as hell are ringing in a high-pitched sound in the aftermath. Feeling detached from myself, as if this isn't really happening, I watch as this man who once had a living, breathing heart collapses lifelessly to the floor like a sack of potatoes.

Oh. My. God. I've just shot and killed another human being. All of my limbs lock up as I freeze with shock and disbelief. I'm paralyzed, and I sure as hell don't want to peer over the mattress to see the final outcome.

My brows furrow in confusion as Travis is suddenly in my face, his lips are moving, but I can't hear what he's saying. He grabs my shoulders and starts to roughly shake me. I begin to hear his voice as it breaks through in segments. He sounds muffled, as if he's talking underwater.

"Now is...time to zone out. We've got...out of here," he yells in dire urgency, but I can't comprehend his fragmented words.

Travis roughly shakes me like a rag doll when I don't respond, repeating, "Jules! Snap out of it! You know the drill; we've practiced this. We've got to move!" I feel paralyzed, the shock and fear locking up all my limbs, rendering me useless.

His eyes become plagued with worry. "Jules, baby. Please, snap out of this," he pleads in an urgent tone. "Our lives depend on it. Don't check out on me now."

I blink my eyes hard several times, trying to come out of my stupor. His fingers work to pry my hand off the gun. When I realize what he's doing, I relax my grip, letting him have it. He then places the gun behind his back, tucking it inside the waistband of his jeans, I'm sure. I've watched him place his weapons there a million times before.

I know I have to force myself to move; however, it's not fast enough for Travis. He takes control of the situation, breaking the spell for me as he grabs me underneath my armpits, lifting me off the bed. He makes me feel as if I weigh ten pounds the way he handles me. I feel numb to the core, an emotionless robot as he holds me steady, with my legs trembling. I hope he doesn't decide to let go of me anytime too soon, or I'm going to collapse to the floor.

"Breathe for me, baby." He slowly inhales a deep breath with me, and we hold our breath together, just the way he taught me. Then we both gradually exhale, holding our lungs empty for a few heartbeats before we repeat the cycle.

"Now, you remember our buzzwords?" he asks, and I nod in response. "Say it aloud for me," he commands.

I breathe through a cycle of air one more time before I recite the mantra he made me learn. I thought it was stupid at the time, but right now, I cling to it like a lifeline as I whisper, "Stay outwardly focused, no introspection, keep calm, and carry on."

"Very good, sweetheart. I want you to keep repeating that in your head. Focus on those words, what they mean, and keep breathing while you get yourself together, okay?"

I grab on to his t-shirt, fisting the front of the fabric in my hands, double checking he's truly alive and standing right here before me. *I almost lost him.* I lean my forehead into the middle of his steel chest and close my eyes; I just want to cry. My hands begin to shake, and my breath hitches as a tear slips out of the corner of my eye.

"Ssh," he whispers as he cradles my cheeks in the palms of his hands, lifting my chin to meet his gaze. "Keep it together for me. Just for a little bit longer, and I promise we'll get out of this alive."

My breath hitches again, my throat is tight, and I can't speak. "Sweetheart," he says almost apologetically, "I have to scope out the rest of the house, and you've got thirty seconds to get dressed, grab my backpack from the closet, and be ready to move out." His eyes plead with mine to not let him down.

I nod in acknowledgment, and then Travis slowly releases me, making sure I can stand on my own two feet first. When I slightly sway, he cocks his head to the side and eyes me warily. I can't let him down. We need to get out of here, and I sure as hell don't want to pull the trigger on a gun again.

I don't recognize my own voice, because I sound all throaty when I assure him, "I got it. I can do this."

"That's my girl." His eyes soften as his lips curve up in an approving expression, like he's proud of me. He reaches behind me, grabs his cell phone from the nightstand, and begins to type into it.

"What are you doing?"

"Putting systems in place," he answers, never looking up from the phone's screen. When he's done, he places the phone in his back pocket, and then looks at me. "All right, thirty seconds, Jules." He arches one brow, sternly reminding me. He quietly walks to the doorway with his gun drawn, and I watch as his backside disappears out the bedroom door to begin scoping out the rest of the house for danger.

I find myself still frozen in place, breathing silently through my nose and becoming more alert now that I'm alone as I listen for signs of danger. A chill runs through me with the knowledge I'm all by myself now. What if something happens to Travis while he's checking out our surroundings?

A few seconds of quiet go by. I suddenly realize I'm wasting valuable time. I close my eyes tightly and shake my head, taking in a deep breath, and using the technique Travis taught me to help me stay calm. *Focus, Jules.*

I force myself to move on shaky limbs to the dresser, thankful the dead body lying on the floor is on the other side of the room. I notice my hands are trembling as I open a drawer and pull out the first pair of jeans I see. Everything seems to take twice as long to complete a task as I rummage through a couple more drawers, methodically pulling out a pair of socks and a folded t-shirt.

I get dressed as quickly as possible, and then hunt for one of my elastics to put my hair in a ponytail. I steal a deep breath and continue to repeat the mantra in my head over and over before I have to turn around and get to the sliding closet doors.

Slowly and quietly, I walk toward the closet on the other side of the room while making a wide berth around the dead body. Out of the corner of my eye, I see the man lying on the floor, sprawled out with a red pool of blood beside his head. Blood thunders through my veins while a massive shiver rolls through my body. I squeeze my eyes shut against the horrifying sight.

Keep it together, Jules. Travis will get us out of this; he has to. Reflexively, the palm of my hand slams against my mouth to cover it as I let out a gag. *Oh, shit, no.* I don't have time to vomit. I feel myself break out in a cold sweat and try desperately to use the breathing pattern I'm supposed to use to calm my nerves. To keep myself from tossing my cookies, I begin to quietly hum our buzzwords aloud, trying to stay on task as I slide open the closet doors.

I sink to my knees, feeling like I've crossed the finish line of a marathon and reaching the closet was the prize. I lean forward and reach out into the depths of the closet, pulling out the backpack in which Travis had prepared for us with incredible foresight.

Once I pull the pack out and place it beside me, I sift through the shoes at the bottom of the closet until I find my pair of tennis shoes. Keeping my back turned away from the scene behind me, I sit back on my bottom and put on my socks and shoes.

Travis knew they were coming, and I have no idea why he wanted to rescue me, all the while knowing he'd be wrapped up in a massive quagmire of shit as a result. All I know is I don't want to go back to that prison cell and be trapped with Nick. God only knows what he would do to me now if I were in his dungeon.

I catch a faint whiff of dispersed gunpowder as I sit here waiting for Travis to return. I keep my gaze forward, refusing to turn around while desperately trying to ignore the smell. I look down at my hands to find them still shaking and notice the engagement ring Travis had placed there mere minutes ago. The brand new diamond shimmers and sparkles, even with my back turned away from the light source. What was he thinking proposing to me? *I promise you, I was exposing the real me. I gave you all of me. I held nothing back.*

"Jules." I flinch and lose my breath, startled from the sound breaking through the deep silence of the room. It's Travis. I slump my taut shoulders, thankful he didn't run into more trouble within the house, or at least that I know of. I turn my head around to find him standing in the doorway with his gun drawn.

My jaw drops at the sight of him. How the hell he managed to scope the house and get fully clothed in camo gear, I'll never know. I bet he could give a fireman a run for his money, getting dressed in full gear.

I don't recognize this Travis. Gone is the soft, passionate man I got to know, and in his place stands a real warrior. He looks so dark and ominous; everything about him screams confident, professional, hardcore killer, and it rolls off him like a massive tsunami. His jaw is set, his eyes are hard, and his every movement calculated. He looks totally in his element as he emits a silent, comfortable sureness, appearing to be in control of all the uncertainties and danger that surrounds us.

His military-style boots quietly echo against the hardwood floor as he quickly makes his way to me. His eyes stay locked on mine while he secures his gun and then holds out his hand to me. I look up from the floor, flicking my eyes back and forth from his hand to his eyes. He stands like a mountain above me. I slowly reach up and take it, and immediately, he pulls me up off the floor. I notice he's holding a vest in his other hand. He lets go of me and begins to slip the vest on my body over my t-shirt. My lungs squeeze with asthmatic pain, the vest reminding me of the perilous danger, and what is about to head our way.

"Travis, I'm scared," I whisper on a shaky breath.

"We're going to be fine, Jules," he confidently assures me. "Stick to me like glue, and we will get out of this alive."

"Where are we going?"

"To the bunker. You know the way blindfolded," he says, and his tone is all business. "You also know the code to gain access, should something happen to me."

I shake my head. "No, I'm not leaving you." A shooting pain stabs at my heart, knowing something could very well happen to him.

"We don't have time to argue, but you will do as I say." His tone is hard and cold, and brooks no argument. Yes, this Travis definitely scares me, and I'm glad to be on his side. His eyes narrow as he holds up his index finger in front of my face. "Discussion is over." I swallow hard as I stare into his impenetrable eyes.

He then leans down and grabs his backpack from the floor, quickly putting it on. He secures the nylon strap in the front with a plastic snap lock. Then he looks to me while taking my hand, giving it a light squeeze. "You did good. I'm proud of you," he says in all seriousness, and then takes a step backward, pulling me along with him. "Come on, we gotta roll out now."

He's on high alert as we make our way through the cabin, and when we reach the back door, he pulls us both to the side of the window to keep us out of sight. While focusing his gaze on our surroundings, he looks through the edge of the window as he talks. "You remember what to do if we get separated, right? If I go down, you'll have to go on without me."

"Travis, I'm so scared."

"I know, baby. C'mere." He steps back from the window and pulls me into his arms. "You can do this. We both will make it," he says with confidence. My God, how is this man always able to hold himself together? I'm astounded at the amount of inner strength and fortitude he carries. He looks so indestructible.

He leans down and captures my lips, and I pray it won't be our last as I kiss him back. His lips are like a balm to my soul. I breathe in his familiar musky scent and savor it. He makes me feel so protected as he looks so invincible. The kiss is over quickly, and then he pulls away to place a pistol in my hand.

"You cannot allow yourself to get caught. They want you alive, but they want me dead." I shake my head in denial, and before I can say a word, Travis places two forefingers over my lips, preventing me. "If for some reason I go down, you're going to have to go on without me," he repeats. "Don't stop until you're safe." My eyes begin to water, and I feel shaky all over again. "Promise me that you will."

"I promise." *I will never leave you behind.* He seems satisfied with the half-sentence I spoke aloud, and curtly nods.

"Remember, we're going to duck and weave together, and

whatever you do, don't let go of my hand, all right?"

I take a deep breath, filling my lungs to capacity, and hold the air in for a minute, psyching myself up for the unknown dangers that lay ahead. I can't help but think the moment we step out from the walls of this cabin, *we may be leaving together, but it feels like a farewell.* I don't think things will ever be the same between us again. I'm sure of it.

CHAPTER 2

My stomach plummets, and I feel like I've been punched in the gut. I lose my breath over the sensation and grab my stomach, wanting to double over and heave.

"Uh-huh, baby. You can tamp that shit back down right now," Travis commands in a militant voice. He grabs my hand from my belly and squeezes it to the point of pain as he pierces me with a no-bullshit glare. I've never seen a man look so battle-ready before, but if this is the look, he is wearing it in spades.

He's able to turn the doorknob with the pistol still gripped in his hand. His eyes then scan the perimeter of the outside as his jaw muscles flex. "On the count of three, be ready to bolt." He never counts to three. He immediately gives my hand a hard tug, pulling both of us out into the bright sunlight. We both burst into a full-on sprint, and I know without a doubt we could run faster if he would just let go of my hand, but apparently, he's not going to take any chances of me slipping through his fingers. Everything becomes a blur around me, and all I can do is focus on moving my legs as fast as humanly possible.

I hear the first shot ring out as it makes a whizzing sound, slicing between Travis and me. He yanks me hard into his side, forcing me to move with him. I almost lose my balance, stumble, and fall. My heart is pumping out a ridiculous amount of adrenaline, and I feel nothing but terror.

"Weave, baby," Travis yells.

Shit, I am weaving! I want to scream, but each breath is consumed with the task at hand. With every leap forward I take, my feet fumble over the uneven ground. Even though we've practiced this a million times, I feel clumsy.

Suddenly, Travis' hard body pushes back into mine, forcing me to the left as he yells out again, "Keep the pattern! Focus!" Somehow, I gain my bearings, and all the training finally kicks. We continue to move in a zig-zag pattern over the open stretch of ground until we reach the edge of the forest.

The morning sun coming up over the forest is almost blinding as we reach the edge of trees. I grit my teeth as my left arm snags and scrapes over a thicket of thorny vines. I feel hundreds of tiny needles digging into me, tugging at my arm as if they want to hold me back. I let out a loud grunt, but I don't have time to look or think about how much skin I left behind on those vines.

I almost feel relieved when we enter the thickness of the wooded trail, thankful to have some cover. Hopefully, we'll make it to the bunker unscathed.

His death grip on my hand keeps my momentum moving forward at an ungodly pace. He doesn't even grunt when his big body rips through a set of vines. He's like a human machete, and it's all I can do to keep my feet landing on solid ground as he pulls me along. There are so many dips and unforeseen potholes in which either one of us can slip and twist our ankles, but somehow we're able to avoid them.

We're about to the halfway point in reaching the bunker when I hear a loud thud, and then Travis begins to lose his balance. His feet begin to falter, and before I know it, he's pulled me down to the ground with him. I grit my teeth together, expecting the impending fall to hurt like hell.

We both plummet to the ground, colliding against the forest floor as a loud *oomph* escapes from my lungs, stealing the last bit of air I had. The only good thing about the impact is it's layered with dead foliage to help break our fall.

I'm not sure what's happened other than Travis could have possibly tripped, but from the looks of how he went down, he didn't try to break his fall the way I did. He didn't even utter a word as he hit the ground. *Oh, God, please don't let him be shot.*

The pine straw pokes into my arms and the leaves rustle underneath my movements as I scramble up on my knees to hover over his body. I frantically begin checking for any wounds as I run my hands all over his upper body, but all I feel is his thick, heavy body armor. For a second, I think he got lucky, and exhale a breath of relief, but the relief quickly dissipates as I realize he's not conscious.

"Travis!" I scream, pulling on his shoulders, trying to turn his heavy body over onto his back so I can assess him. I have tunnel vision as I can only seem to focus on one thing, and that's seeing to Travis' wellbeing. I grunt and pull back on his shoulders with all my might, but his body is all dead weight and he won't budge. Not knowing what to do at this point, I start to panic.

An adrenaline boost must be rushing through me as I try in one last-ditch effort to roll him over, and succeed. Once I get him on his back, I cradle his cheeks with my palms and search for breaths of life. "Travis!" I scream again while tapping his cheeks, trying to rouse him.

A glistening sheen of perspiration across the top of his forehead glistens in the light, and I wipe it away with my hand. I don't know what I think that will solve, but I'm so frazzled I don't know what else to do. I lean down and kiss his damp forehead, choking back tears. I feel stupidly helpless as I softly begin pleading with a feeble, croaky voice, "Travis, please wake up. I don't know what to do." There is no way in hell I can leave his side. I know he's told me to, but I just can't leave him like this; it's just...wrong. Anxiety grips me around the neck with a painful squeeze, and I close my eyes as the impending breakdown of tears takes over.

"Oh, *fuck*," he wails out. Startled from the outburst, my hand covers my mouth and my eyes bolt open wide. A deep, guttural sound leaves his lungs as he makes a huge effort to catch his breath. His eyes look distressed and in pain. Waves of relief roll through me. He's alive!

"It feels like someone punched the holy shit out of my back." Lifting his head, he drops his chin to his chest, looking down to investigate himself. He feels with both his hands all over his upper body, looking for a bullet wound. "Shit, even though I'm not seeing it, I'm not sure there isn't a gaping hole going through me." His voice is so intertwined with pain that his agony then becomes mine. My stomach twists in a knot, as I feel so helpless for him.

When he wails out in a distressed groan again, the sound grips at my gut. It's almost as if I can feel his pain, and I die a little on the inside. "Are you shot anywhere?" I ask as I run my fingers through his thick, tousled, and sweaty hair. He jerks his body away from mine, pulling is head away from my hands, looking startled to find me, of all people, kneeling beside him.

He shakes his head and blinks his eyes rapidly in a confused state, just now realizing I'm here. "Jules, are you okay?" he asks as he huffs and pants through his pain.

"I'm fine. Are you shot?" I worriedly ask again.

"No, but it sure as fuck feels like it. Thank God for bulletproof vests." Then his eyes narrow on me as if he's thinking about something. "Dammit!" he bellows, his angry voice taking me off guard. My eyes flinch, and I jolt backward. "What the hell are you still doing here then?" He flops his head back down in the pine straw in defeat, and then he squeezes his eyes shut while visibly fighting against the pain wracking his body. "You promised me," he adds through gritted teeth.

My heart sinks at the sound of his disappointment in me, but I didn't have it in me to leave his side. I couldn't. "I'm sorry. I just couldn't leave you like this." I watch as both his hands clench into fists, and then he makes painful grunts as he pulls himself up into a half-sitting position, coming to rest on his elbows. He looks rather pissed off at this point, but I don't care. I ask him again, "Travis, can you get up?"

He shakes his head in anger and snarls at me, "Go now. Run to the bunker and don't stop."

"Not without you," I argue back.

"*Sonofabitch*, you hard-headed..." his voice trails off, and I watch as his left hand reflexively brushes at the back of his neck at lightning speed as his head recoils off to the side. He acts as if he just got stung by a swarm of bees.

"Fuck!" he shouts out. I'm confused as to what's going on until he brings his hand back around from his neck and it's painted in blood. I gasp, horrified to see him bleeding. He doesn't give me time to process what just happened, because in that very second, he slams his body over mine, protecting me from a spray of bullets, which whiz by overhead. His arms wrap tightly around my body as he traps me underneath his heavy weight, pinning my arms to my sides.

His lips rest against my ear, his breathing heavy as he tells me in a gruff voice, "I'm so going to have your ass when this is over." I don't know how he can be so confident in a time like this. I feel as if my ass has already been hung out to dry. I've already said my prayers.

"Travis, are you okay?" I'm so rattled my voice shakes, and my words rush out in a string of panic. "Please, tell me you'll be fine."

"Never been better, sweetheart," he states brusquely. "Just a graze."

My God. *Just* a graze, he says. I'm not trained for this high intensity shit. I've only been trained to shoot and run. They could've killed him.

Could've? They still can. I begin to hyperventilate, and I realize I'm so scared; I literally *could* pee my pants.

The firing overhead ceases just as quickly as it started, and I'm thankful for the weight of Travis' body on top of mine to keep my heart from exploding out of my chest. His faint breathing against my ear gives me some comfort, knowing we are both still alive. I'm thinking with the cease-fire, this would be the most opportune time to get up and run, but Travis doesn't move as he continues to hold me tighter in his arms, which worries me.

"Travis," I start off. I'm about to tell him we should get up and make a break for it.

"Shh, baby," he interrupts, whispering into my ear. "Trust me. We need to stay down now."

My ears perk up over Travis' heavy breathing, and I think I hear a set of heavy footsteps approaching. Maybe it's all in my head. Ah hell, who am I kidding? Shit's about to get real ugly again; I can feel it.

I squeeze my eyes tight as panic grips at my heart, seizing my last breath. When I do finally inhale, I draw in a breath that is all Travis. I take comfort in his familiarity, his touch, and his strength. His body weight provides me with a consolation that is hard to describe, despite the circumstances at hand.

A set of quick footsteps sound out to my right. Leaves crunch and pine straw snaps under the weight of those feet, and a sickening feeling begins to wash over me. As the footsteps come to a halt, a deafening silence fills the air.

"Well, well, well...what do we have here?" a male's deep voice laced with evil rings out against the thickness of the forest. "Looks like we've got a little love nest going on. Thought you were a little more high-class than this, Travis," the man taunts. Travis holds stock-still over my body, and I can't see over him to tell who this man is.

I find it odd, however, that his muscles don't tense like they did back at the cabin. It's like he's actually keeping himself loose and limber on purpose, trying to ready himself for a fight. His lips brush behind my ear as he gives me a chaste kiss before he rolls off me and faces the dark voice head on.

I watch Travis as his eyes narrow on the man, who's standing before us. "Mitchell." Travis says his name as if he's spitting out vile vomit. I shift my eyes between Travis and Mitchell, their heated exchange making my blood run cold.

It's quite evident these two men have shared a past, and judging by the animosity radiating off both of them, it isn't a good one.

Mitchell stands tall and strong, arrogance evident in every cell of his body as he speaks. "What were you thinking, Travis? Did you think we couldn't find out about this place?"

"One can only hope, can't they, Mitchell?" Travis asks through clenched teeth. Something about this man seems familiar to me, but I can't place him.

"Hope is all you'll ever do, Jackson, especially once Nick gets his hands on you."

I force myself to breathe as this horrifying scene unfolds before me. I'm scared out of my mind; I can't see straight. There is no stand-off here. This Mitchell guy holds all of the power as he's the only one with a pointed gun, and here I am at an impasse again.

These fluctuating emotions are enough to send me to an

early grave. I'm sick of bouncing between them all, and how my emotions are always in reaction to someone else's doing. Small things I've always been able to ignore, but abduction, guns, and threats always deserve a backlash of fury, and I feel the unleashed wrath snap within me.

I've had way more than enough, and I'm sick of continuously being the victim, especially a shooting target. My life has been constantly on the line at every turn. My fear has faded, and in its place, anger and retaliation take place front and center. With my life hanging in the balance, I become determined to get the upper hand once and for all.

As heated anger begins to pool inside the pit of my stomach, I flick my eyes around, looking for my dropped gun. As the men continue to be distracted by exchanging heated words, I slowly inch my hand behind my back, and quietly sift through the pine straw. My heart leaps for joy when my fingers come into contact with the hard steel.

With my hand already being in the most opportune place it can be, hidden from sight, I calculate what it would take to get the grip of the pistol totally in my hand, and at the same time, be able to whip it around my body to shoot.

"Not so quick, young lady," Mitchell says as his deep voice cuts through me, making me go numb from head to toe. I bite the inside of my cheek as I look up at him. He points his gun at me, and my pulse spikes sky-high. "You're a tough little shit, aren't you?" he asks, sounding half impressed, and then he flicks his eyes between Travis and me. "You've wasted no time, I see."

"I don't waste my time on trash, like some people do,"

Travis states with a smooth, scary calmness.

Mitchell shifts his pistol, pointing it directly back at Travis, and says, "Neither do I."

The loud thunderous bang of a gun goes off, and I scream at the top of my lungs. I look to Travis, expecting to see him bleeding out, but am surprised he's sitting tall wearing a satirical grin on his face. I whip my head in Mitchell's direction and realize I'm not the one screaming anymore; he is. Mitchell is down on the ground, rolling around in the pine straw, in some serious agony.

My heartbeat thrums in my ears as another man approaches out of the hidden foliage from between some trees. His face is unreadable, and he's powerfully built, like a Mack Truck. Black streaks of war paint decorate his face as if he just came off a football field, except he's wearing camo gear instead. His weapon is huge, and the way he's holding it with such confidence and skill, one would think it is an extension of his arm. Everything about this man reminds me of Rambo, from his imposing stance to his muscular build.

I shift my eyes to Travis and watch as he gives the man an icy look. This shit is just too much, so I reflexively make a go for my gun. I'm not quick enough. The approaching man sees what I'm about to do, and with his gun being at the ready, he merely lifts it and holds me at gunpoint.

"Don't do it, Jules." His hard, rough voice freezes me in my tracks, and as he nears, I almost piss my pants. He is freaking huge. *How does he know my name?*

"About fucking time, asshole," Travis says with ungrateful scorn.

The man has the sudden audacity to smirk at Travis as he says, "The Travis I know wouldn't have fallen to the ground in the first place. Looks like your ball-and-chain took you down."

Travis lets out a puff of air in a half-laugh. "Fuck you, man."

Rambo starts to chuckle as he secures his gun and steps toward Travis, offering his hand.

Confusion begins to take place over their exchange. My brows furrow, and I doubt my sanity. Didn't Rambo just have his M-whatever gun pointing at me? Travis gets up and stands to his full height, and I angle my head back to stare at the two giants. I'm guessing this guy is on our side, especially when they do a quick, back-slap man-hug. I thought Travis was a big man, but Rambo definitely has him beat. My mouth is left gaping wide open as I scope out the muscles on the hulk. They are insane.

Travis breaks through my confused state and holds out his hand for me to take. "C'mon, Jules. We have to keep moving." I glance at Mitchell and see he is still alive. He's almost unconscious now, but his labored breathing tells me his heart still beats. "Jules," Travis warns.

I look over at Mitchell, who is sprawled out on the ground. "What about him?"

"He'll be taken care of. No worries," Rambo pipes in. Then he reaches into his back pocket as he kneels down on one knee, pulling out a few zip ties before he starts to secure Mitchell with them. Mitchell makes an ungodly guttural sound of pain when Rambo rolls him onto his stomach so he can tie his wrists together behind his back. I sit here stunned, in a daze. Travis squats down to get in my line of vision, blocking my view of the spectacle in order to gain my attention. I stare at Travis wide-eyed while searching his face for answers.

"It's okay, baby," Travis says softly, as if I'm a scared and frazzled little kitten. I probably am. He extends his hand out for me to take. All I can seem to do is stare blankly at his hand like it's a foreign object. Taking matters into his own hands, he slips them underneath my arms and lifts me up. My legs tremble and shake as he makes me stand on my own two feet. I begin to sway, and my eyes close reflexively. I'm feeling a tad dizzy. All the crazy has finally caught up with me.

"Whoa, there." He quickly holds me in a tight embrace, and I lay my head on his hard chest. I can't hear his heart beating through the bulletproof vest, and I want so badly to hear the relaxing sound of his strong heart. "Are you okay, Jules?"

"I think so," I mumble into his shirt. "Very freaked out, but I think I'm okay."

"We will get through this. I promise," he solemnly whispers over my head while keeping me within his protective hold.

"All right, Travis. Mitchell's all tied up," Rambo says from behind me all matter-of-factly, as if he didn't just shoot somebody. "I have Stryker and Chase on clean-up duty. We need to move to the bunker and regroup."

Travis bends his knees slightly and slants his head to the side with a worried look on his face. "Can you walk, baby?" I blink a few times, take a few deep, calming breaths, and then nod. "All right then, let's get going."

I must be in shock, as I don't remember the walk to the bunker. It's not until the steel door slams shut with a loud resounding clang that I come to my senses. Standing in the middle of the living room, I begin to find my anger again. I take out my shitty morning on the man who saved my life; I can't help it. I turn around and narrow my eyes on Travis, and he stops in his tracks as he pauses to decipher my mood. It must be written all over my face.

"Travis, mind telling me just what the hell is going on?"

He lifts a brow, studying me for a moment, and to his credit, he doesn't get flustered with me.

"Jules, just calm down," he replies calmly.

I feel hysteria coming on, and he tells me to calm down? The pitch of my voice could break glass I'm so irate. "I've just killed someone. Bad men are gunning us down. I thought you were shot, and you're telling *me* to calm down?" I pause and point at my chest. "Why me? I don't understand any of this!" I turn around and wave toward the hulk of a man who's standing in the kitchen, rummaging through some cabinet drawers with purpose, and then my voice goes deep and low. "Then there's freaking Rambo in here who just appears out of nowhere to save the day. What the fuck, Travis?! Mind letting me in on your little games?"

"Jules, calm the fuck down," Travis growls, his temper sounding just as short-fused as mine. "Just calm down and I'll explain."

I take a deep breath, even though I want to yell and scream, but I'm flustered for words right now. I feel shaky and distraught, and I suppose it's because I'm out of harm's way.

"Your adrenaline is running wild." He steps toward me to hold me tightly against his chest. I tremble in his arms as I start to hyperventilate. "Shh, sweetheart. Easy breaths," he commands softly. How the hell he continues to stay strong and put together through all this, I'll never know. He acts so unaffected from our circumstances, and it baffles me.

I startle when Rambo sneaks up behind me and whispers in my ear, "By the way, my name's not Rambo. I'm Quinn. I'm saying sorry on the front end, but I have to do this." My forehead wrinkles in confusion. That's an odd statement, and before I can turn around to see what his deal is, I feel a needle jabbing into the side of my arm.

"Ow!" I jolt back reflexively, but I don't move as Travis catches me in a vice grip. I'm stuck. "You bastards!" I hiss. I can do nothing but stand here in shock and dismay, all the while feeling helpless against the stinging sensation in my arm. God knows what kind of drug is getting ready to run the gamut through my veins this time. The prick of the needle and pain subsides only when Quinn pulls it out of my shoulder.

"You sorry sons of bitches." My lip curls in contempt as I narrow my eyes on Travis with a mixture of anger, pain, and betrayal while my head grows fuzzy.

I blink my eyes several times, trying to shake off the effects of the drug before I lean my forehead into Travis' chest. Whatever this shit is, it's working damn fast. I claw and clutch onto Travis' shirt, grasping at straws to stay upright and alert, but I'm failing miserably. I'm so tired; my eyelids begin to flutter, and then they finally close as my consciousness begins to dissolve into a sea of oblivion. The last thing I remember is Travis bending down to scoop me up into his strong arms.

CHAPTER 3

~Travis~

After Quinn injects Jules with a healthy dose of sedative, I'm met with a string of heated expletives. As the drug begins to take effect, I can see her trying to fight it, but it's useless. Now that she's going down for the count, her anger has quickly faded, and in its place is the look of utter betrayal.

She clutches at the fabric on my shirt, holding on tightly as her eyes begin to flutter closed. She lets a few choice words slip from her lips before she passes out and goes limp in my arms. Immediately, I scoop her up to hold her in my arms, and then I give Quinn a death glare. "What the hell did you do that for?"

He stands in front of me unaffected, as if it was no big deal he just rendered my girl unconscious. Still biting the needle cap between his molars, he speaks through his clenched teeth, "I couldn't think with her freaking out. She needed to settle down, T."

Taking the cap out of his mouth, he carefully inserts the needle back into its plastic sheath and then shrugs his broad shoulders. "We've got plans to make, and she was slowing us down." He feels for her pulse, and then continues, "Trust me, she needed to check out for a while."

His assessment of her emotional status is most likely correct. She was in emotional overload, and if I wasn't emotionally attached to her, I'd probably have done the same thing.

"She is going to be pissed off when she wakes up, man," I warn Quinn.

"If I don't have at least five women pissed off at me at any given moment, it means I'm doing something wrong." He turns around and throws the used needle on the kitchen counter, and then turns back to me with his hands on his hips. "Look, she's going to be pissed off either way. Rather her be pissed off later than now. We've got other pressing matters to take care of, wouldn't you say?"

As much as I hate to admit it, he's right. I don't have time to pamper her ass. I shake my head and close my eyes for a moment, not looking forward to the thought of her wrath when she wakes up.

"You just poked a sleeping tiger, dude," I mumble under my breath as I sidestep Quinn, making my way to the larger bedroom on the left. When Quinn lets out a round of successive chuckles behind me, I add, "You think it's funny now, but just you wait and see when her fury falls on *you*. You won't find it so amusing then."

I gently lay her down on the full-size bed and grab a blanket from the small closet to lay over her. Her hair has started to come undone from its ponytail and is all over the place, with pieces of pine straw matted in. I sit on the edge of the bed for a minute, smooth out some of her tangled hair, and remove the debris. She looks so peaceful like this. I'm really dreading the impending fallout once we have a minute to catch our breath. I don't even want to think about what will happen if she doesn't want me.

I sit back for a moment and look upon her with admiration. I still can't believe she killed a man to defend me today, and she was ready to do it all over again with Mitchell, and then again with Quinn. I shake my head in disbelief. The sheer strength of this woman is off the charts. My heart hurts for her, though, and all the pain she's been through, and I cringe to think about the trials and tribulations she has yet to go through.

I pray to God I've prepared her enough to emotionally be able to withstand the aftermath from the act of killing another. The magnitude of the effects from such a psychological trauma can be so damn debilitating. I need to be the one to help her pick up the pieces, and make sure she's good with it. I lean forward and press my lips against her forehead, leaving them there against her warm skin. I close my eyes and catch the brief lingering scent of her strawberry shampoo.

"You were so brave today, sweetheart. So...so brave." Before I pull away, I kiss her cheek reverently, wishing she were awake right now so I could tell her so. I continue talking softly to her as the back of my knuckles tenderly stroke her cheek. "I've been dying to say this to you, but I could never seem to find the right time. I love you, Jules. I love you so damn much I can't stand it, and I don't know when I can tell you this and have you believe it."

My gut clenches at the thought of her never believing anything I tell her from here on out. "It's going to take a while for you to trust me again, but I'm not going anywhere. I will prove myself to you, and I might not be able to tell you the words for a time, but I'll sure as shit show you how much you mean to me."

I stay with her a few more minutes, wanting to make sure she's okay. I cradle her face as my thumb strokes over her lower lip. Her breathing pattern has smoothed out and it's steady now.

I know Quinn is waiting on me to help him formulate a new plan, but all I want to do is stay holed-up here with her for however many days it will take to make this right between us. I lean down and tenderly kiss her soft lips, murmuring solemnly over her lips, "I was serious when I asked you to be my wife." Before I pull away from her sleeping form, I give her one more chaste kiss. I have a feeling it will be a cold day in hell before she lets me get this close to her again.

I let out a sigh and begrudgingly leave her side. Out of habit, I shut the bedroom door on my way out, and then make my way to the large dining room table where Quinn sits, patiently waiting for me. His elbows rest heavily on the wood table, and his fingers are threaded together. He looks deep in thought, as he seems to stare right through me.

I pull out a chair from the table and sit down directly across from him. I have crazy adrenaline running through my veins right now, and I can't seem to sit still. My right leg begins to bounce up and down underneath the table as the aftermath of the most fucked-up morning of my life begins to sink in. I look up into my friend's eyes to see worry etched across his face.

"Travis, I need to look at the back of your neck," Quinn states with concern. Shit, I had forgotten all about it. I swipe the palm of my hand over the abrasion at the back of my neck, and then look at my hand. "There's no fresh blood; I'm good right now. I can clean it up later."

Quinn scoffs at me and shakes his head. "Do you even *feel* pain?" he asks with wonder. I've always had a high tolerance for pain, but right now, my adrenaline is going a hundred miles an hour, so I don't even feel the wound.

"There's too much other shit to settle first. I don't have time to feel pain. The first thing we need to figure out, being that we're in Hyde County, is how the fuck they found us."

Quinn shakes his head. "I don't know, but it did take them a good while, didn't it? All of our signals are meant to be boosted for output only. We're out in the middle of bum-fuck Egypt, so there's no way in hell they could've spotted us with incoming signals." Quinn then leans back in his chair and crosses his arms, and then asks me a point-blank question. "What about Mitchell? Could he have known about this place?"

I shake my head with earnest conviction. "No. I'm positive, but at least now I know where his loyalties lie. The motherfucker tried to kill me, Quinn." The very thought that I could've died today out in the woods just pisses me off. "I want blood. When this is ironed out, I want to be the one to deliver due justice to him."

Now I know for certain it was either Mitchell or one of his men who T-boned me in Charleston. I couldn't be any more pleased that it was Quinn who took him down. The way he was spraying bullets overhead, I knew then Mitchell had his own agenda. He couldn't have cared less about sparing Jules' life, and that infuriates me. She's an innocent in all of this. She didn't deserve that.

"Look, let's just handle one thing at a time, okay? Stryker and Chase will put him in a safe place until we're ready to deal with him, but right now, we need to be concerned with a second attack. We need to get the upper hand and increase our defenses."

"Not until Jules is out of harm's way, Quinn," I sternly argue back. I feel my blood pressure spike at the thought of her getting mixed in with more of the crossfire.

Quinn leans forward as his eyes crinkle at the corners, his features giving off a serious and determined look. "We don't have a choice. She's part of this now." He shakes his head, frustration evident. "And just where is *out of harm's way*, Travis? She's the reason why all this exists. They want her, and even though we're all under fire, she's safer with us. Not to mention, you'd go fuckin' nuts worrying about her every second she wasn't in your line of sight, and you know it." I stay silent, but nod, acknowledging him. He's right. "Your attention would be anywhere but on the task at hand. You'd be thinking of her the entire time, worrying if you weren't there to protect her they would somehow find her and recapture her."

I'm so fucking fired up it's unreal. I have a million strategic war scenarios spinning around in my mind on top of trying to figure out how I'm supposed to make my relationship with Jules work. Memories from my past try to creep into my thoughts, and I have to remind myself I physically have her within my grasp. I will not let her slip through my fingers. I can't. I let out a long-winded sigh and run my fingers through my sweaty hair. "I knew they were coming, but I didn't think it would be this soon," I admit.

"We all knew they would eventually come. You can't beat yourself up about that, but you need to get your head in the game."

I look at Quinn disbelievingly. Has he gone crazy? "What the fuck? I am in the game," I state offensively.

Quinn holds up his hands, palms out, trying to calm my temper. "All I'm saying is you need to prioritize all the shit running through your head right now. I see the wheels spinning in that mind of yours, Trav. We all know you've been down this road before, and I don't need you getting sidetracked. You need to keep the main thing the main thing here, and that's seeing to everyone's safety." He holds up his index finger to make a point. "Since we still have the upper hand, the next thing on the list is to finish those bastards off. Once all that shit is done, *then and only then* can you worry about your Sleeping Beauty."

I place my elbows on the table and rest my head in the palms of my hands, trying to think. I'm letting my emotions rule over me while trying to prevent history from repeating itself. I need to think about our next step, but I come up empty-handed.

No matter how hard I try, I can't seem to focus on what that next step should be. I keep thinking about the possibility of Jules being captured and getting placed back into the wrong hands again. Growing more frustrated by the second, I act on impulse and reach into my back pocket to pull out my cellphone.

"What are you doing, Travis?" Quinn asks with growing suspicion.

"Getting ready to stir some shit, you know, poke the tiger," I say while typing a number into the phone, one of which I know by heart.

"Travis?" Quinn questions again, with uncertainty lining his voice.

"Relax. I'm just going to personally let the bastard know his mission failed. I'm sure he's pacing the floor right now wearing a hole in the carpet, hoping against hope Mitchell has some good news for him."

I look up after dialing the number, and smirk at Quinn as I put the phone to my ear. I actually feel a little proud I have the opportunity to get under his skin. I want to be the one to personally let him know I still control this situation, and I want to listen to him lose it as he realizes she's slipped from his hands and into mine.

Picking up on the second ring. "What's the news?" he asks, his voice coming through loud and clear, and I can hear the eagerness in his tone. He probably thinks I'm one of his men calling him to touch base, especially since my cellphone is encrypted.

"Nick." I breathe the word like thick venom, and somehow he doesn't miss a beat.

"Travis," he says silkily, "I can hear you're still alive. Such a shame."

"You should know by now it would take more than just a few of your cronies to take me out." I pause for effect and smooth out my voice. "I'm surprised at your lack of judgment, Nick. Three men, really? Is that the best you've got?"

"I want her back, Travis," he barks out, cutting to the chase.

"If you would've known how to treat her from the get-go, you might have never been put in this predicament," I taunt.

"Somehow, I doubt that, Travis." He hesitates for moment, the silence deadly between us before he asks, "What do you want?"

I shake my head even though he can't see me as smug arrogance lines my voice. "I already have what I want, Nick."

"You bastard!" If Nick could breathe fire, my ear would be singed right now. He's that pissed.

"I've been called much worse," I calmly state.

"You're not going to keep her. I'm all over your ass, Travis, and I'd quit while I'm ahead if I were you. Turn her over, and I might spare you," he warns.

"I don't need sparing, and I believe since I've already got her, the *finders keepers* and all that shit applies."

He chuckles menacingly into the phone. "Why are you really calling, Travis? Did I stir up your little love nest? Are you upset you got blindsided by my men? I'm one up on you, and I plan to keep it that way."

"Nope, not upset at all. Give me your best shot, Nick," I say nonchalantly. "Oh, wait, you already did, and you failed." I then think of Jules and how she almost got shot down. "By the way, just so you know, tell your dipshit men to aim at me next time, and not Jules."

"What? Was she shot?" he asks with sudden panic.

"Near misses, Nick," I spit out angrily. "Of course the men

you sent couldn't hit the broad side of a barn." I know the bastard isn't going to tell me how he found us, so I don't even ask. At minimum, however, I want to take a jab at him, get under his skin, and let him know more than just his mission failed. "You know, a real man would've come after his woman, but instead you sent a team of dysfunctional dumbasses. What does that say about you, Nick?"

"You have to know your days are numbered, Travis," he hisses.

"Everyone's days are numbered, Nick. Some have larger numbers than others. Since your men fight like pussies, I'll live to be a ripe old age."

I hear a string of curses come through the receiver. He is so pissed off on a rant that I hold the phone away from my ear and his voice fills the room. Quinn shakes his head at me in amusement while he starts to chuckle.

"Travis! Travis! Do you hear me?!" Nick bellows. "I want her back, dammit!" I hear the desperation growing thick in his voice as he adds, "Name your price."

A grin forms across my lips as I taunt Nick again. "Mmmm...you can't put a price on her pussy. It tastes too sweet to give back or sell. Not to mention, her pussy has been molded to fit my dick perfectly now, just like a glove." Then I hang up on him abruptly, happy I was the one to get in the last word. He would've only had a string of curse words for me after that anyway.

The sardonic smile dissolves from my lips as I look at Quinn in all seriousness. "Well, I stirred up the hive for us. We'll be drawing them out now, 'cause he's madder than a nest of wet hornets, and after that, I have a feeling he is going to unleash every last resource he has on us."

Quinn leans back in his chair and runs his fingers through his hair, and then interlocks his fingers, holding his hands at the back of his head. I can tell he's formulating something in his brain as he stares at the ceiling. Since I've pissed Nick off, I feel a little better now and can think clearer.

Quinn speaks toward the ceiling as he tells me, "We need to get back to my house."

I shake my head at him. "Negatory, man. It's not safe to go to your place just yet. We have to find out how they found us first. Otherwise, it will be like leading a kid to candy again." Quinn's house is north of Raleigh, a little ways outside of the city limits. He lives on a few acres of land in a rural area, with a shitload of armory. Plus, he has more electronic resources there than the government. "I say we head into the city first, stay in plain sight. We need to be around a mass number of people and try to mingle in until we can figure out how he's tracking us."

Quinn drops his gaze from the ceiling to mine, and then wrinkles his forehead in thought. "Yeah, let me make some phone calls and get some backup in place. I know a hotel we can hunker down in for a day or two until we get this figured out."

"Do you think we got them all?"

"As soon as you texted me from the cabin, I made my way toward the front drive and saw there was only one vehicle. Figured on three men. So yeah, we got them all. I took down one man who was standing guard at the vehicle, and of course I got Mitchell, and then you took the other."

"Correction, Jules took that man out all by herself."

Quinn's neck snaps back in surprise with both eyebrows lifted high. "Damn. That's one hell of a woman."

I give him a sly grin. "That's why I told you not to piss her off." Now that I've calmed down some, I can see it was best to have sedated her. What she just went through was some serious action. "It's probably for the best you knocked her out. I think she was on the hard and fast road to a major meltdown."

Quinn opens his eyes wide in mock surprise as he sarcastically comments, "You think?"

"My concern is when she wakes up." I pause, shaking my head, and let out a sigh. "She's never killed anyone before, and I'm seriously worried how she's going to process all of this. This whole scenario is going to change her, Quinn. We all know she'll never be the same after this, and she won't want to hear that."

Quinn's lips form a thin line before he speaks. "That it does, my friend. That is does." He quietly contemplates his thoughts for a minute before he speaks again, and when he does, his eyes pierce mine with utter resolution. "We have your back on this, you know? All of us will do what it takes to help pull her through the aftermath."

"Thanks, man," I say, looking at Quinn through the eyes of Jules. The corners of my lips lift in a smirk as I eye him up and down. I guess he does look like Rambo, in all his getup and gear with war paint on. It's something I'm so used to seeing, so I've never thought twice about it. I can only imagine the thoughts that ran through her head at the first sight of him. The thought strikes me funny, and I start to chuckle.

"What are you laughing at?" he asks skeptically.

I shake my head at him and tease, "Rambo. Of all the names for someone to come up with, she comes up with Rambo."

He chuckles himself, and then shrugs. "Hey, I'll take that as a compliment."

"So what's next?"

"Given the fact they know where our vicinity is, they're probably sending out more men as we speak. Once Stryker and Chase get here, we can head out. Chances are excellent we won't have a tail," he pauses, "for now anyway. At least we'll have a head start. I'm parked about a quarter mile out." He jerks his chin up and to the left, as if I know where he's indicating.

"Lovely…just fucking lovely." Sarcasm drips from my voice as I think about having to carry a very sedated Jules for a quarter mile. "You just had to drug her, didn't you?"

He holds his hands up in the air in protest. "You just agreed it was a good idea."

"Mmmm, I think we all need to see what this Rambo is made of. I believe you should be the one to carry her ass out to the truck," I stand up and reach across the table to give his arm muscle a manly squeeze, "since you're the one who drugged her and all."

A smooth smile spreads across Quinn's lips as he rags on me. "Why, Travis, I do believe you're getting old and feeble on me. Why don't you just admit it; you've gone soft and can't handle carrying the extra baggage."

"Shut the fuck up." I let go of his shoulder and he starts to laugh.

CHAPTER 4

~Jules~

My eyes flutter open, and confusion overcomes me. *Where in the hell am I?* I rub the sleep from my eyes, narrowing them to focus, and I realize I'm in another friggin' hotel room. A cold chill runs down my spine as bad memories roll through me, my pulse picking up speed. I catch the scent of Travis and my stomach dips. I'm not caught; I'm with Travis. A huge gust of air leaves my lungs in relief.

When I peel the blankets back, I raise a brow. My legs are bare. Looks like Travis had put me in one of his oversized t-shirts, and thank God I'm in my panties. The clock illuminating on the nightstand reads seven. *Is it morning or night? I can't tell.* The curtains are drawn shut, and I'm not about to look behind them and tempt fate.

I make my way to the bedroom door, still in a disoriented stupor, and step out into the carpeted hallway. The sound of men's voices carries from down the hall. It looks as if I'm in a large hotel suite. I follow the voices and find myself in front of a table full of men. I stop in my tracks. I don't recognize any of them except for Stryker and Quinn.

All of the men abruptly stop talking, turning around to look at me as if I just interrupted a secret meeting. I spy a huge spread of breakfast food stretched out across the table, and at that moment, I know I've slept into the following day. Quinn is sitting off to the right, and I narrow my eyes on the bastard for drugging me like that.

Someone clears their throat, and out of the corner of my eye I see Travis scooting his chair away from the table. He hastily makes his way toward me as he speaks in a gruff voice, "Guys, give me a few minutes. I'll be right back." He reaches out and gently takes me by the elbow, and leans in to whisper in my ear, "Babe, you can't come out dressed like that." Oh, crap, I didn't even realize that. Thank goodness his shirt comes down to my knees.

He ushers me quickly back down the hallway, out of sight. When we reach the bedroom door, he pauses to ask, "Can I get you some coffee or something to eat?" I look into his eyes and they seem a little off, like he's hiding something.

"I am thirsty," I softly reply.

He leans his head out the bedroom door, then shouts out toward the dining room, "Stryker, need you to bring Jules some OJ."

He guides me into the bedroom, and sits down on the edge of the bed. He pats the empty space beside him, silently telling me to have a seat. I sit down on the edge of the bed with him, and for some reason, I feel unsettled. Maybe because there is an army of men out there and we're on the run, but Travis is acting different.

"How are you feeling?" he asks.

"I'm doing fine," I respond flatly, staring at the floor.

"I hate that answer, you know that? Fine means you're doing shitty," he retorts, leaning in close to me.

I pull away and turn to look at him with a scowl on my face. "What do you want me to say, Travis? Too many things have unfolded in the past twenty-four hours for me to process anything. Not to mention, I was knocked out with God knows what drug since noon yesterday."

He looks away from me, and hopefully it's shame that fills him. "I'm sorr—"

"Save it." I hold my hand up, interrupting him. "I want answers, and I want a phone call," I demand.

He narrows his eyes, looking at me as if I've lost my mind. "Yeah, I can't let you have either," he says sternly.

"No? What the hell, Travis? No?!" My voice escalates with indignation as he raises an eyebrow at my outburst. "I can't believe you're going to deny me." My throat constricts, and my upper lip snarls. "You're a real bastard."

At that very second, Stryker loudly clears his throat, purposely interrupting, and we both turn to look at him as he stands in the doorway holding my glass of orange juice.

I give him the evil eye, and at least he has the regard to act a little penitent for being part of Travis' game. He walks into the room and hands the orange juice to Travis, which is a smart move. I have the desire to toss the drink in their faces. It's a coin toss at the moment as to which one.

I turn to face Travis with a heated scowl. "My father needs to know I'm safe. This is *my life* we're talking about here, my own flesh and blood, and you won't even give me the courtesy of a phone call?"

Stryker's lips thin as if he wants to say something, but he holds back, letting Travis handle the situation. Travis grabs my hands and looks at me with pleading eyes, which is odd. Since we had been invaded, he's been in warrior-mode the entire time, not showing a speck of his soft side.

"Nothing is safe right now, Jules," he explains. "The only safe place for you right now is here with me, by my side 24/7."

I scoff and jerk my hands out from under his. "Is that so? How convenient," I mock. "I'm surprised you're not drugging me with more Blyss right now...or did you forget to put that in your backpack?" I hiss. I look at my wrists and make another snide remark. "What? No restraints? You're slipping, Travis. I'm surprised there's not a dead bolt on the door, too."

Stryker steps in front of me, coming to Travis' rescue, and interrupts, "Jules, you're not being fair here."

I raise both brows, staring indignantly at Stryker and his audacity. *Who the hell does he think he is?* I cross my arms over my chest defensively. "Well, do tell then, Stryker. I'd seriously like to know what you think is fair. How about I rip *you* apart from everything you've ever known and loved, and then drug you. Oh, yeah, then let's top that scenario off by having you shoot and kill another man, all for a criminal you already know is going to keep holding you hostage."

He bites at the inside of his cheek, his lips puckering off to the side as he keeps his mouth shut, not having a decent retort.

My bare foot begins tapping on the carpeted floor, with my lips pursed while I stare Stryker down with a heated glare. *Is what I'm asking for really that unreasonable?* Maybe I shouldn't be so obstinate, but nobody is giving me answers, and it's like the minute I got my memory back, Travis has been the very man I knew him to be at the facility, and I don't like it. He's played me for a fool the entire time. Now I know how Nick felt when I did it to him.

Travis' deep voice breaks through the silence in the room. "Stryke, I got this. Just shut the door on your way out," he commands in a low and ominous tone as he jerks his chin toward the door. I don't like where this is going. I watch in silence as Travis bends down to put the juice on the floor. His jaw muscles are taut, and as he sits upright, the look in his eyes has me holding my breath. *Uh-oh.*

Once the bedroom door clicks shut, Travis clenches his fists tightly, and then spreads his fingers out wide, releasing obvious, pent-up tension. Frustration is evident as he leans forward, mere inches from my face, and grits out through clenched teeth, "When I say no, I mean fuckin' no. I'm not going to deal with your tirades of childish behavior. Not now, not ever. My patience is hanging on by a thread here, and I don't think you want to push me over that edge, do you?" His steely words cut through my soul like a sharp knife as his eyes flare at mine. "So tell me, Jules, just what the fuck don't you understand about the word *no*? Or do you need a lesson in the meaning?"

The blood drains from my face. The icy tone in his voice emits the same viciousness as when I was captive at the facility. I remember this Travis all too well. Now that the jig is up and my memory is back, there's no need for him to play nice. Every one of his words from not too long ago comes back to haunt me. *"This is where the shit gets real, Princess. No one is going to hold your hand anymore, especially me."* And the worst one, *"That's none of your concern; you're a slave. How's that for a different perspective?"*

I don't know what the hell he wants from me, but I'm not going to take it from him. *I just saved his ass, and this is how he treats me?* I haul my hand back, getting ready to slap him across the face, but he catches my wrist.

"Son of a bitch," he spits out angrily. "What the fuck, Jules?"

"I'll tell you what the fuck," I start to rant, but he cuts me off by crashing his lips against mine. I fall back on the mattress, fighting his kisses as his heavy body topples over mine. He grabs my other wrist, manhandling me, and I lift my hips to buck him off, but it only serves to place his cock between my legs.

"You wanna dirty fuck, Jules?" he breathes over my lips. "The way you're grinding on me, I think you do."

"Get off me, Travis," I warn through gritted teeth.

"You mean, *get you off.*" He smirks then rolls his hips into mine as his lips press hard against me.

I thrash my body, trying to buck him off, but I fail. He slips his tongue over the seam of my lips, and I turn my head to the side to get away, but he just follows, working me over and over until I start to tire from the struggle. Oh, God, his lips are to die for, and slowly I feel myself caving in, my anger dissipating. My chest's labored breaths change from struggle to lust and passion. How does he do this to me? How does he make me feel like he's a part of my soul and I can't live my next minute without him?

"You know you want me," he arrogantly whispers over my lips. I narrow my eyes, trying to look defiant and not give away my fading resolve. His gaze is heated, and his need is becoming more evident between my legs, causing a rush of heat to spread to my core. He rains hot, passionate kisses down the length of my exposed neck, and shivers roll through me.

"You think you can just get away with distracting me, using your body?" I breathe heavily.

His knee pushes against my thigh, spreading my legs open to him. My nipples have betrayed me already, and I arch my back into his hard chest, seeking friction.

"Yes," he gruffly whispers as his teeth graze my skin along my neck. I can feel him smiling against my skin, and then a deep chuckle follows suit. *Smug asshole.* He works his way to the outer shell of my ear. "So sexy." He breathes his warm breath into my ear, sending goose bumps scattering across my skin.

"Travis..." I whisper in vain. I quickly decide that escaping reality feels better than facing it. I allow my muscles to relax and sink into the mattress as I let him have his way with me.

"That's it, baby. Let me have you," he softly whispers as he releases my wrist. His hand slips into the front of my panties, and I lose my breath. My stomach flutters, swirling with excitement as his fingers brush along the lips of my sex. I stifle a whimper when his fingertips spread open my folds and dip inside. I let out a soft gasp, and grab onto his shoulders, squeezing in response.

"So wet, already," he whispers as he slides his finger deep

inside my wet heat, filling me. I thrust my hips into his hand, silently begging for more. He then pushes two fingers in deep, stretching me, and then rubbing them against my g-spot while using deep, sensual circles.

"Oh, God," I moan, closing my eyes, savoring the pleasure. His fingers are so strong and masculine; they feel like heaven as he brings me to the edge of ecstasy. He withdraws his fingers to swirl my wetness over my clit, and then he plunges his fingers back inside, spreading me open wide. "Travis, we can't..." I trail off with a helpless whimper as he rubs my clit with his thumb. There are people in the next room.

"Kiss me, Jules," Travis softly demands.

My tongue slips out and I run it over the seam of his lips, giving him what he wants. My heart skips a beat as his warm tongue deliciously swipes over mine in reply, and my pussy clenches around his fingers. He tastes so forbidden, and it feels like we're a couple making up after a lovers' spat. The sexual craving he creates in me always turns my resolve upside down. I scrape my nails down the length of his muscled biceps, and they flex as he continues to pump his fingers in me faster and faster.

I whimper as our tongues dance in a heated tangle. I gasp for breath as his thumb relentlessly swirls around my clit with firm pressure, tormenting me, and finally pushing me over the edge. I thrust my hips into his hand as he ignites a fire, my inner muscles pulsating and squeezing his fingers.

"Damn," he groans, and then drowns out my cries with his possessive kisses. I grab his broad shoulders, pulling him into me so I can wrap my arms around him. When my legs stop shaking and I've come down from my high, he breaks the kiss and pulls back, with his lips hovering over mine. "I want nothing more than to fuck you right now."

"Please do." I'm shameless.

He groans as he removes his fingers from my sex, and I immediately miss his touch. He then rests his body back over mine and holds my face in the palms of his hands. His desire is still evident as his erection throbs between my legs, but he ignores it. "I have important business to work out right now, baby." His eyes search mine before he softly says, "Look, you will get your answers, and I'm not saying you can't call home... just not right now, okay?"

I nod, agreeing with him. With the oxytocin released from my orgasm, the hormone is humming happily through my veins. It's left me calm and sated. We both fall silent for a moment. He gently caresses along my cheek with the back of his fingers as each of us gets lost in our own thoughts.

I'm sure he's just trying to placate me, because really, when all this mess is said and done, I'm still somebody's captive. With the thought of being his captive, his marriage proposal comes to mind. The happy hormones come to a screeching halt, and I feel confused all over again. I glance at my left hand resting on his shoulder, the glimmering diamond catching my eye. *Why did he ask me to marry him? What is his motive? With there being so many secrets, how am I supposed to know if he was being genuine or not?*

I bring my hands to my chest and nervously begin to twist the ring around my finger. As I do, I contemplate the questions that are swirling around in my head. Decision made, I nervously bite the inside of my cheek as I slide the ring off my finger. Travis sees what I've done, and quickly places his hands over mine, stopping me. He dips his head to the side to catch my gaze, but I keep my eyes fixated on his hands.

"Don't even think about it, Jules. I know what you're thinking, and I don't want it back."

I lift my chin slightly, peering up at him. His eyes swirl with distress and affliction. "How do you know what I'm thinking?" I softly ask.

He breathes out a huff of air, sounding slightly offended. "You really have to ask that? I've spent damn near every waking hour with you for the past six weeks. I know how you think."

"Travis," I clench my jaw and look away from him, not sure if I want to hear the answer, "why did you ask me to marry you?"

His two fingers come to rest under my chin, turning my head back to him. "That's a loaded question," he states as his eyes bore a hole through me, straight to my soul. His voice is serious and full of finality, "but one we will address later, when we have time to work on us. The ring stays on."

Wow. He's seems so sure of this...of us. It would have been nice to hear an I love you.

"What does keeping this ring on until things blow over have to do with anything?" I whisper, confused. I slip my hands out from under his, and despite his protest, I hold the ring out for him to take back. He shakes his head adamantly, refusing it.

"No, Jules," he breathes in a low voice, and he looks as if I ripped a piece of his heart out, but I continue to hold the ring out for him to take anyway, remaining silent. "This isn't going to happen right now," he insists, his tone hell-bent with determination. As if he's in denial, he wraps his hand back around mine, closing the ring inside the palm of my hand. His eyes search mine for answers, but I don't have any. He's the one who popped the question, and like everything else, he remains elusive as to why he does the things he does.

My voice comes out croaky and downhearted. "Relationships are built on communication and trust, not on lies and deceit. Have you forgotten the fact I'm already engaged to someone else, Travis?" He briefly closes his eyes, and his jaw muscles flex with tension.

"We are not discussing this right now," he states firmly, and the discussion is over. There's a war going on between the two of us, an unspoken one with our eyes. With renewed determination, he takes the ring from my hand and slips it back on my finger. I look from the ring back to his eyes in disbelief. "This ring belongs here, right on your finger. Even if I were to take it back, which I won't, I have nowhere safe to keep it right now. First, let's get through this ordeal alive...then we'll talk," he says adamantly. It's obvious I've upset him. Maybe he does love me and doesn't know how to say it. "We're also going to need to sort out the battle scars in your head before you even think about handing that ring back."

"I don't need to sort out anything, Travis. I know what I need. I need to go home."

I watch as he forces himself to relax, battling to keep his voice calm. "You can't do that just yet. We've already discussed the reasons why you can't go home right now. You need to trust me when I tell you the full magnitude of the past two days hasn't hit you yet. The amount of emotional turmoil on your psyche is going to bowl you over," he says with concern.

"I'm fine," I whisper, looking down at my hands.

"Unfortunately, I know better." He lifts my chin, forcing me to meet his somber gaze. "I've been through this hell before. Shit, I've been trained for it, but even that doesn't stop the consequences that follow the act. Even the most highly trained men and women struggle with the aftermath of battle. It's a basic fact. Something happens on a subconscious level when you pull the trigger."

"I don't want to talk about this right now, Travis." My heartbeat accelerates just from the mention of the word trigger, and I squeeze my eyes tightly, wishing it away. He tucks a stray piece of hair behind my ear in a tender show of compassion.

"Hey," he says in a soft, husky voice, "don't check out on me." I search those beautiful eyes of his, and all I see is genuine concern. "I have to wrap up some plans with my men out there, sweetheart. They're waiting on me." He brushes his lips over mine in an endearing kiss. "I want you to take a nice, warm shower while I finish debriefing my men, and then after that, I want you to eat something."

I clear my throat. "Why can't you tell me what's going on?"

He rests his forehead against mine and softly sighs. "The only thing I can tell you is shit's getting very intense. I need you to listen to all my orders, and follow them to the T. I can't afford you doing something off the cuff right now. I'm serious, Jules, because doing so will inevitably put yourself and my men at risk, and it will all be on you if you decide to buck my authority," he firmly states.

"All right," I whisper, agreeing to listen.

"By the time you get out of the shower, I'll have some breakfast in here waiting for you."

"Okay," I softly reply.

Whatever is going on with his men, it has him wound up in a bad way, because he schools his facial features again, turning them back into his infamous stone wall. "Good girl," he murmurs, and then gives me a tender kiss on my forehead before he gets up to leave.

This must be what it feels like when love and hate collide, and then intertwine, creating mass confusion and mixed-up feelings. I feel so discombobulated over my unsorted feelings. *He's a criminal for God's sake, Jules! One who stole you, and has not only kept you captive, but continues to do so.*

This situation of me having feelings for him is really screwed up, and I wonder where this leaves Adam and me. Hell, is there even an Adam to return to? And if there is, could it even work at this point? There is no way either one of us would be able to ward off this type of danger chasing us. Both of us are simply too inexperienced in the department of guns and street battles, let alone being able to hide ourselves effectively. Is it even fair to pull him into this perilous world? We'd forever be on the run, looking over our shoulders. Where would that leave his job and our future?

I'm precariously teetering on the edge of a cliff, and I don't know how hard I will fall when I hit rock bottom. I feel a sinking depression coming on, and my hope is waning. I chastise myself for wanting to give up hope. Maybe I'm just simply tired and worn down. Perhaps Travis is right; I'll feel better after a much-needed shower, and then once I eat something, I'll gain a little strength and a fresh outlook. I force myself to get out of bed and head for the shower.

CHAPTER 5

~Travis~

When I left Jules alone to take her shower, I made her a nice spread of breakfast food and placed it on a tray. I left it on the little table in our room for when she got out of the bathroom, because I knew once the men and I started discussing strategies again, I'd forget to feed her. None of us slept well last night, and we're all tired. The mental strain of figuring out what our next move needs to be just adds to our exhaustive state. Even though we're used to working under pressure like this, especially on very little sleep, I find myself more on-edge than usual. Maybe because I'm worried about Jules.

After talking and working out the final logistics for another half hour, the guys then split apart, each man having their own task to carry out. They've left Jules and me to ourselves for a little bit so I can make sure her volatile mood is truly diffused. Plus, I need to brief her on what's about to go down, and what's expected of her. I don't think they wanted to be around for when I have to break the news to her anyway.

Of course, after I lost my temper earlier, I imagine she'll think twice before copping another attitude with me or the men. I don't have time to play games or sugarcoat shit. These are real bullets with real-life repercussions, and I need her to stand in line and be subordinate, or it could cost someone their life. I'm sure as shit not willing to risk any of my men over a temper tantrum.

Chase is the last man out the door with his gear, and when the door slams shut behind him, I head to the bedroom to check on Jules. It's quiet, and I find myself tiptoeing down the hallway to see what she's up to. When I peek around the doorframe, she's sitting in a chair by the small table still wrapped up in a bathrobe, and wearing a towel wrapped around her head like a turban. I'm pleasantly surprised to see her breakfast plate has been cleaned off. I internally smile; I'm glad she's not mentally checked out on me. Her eating means she still gives a damn and she's still in the game.

She's gazing rather serenely out the window as she takes in the city scene below. We're on the highest floor in this Raleigh hotel. It's damn near a skyscraper, so it's safe for her to have the curtains drawn back. It's impossible for anyone to spot us from down below. I shake my head in awe of her. She has constantly impressed me with how she's been able to handle one fucked-up situation after another, and how easy she rolls with the dice every time...or at least it seems that way.

I was not happy she slept into the next day the way she did. I'm sure the mental stresses combined with the drugs Quinn gave her must've been too much for her petite body to handle.

I'd also bet ten-to-one the sedative she got was meant for a man twice her size, hence her being out of it for a lot longer than she should've been. That thought pisses me off all over again. Thank God for Stryker. He kept monitoring her heart rate and blood pressure constantly, and he had other meds to give her should something have gone wrong. Quinn and I had terse words over him arbitrarily deciding on his own what he thought Jules needed. After our talk, I don't think he will ever give her anything ever again, not even an aspirin.

She must have sensed me staring at her, because she turns around and meets my gaze. She looks tired despite the vast amount of sleep she's just had. Maybe tired is the wrong word; defeated and mentally worn down is a better description of the Jules I see. My chest tightens with remorse, because I know this is the beginning of the chaos to come. She probably thinks we're having a reprieve from the battle, and she couldn't be farther from the truth. I know she's a tough girl, but even some of the toughest men I've known have met their breaking point, and she's no different.

I enter the room at a slow pace, paying close attention to her mood. She's been through too much to stay even-keeled. I can deal with grumpy on occasion, but becoming a loose cannon is unacceptable, especially right now. I'm prepared to put her in her place if need be.

"It's quiet. Where is everyone?" she asks in a low voice. She appears to be calm and at peace with her situation right now, and that's a good sign.

"They left a few minutes ago." I pull up a chair and sit down beside her, still studying her. "Why are you still in a bathrobe?"

"I didn't have any clean clothes to change into, and I couldn't find the clothes you took off me last night. I didn't want to disturb your meeting, so I was just waiting in here until you were done."

"I had a runner go pick up a few things for us. I'll go get them." I start to get up, but Jules stops me by grabbing onto my forearm. I look from my arm to her face in confusion.

"Travis," she softly begins, but then stops, hesitating to continue. I can see all the emotions running through her baby blues: fear, worry, betrayal, and God help me, hopefully a little forgiveness is in there. My heart grows heavy from all the turbulence swirling around those sad eyes. She looks so desolate and lonely, and it guts me.

I sit back down and look at her with some much-needed compassion. "Baby, I am so, so sorry." I reach out and caress her face, not knowing if she wants to punch me or have me touch her.

She leans forward into my touch and places her index finger over my lips to shush me. "I promise I will try to be patient and listen to you. I'm in an odd place right now in my head, you know? I have so many questions, and I'm still not getting any answers. One question in particular keeps circling around in my head, and I have to know." She hesitates to continue, but I stay silent as I wait for her to find the courage to ask. "I know you said I wasn't your slave, but you never denied the fact I'm your prisoner. Am I...your prisoner?" she asks, looking me square in the eyes.

Her question is like an electrical shock to my heart, and I feel the voltage shoot through me. No matter how I slice it, she will not be able to understand the complexities of her circumstances, even if I had all day to explain them to her. Nick did a fantastic job of pinning her down, cornering her in like a hunted fox. There is no way out for her. How do I tell her that?

I try my best to downplay her question, cupping her cheeks as I search her eyes imploringly. "Prisoner? No," I shake my head several times, "but it's a little more complicated than that."

"I thought so," she softly murmurs, interrupting me before I can finish. Her eyes shift away from mine, falling to the floor in defeat.

"No, Jules, look at me." I patiently wait until she looks up. "You're right. I can't let you go, but what you need to understand is that what we had at the cabin wasn't a lie." Her eyes start to turn glassy, and I don't know what to do to fix this. "What we have, what we felt for each other...it's all real."

"I don't know what's real anymore."

"Yes you do, baby," I softly urge. I slip my hand inside the V of her bathrobe and rest the palm of my hand over her heart. I close my eyes and feel the tempo it's playing. It's fluttering fast against my touch, and I know I'm affecting her. "As sure as I feel your heart beating, you feel this thing between us."

The edge of my hand is only inches from touching her nipple, and I clench my jaw, forcing myself not to stray. My thumb didn't get the memo as it drifts, slowly stroking her supple skin over her breastbone. I notice her chest silently rise and fall with excitement as I caress her with a feather-light touch.

Her gaze turns heated as she pleads on a whisper, "Travis,

take away this pain inside. Make me forget."

I lean forward, only inches away as I huskily whisper over her lips, "Let's get one thing straight, Jules. I'm not your escape from reality. I *am* your reality, and if it's a fuck you want, it's a fuck you'll get." She gasps, taken aback by my dirty mouth, and her reaction makes my lips quirk in an arrogant grin.

I slowly remove the towel from her head, and her damp blonde hair spills out all around her. The strawberry smell is gone, replaced by the hotel's cheap shampoo, but I don't care. I'd take her in a gunnysack; she's that priceless to me. The silence in the room is filled with a potent mix of longing and heart-pounding desire.

Her breathing picks up when I untie the belt to her bathrobe. I take my time, drawing out the sweet torture of anticipation. It's been a few days since we made love, and I for one will not turn down a chance to keep ruining her for all other men. I know she's confused about her feelings, and I'm a real bastard for taking advantage of her weakness, but my plan is to sway her any way I can. I've never claimed to play fair, or be her Prince Charming. I slowly push aside the fabric of the bathrobe, exposing her bare breasts, and the sight of their creamy fullness spilling out before me has my mouth watering.

When I graze my fingertip over a nipple, she inhales a sharp breath and arches her back, pushing her breasts firmly against my hand. "I think my girl likes the dirty talk."

Instead of taking her nipple into my mouth, like she thinks I'm going to do, I surprise her by lifting her up out of her chair in one quick motion. She squeals as she's lifted into the air. Her chair falls backward against the carpeted floor as I push her a few steps back, flattening her body against the hotel window, and then lean in to brush against her lips with mine.

"Why do I have such a hard time resisting you?" she asks in a breathy whisper.

A low chuckle resonates deep within my chest as my fingers find their way to her erect nipples, and I gently pinch them as I reply, "Because you know we belong together. Your body screams it loud and clear; it's your mind that needs to get the message."

I slide my hands toward the outside of her breasts to slip the bathrobe off her shoulders, and down her arms, never letting my hungry gaze leave hers.

Tiny rivulets of water drip from that luscious blonde hair of hers, sliding down to her chest. I lean in to lick the cool water off the swell of her breast, and a visible shiver runs through her. "Are you cold?" I ask, peering up at her out of the corner of my eye. She inhales a sharp breath as her eyes flutter closed. "You won't be cold for long," I promise just before I take her hardened nipple fully into my warm mouth and lightly suck. "Mmm," I moan while palming the weight of her full breasts in my hands as I savor the feel of her nipple against my tongue. I think my dick just grew another few inches.

I let her feel the strength of my thigh muscles as I nudge myself in between her legs, gently prodding them apart.

She's breathing excitedly, and places her hands on my shoulders to steady herself.

"Are you wet for me, baby?" I huskily whisper. I settle my straining erection against the apex of her thighs, and then roll my hips into hers. She moans when I let her feel all of my fullness as I apply pressure against her sweet pussy using my body weight.

"Travis," she murmurs as I kiss my way up her neck, leaving behind a blazing trail of fire to her jawline. Her skin smells clean and fresh, and I love the way she tastes on my tongue as I kiss my way to her ear.

"Tell me what you want," I pant huskily between kisses, and then lick the outer shell of her ear. Using the back of my fingers, I make a slow, winding trail down to the curves of her hips before I run the pads of my fingertips over the little patch of hair between her legs. Her skin is soft and smooth, and I stifle a groan knowing she's shaved for me, having me in mind when she did it.

"Is this what you need?" I whisper before I coax the lips of her sweet sex open and slip two fingers in, sliding deep into her slick heat with ease.

"Oh, hell, you're soaked," I rasp, "so wet and ready for me." I slowly pump my fingers in and out of her warmth, my fingers coated in her juices. I curl my fingers upward and stroke that special place inside.

As she rides my hand, her hips thrust in rhythm and her pussy squeezes around my fingers. I use my thumb to rub against her clit in small, firm circles as I continue to fill her. I'm rewarded with a strained cry as she arches, exposing more of her neckline for me to devour.

Her nails dig into my biceps as I add a third finger into her core, stretching her wide open. Her head falls back against the window as her eyes flutter closed. "Travis, ohhh, God," she moans out in pleasure.

I know what she's doing in her mind. She's using me as an escape from reality right now, using me to forget, and I have no intention of letting her forget me or what we had. "I'm not big on promises, sweetheart, but I can promise you this: when I bury myself deep inside your sweet sex, you're gonna know I've been there for the next two weeks." I nip at her bottom lip and thrust deep while putting pressure against her G-spot. "Look at me, Jules," I command, and as I look into her eyes, I can see I don't have to wonder if she's thinking of anything or anyone else but me, but I want to hear her confession anyway. "Who owns this pussy, Jules?" I growl as my thumb rubs along the outskirts of her clit, avoiding her hard nub on purpose, driving her crazy with need.

I'm glad when she doesn't hesitate to answer me back. "You do, Travis. You own this."

"Don't ever forget it either," I warn with a stern voice.

She whimpers, reassuring me, "Yes, Travis, you have me."

"Damn right, I have you." Her legs begin to quiver, and I know she's close, but I'm not going to let her come this way. I need to feel her sex squeezing around my cock. I withdraw my saturated fingers from between her wet folds, and take a step back. With a heated stare, she watches me slip my fingers into my mouth as I slowly suck her juices clean off my fingers. I close my eyes briefly, savoring her taste. "Damn, you taste fine."

With the floor-to-ceiling windows behind her, the morning sunlight streams in, casting a golden glow around her entire body. She looks angelic, and the light catches some of her blonde hair just right, giving her a halo. I need to bury myself deep into this divine creature of mine...now. I hastily slip off my jeans, not taking the time to remove anything else, and then I stand to my full height in front of her while I wrap my hand around my thickness, and slowly stroke the length a few times, making a show of what she's about to receive.

The ring on her finger catches my eye as it glistens in the sunlight, and a fierce, protective, dominant feeling falls over me. I figure if she keeps the ring on her finger long enough, she'll get used to seeing it there, and then she'll accept the fact that there is an *us*. I notice her gaze hasn't moved from my dick, and I grin. I purposely squeeze it, and then stroke my length one last time in front of her, letting her know, "You're mine, Jules. No matter what comes between us, we will overcome it. There's no denying what we have. We belong together."

I let go of my erection and step forward, nudging her legs apart with my knees as I press her back against the coolness of the glass. God, her bare skin feels so good against my straining erection. I cup her breast with my palm and squeeze.

I narrow my eyes as I look down at her. "You understand me?" I wrap my other hand around the back of her neck as I thread my fingers through her damp hair, pulling her mouth only inches from mine. I lean in, grinding my hips into her, and nibble over her lips, whispering, "Tell me that you can deny this."

Her breathing turns shaky as her body molds to mine. "I *can't* deny this, Travis," she whispers. I smile to myself. I know I've ruined her for any other man, and the way she so easily surrenders to me tells me I have her.

"You're about to be fucked against a window, Jules, for the

entire city to see." The dawning of realization flits across her eyes; she tenses, and a deep chuckle escapes me. "In a minute, you'll be so wanton, you won't care where we do it," I whisper arrogantly as I spread my fingers out, stroking the length of her toned body before I roughly grasp the back of her thigh. She nervously licks her lips, but before she has a chance to think twice, I assault her senses with everything I have.

I crash my lips over hers, letting the heat of my tongue inflict her with blind desire. She softly whimpers while I roll one of her nipples between my fingertips and slip my hardness between her legs.

I'm making her so dizzy with lust she can't see straight, and I have her right where I want her. She pulls away from my kiss to run her tongue over the ridge of my jawline while reaching down to cup my balls in her hand, giving them a light squeeze.

"Oh, hell." My girl wants to play dirty. I close my eyes and a shudder of explosive passion rolls through me. All the blood drains from my upper body, rushing to my cock, and I swear I'm going to explode. I quit screwing around with taunting her, and dig my fingers into the cheeks of her ass, hoisting her legs up and over my hips. Her legs immediately wrap around my waist as I flatten her backside against the window, positioning the tip of my head right in the seam of her opening. I catch her lips in a fiery kiss, slipping my tongue into her mouth.

She grabs my shoulders as I slowly let the weight of her body slide down over the length of my shaft, and she gasps for air. *Sweet Jesus...I'm not going to last long.*

Her warm, tight pussy envelops me, and my eyes close tightly as I try to focus on not blowing early. I will never tire of this feeling she gives me when I'm deep inside her. I slide my hips back, getting ready to slam into her, but before I can, her hips buck forward into mine, forcing me back into the depths of her slick heat, and I groan.

"Two can play at this game, sweetheart." I force my body weight into hers, rotating my hips as I rub my pelvis against her clit, staying balls-deep inside of her.

"Oh, God, Travis." A breathless, shaky whisper is all she can muster as I pick up the pace and begin pumping my hard length in and out of her, mercilessly thrusting myself into her tight pussy with everything I have. All she can do at this point is helplessly take it as her ass makes a lasting imprint on the glass.

While her fevered whimpers get swallowed up in a frenzied kiss, Jules' grip on my shoulders tightens as she digs her nails into my skin. My thigh muscles begin to burn, but I ignore the pain. I want to be able to fuck her for hours like this.

"You feel so good, baby," I pant on a labored breath. I'm coated in a sheen of sweat as I thrust rhythmically, in and out, swirling and grinding.

Her whimpers grow more frantic, and I know just by the high-pitched sounds she's making that she's not far from reaching her pinnacle.

I can feel the minute she begins to pulsate around me, and her legs tremble and quake in response. She tries to pull her lips away from mine, but I'm not having it. Wanting to swallow her cries of passion whole, I cover her with my mouth as our tongues tangle. Not being able to hold off any longer, I let go.

My cock throbs and pulsates within the tight walls of her pussy as I spill my seed into her womb. My thrusts become erratic, and I pull away from the kiss, burying my face in the curve of her neck as I come with a fierceness that makes shudder. I'm breathing heavily, and my eyes water from the intense orgasm. I don't want this connection between us to end. I just want to stay holed up in this room for days as I make her see that we are meant to be.

Once we've both come down from our high, I hold her in place, staying buried deep inside her warmth. I don't want to pull away from her body and face the realities of the day, because I know within the hour, we'll have to be out on the streets, acting as bait. There's a pang in my heart at the thought of something bad happening to her. I'll never be able to forgive myself if something does. It will ruin me. I breathe in her scent, and exhale slowly. Those three little words hang precariously on the tip of my tongue. She has no idea how many times I've come close to telling her how I feel about her.

CHAPTER 6

As both of our breathing patterns calm down, her legs unwrap from around my waist, and I reluctantly let her body slide off my hips and onto the floor. "I don't know how you held me up like that for so long," she softly comments.

"Hey, if I can't hoist my girl up against a wall or a window, then just go ahead and check me into a nursing home," I reply with a grin. She returns my smile, still able to partake in a little light humor. I kiss her forehead and hold her steady until I feel she can stand on her own.

My lips twitch, lifting in an arrogant, lazy smirk. "You can scratch being fucked against a window off your bucket list now," I tell her, and her face flushes a beautiful shade of pink as she coyly looks away and I chuckle. She tries to take a playful swat at me, but misses.

"What makes you think I..."

"Babe," I interrupt, lifting a brow, "being fucked held up against anything is every woman's dream."

"So you say." A haughty arrogance lines her voice, and I smile. I know she's full of shit.

"Oh, I do say." Then I tilt my head to the side and tease her, using a feminine voice, "Travis...oooh...God...don't stop."

I pull away quickly, avoiding her quick swing, and laugh aloud. She tries to hide her mirth, but fails miserably. "You're so bad."

"You like me bad, baby," I say with a grin as I bend down and grab my jeans, slipping them back on, but leaving the top button unfastened at the waist.

I turn and make my way to the bathroom to grab a washcloth. I douse it with warm water, and as I do, my grin fades. Jules' silver medallion gleams on the countertop underneath the bathroom lights, catching my attention. She has to be more careful with this piece of jewelry now. I don't want her taking it off for a split second, because that would be all it takes for shit to go from bad to worse. Then I'd have a hell of a time trying to find her.

I grasp the necklace in my hand and close my fist tightly around it as I'm reminded what this necklace stands for. *Eternal Love.* I remember the exact words she said to me when I noticed her necklace for the first time too. *Family, where life begins and love never ends.* I wasn't able to fully grasp its meaning then, not like I do now.

I slip the necklace into my pocket, and then wring out the wet rag. I'll need to have a chat with her about keeping this on 24/7. When I walk into the bedroom with the warm washcloth, she's sitting on the edge of the bed with her bathrobe wrapped tightly around her body, looking lost.

When I narrow my eyes on her in question, she turns her gaze away from mine, and I suddenly get the feeling we somehow took ten steps back from the intimacy we just shared. "What's the matter?" I ask as I kneel down before her and gently use two fingers to turn her chin, forcing her to meet my gaze.

"Nothing's wrong," she says solemnly. My brows furrow at her odd behavior.

I'm not sure what the hell just happened between us, and I don't like it. "That's not a *nothing's wrong* look to me, sweetheart."

She softly sighs in defeat, her blue eyes full of grief as she asks, "So, what now?"

I squint my eyes, and raise a brow at her. "That's a pretty vague question. Care to elaborate?"

She waves her hand around in a swirl through the air while she speaks. "You guys were having a secret meeting out there this morning. I'm just wondering about the plans you came up with."

My lips thin in thought as I ask myself just how much to tell her to keep her appeased. "The plan is to stay in plain sight for now. Somehow, they found us at the cabin, and until we know how they did it, we can't disappear fully, because if they found us once, they'll find us again."

I watch the wheels in her little head turn as she thinks about what I just said and then tries the word out on her tongue. "Disappear?" She swallows hard at the thought, her voice turning croaky, "You mean...*really* disappear? But what about —"

Cutting her off, I quickly explain, "I mean slip away to a safe hiding place...like what we had at the cabin, but we need to throw them off our trail first." She doesn't need to know any more of my future plans at this point. It'd only freak her out anyway, and we have a pressing task at hand. I set the warm rag on the bed and pull out the necklace from my back pocket. As I place it around her neck and clasp it, I warn her, "Jules, I know how much this necklace means to you, and with us being on the run like we are, we might have to leave in a second's notice. That means you'd lose something very special to you forever if it's not on you. Promise me you won't take it off until I tell you that you can. Don't even take it off to shower, okay?"

She clutches the medallion in her hand as if she had already experienced the loss of it. "Okay," she softly agrees.

"Good." Now that I've cleared that up, I pick up the washcloth and carefully peel open her bathrobe. She's looking shy, and I see she's not going to be any help, so I nudge her legs apart. I gently wipe her clean with the warm cloth. Looking at her flushed body as I wipe away my cum off her toned thighs, *shit*...I could take her again right now.

She cuts through my lascivious thoughts and asks, "Do you think they can find us by the microchips in our hands?"

I toss the rag aside and place my hands on her bare thighs, giving her a look of concern. "No, baby, I've already told you those memory chips are read-only. They could never be a tracking device; they would have to be the size of a quarter, and then implanted..." I abruptly choke on my own words as I remember less than a month ago, presenting new tracker technology to Nick. In fact, it was the same week Jules was brought into the facility. *No fucking way.* The company hadn't finished working out all the logistics. They were still working out the kinks and battery life. Plus, the satellite range hadn't been fully developed yet.

"Travis?" Jules asks warily, breaking into my thoughts. "What are you thinking about?"

I ignore her growing apprehension as I shake my head in disbelief. The fucker couldn't have, could he? I stand up, grasping Jules by her shoulders, and force her to lie back down on the bed. She immediately grows on edge, tensing all her muscles, and her eyes go wide with fear.

"What's...what's wrong? What are you doing?" she asks with panicked confusion.

Being intent on one thing only, I ignore her questions. She starts to squirm, and I sternly warn her, "Stay still." I open her bathrobe to further expose her hips, and she twists her body, trying to get away. I grasp tightly at her thighs, growing frustrated. "Stay the fuck still, Jules!" I bark firmly. She flinches at my harshness, but this time she listens. As if my words were ice, she lays frozen on the bed, not moving a muscle.

I bend down and hover closely over her left hip, inspecting her flesh closely with my eyes while skimming her skin with my fingertips, feeling for any kind of a lump. I hope against hope I find nothing, but as I move my fingers a little to the left, I feel a hard nodule. I lift my head back toward the ceiling and bellow out, "Fuck!"

I bend back down and feel for the device again, praying to God it was a fluke, but it's not. My breathing picks up as I feel the circumference of the quarter-sized tracker lying underneath layers of her skin. I can make out the tiniest scar where an incision was made, a mark so small one would have to actually be looking for it to find.

My outburst and odd behavior has her eyes full of alarm, and her hand flies to her chest in a panicked gesture. "You're scaring me," she hoarsely whispers. I glance at her face; her eyes are glassy and full of confusion. I let loose of the grip I have on her hip and take a few steps back from her. Running both hands through my hair in frustration, I begin to pace the room, trying to think. I'm so damn infuriated at myself for not thinking two steps ahead of Nick. Of course, I didn't think in a million years I'd be stealing his woman out from under him at the last minute either. I should've known he would have taken these precautionary measures, going overboard, even though the tracker isn't fully developed yet.

I have to think...*shit*. This changes everything. All of the plans my men and I made this morning have gone out the window. We're going to have to rearrange, regroup somehow, to come up with a new plan, and quick.

"Travis?" Her soft, trembling voice pulls me out of my deep thoughts. With the side of my body facing her, I don't turn to look at her. If I catch sight of her helpless blue eyes, it'll gut me and I won't be able to think straight.

I hold up my index finger, indicating for her to give me a moment. Valuable minutes are ticking by, and I don't have time to explain things to her right now. I need someone with know-how, and who can provide a solution. I pull out my cellphone and call Quinn.

"Trav?" Quinn questions with consternation.

"Quinn, we've got a big problem."

"Let it roll, man."

"Just found a GPS tracker in her hip." Jules lets out a loud gasp, and I turn to look at her as she covers her mouth with her hand. Her sweet blue eyes are drowning in foreboding terror. I try to stay detached from her emotions, and continue, "It's brand new technology, hot off the press, and it wasn't supposed to be on the market for another month or two, but I guess Nick pulled some strings to get his hands on it early."

Quinn whistles low into the phone. "Well, that is one hell of a monkey wrench thrown into the mechanics of our plans, isn't it?" Despite Quinn's muscle power, out of all of us, he's actually the best technical guru to handle all electronic devices.

"I thought you said incoming signals were damn near nil out at the cabin." I grow irritable with an accusatory tone while I walk toward Jules and sit down beside her. I grab her hand, giving it a gentle squeeze, trying to give her some level of comfort while I work this out with Quinn.

"With that type of new technology, Travis, I'm sure they received a lot of false positives over the last few weeks, meaning those signals had to have been extremely weak, especially given where the cabin is located. I think maybe that's why it took them so long to find you."

"So what now?"

"I'll let the other guys know, and we'll reassemble while you calm your woman down. I'm sure she's a wreck over the news."

"Yeah, shock is more like it right now."

"You know, since we did want to draw them out, knowing what we know now...well, it can give us the upper hand. We'll just have to be more vigilant, because once you step out into the streets, it's fair game. I can only imagine this will unfold very quickly." He pauses for a brief moment, saying something in the background to Stryker before he returns to me. "This does put her at more at risk, you know. Are you willing to expose her like that?" A deep sigh escapes me as I close my eyes and think for a long moment. "Travis?" Quinn prods, trying to get me to respond.

"I'm here," I reluctantly reply. I force myself to come to a hard and fast decision, one that will put Jules back in the line of fire, but it's the only way. "Let's do this," I say with resolve. Quinn and I talk for a few more minutes, working out a few semantics. Some of what we say is in code, so Jules can't decipher all of the conversation, and by the time I hang up, her face has drained of color.

She pulls her hand out of mine and stands up, clutching her robe tightly around her body for false security. She stutters in dazed shock, "I've got something in me?" Her voice escalates in panic, and all I can do is give her a quick nod.

"Oh, God!" She goes weak in the knees, and her legs lose control as she slinks to the floor with a stunned look on her face.

Rushing to her side, I kneel down on the floor in front of her and cup her cheeks with both of my hands. *My poor Jules.* I lean forward and slow my speech, wanting her to comprehend my every syllable. "I need you to listen to me, and pay close attention to my words." The pleading in my voice matches the desperation in my eyes. "I need you to trust me, Jules. I've got you," I implore. I don't know what else to say to convince her of this. I've already shown her that I'd take a bullet for her, and I'd do it again without hesitation.

She breathes short, tight breaths, indicating the beginnings of a panic attack, and if I don't find a way to calm her down, she'll be on the brink of having a full-blown meltdown within seconds. I rest my forehead against hers, and softly assure her, "Baby, to the best of my ability, I'm not going to let anything bad happen to you. They will have to pry you from my dead fingers if that has to be the case."

I lightly kiss her lips and whisper, "I'm here, baby. I'm not going to leave your side for a split second. The guys and I have put a game plan into motion, and you need to calm down so we can go over it together. I need your head on straight."

Taking her by both hands, they tremble in my hold as I carefully lift her to her feet.

I guide her to the edge of the bed and have her sit down as I squat in front of her. Poor thing looks like a zombie coming off crack cocaine. A tear slips from the corner of her eye, and my chest constricts from the sight of her distress.

I don't know how to calm her frayed nerves, and I have to be careful how I approach the sensitive subject of the man chase at hand, but I can't sugarcoat the severity of what's going on either. Shit's getting ready to hit the fan at warp speed, and there is no hiding that fact.

Speaking in a gentle, yet serious tone, I tell her, "Jules, I need you to listen to me, and do everything I'm fixin' to tell you to do. I have protective gear here, and both of us are going to wear it, okay?" She squeezes her eyes tightly, which forces two more tears to leak out the sides of her eyes. She takes in a deep, shaky breath while making the most God-awful face, as if she's in pain.

"Shit, baby," I quickly explain, "I never wanted you to be in harm's way. I promise. I knew the cost when I took you, and to be honest, I expected this shit storm, but I thought I could at least tuck you away somewhere safe while I dealt with the repercussions."

"Travis, get it out of me." Her voice quivers as it pitches to a high note as she pleads, "Please, I don't care if you have to use a pocket knife; just get it out of me." Her hands ball into tight fists, expressing her extreme anxiety.

"Unfortunately, now is not the time," I state calmly as I shake my head. "We have a window of opportunity to gain the upper-hand on these guys, and catch them off guard."

"No...no...no..." she chants, not understanding what I'm trying to say.

"Listen to me," I urge, cradling her face in my hands. "If they suspect we know nothing and we act oblivious to the tracker, they will think they're still in control. In fact, the more natural we act, the better. I guarantee you they've already located us, sweetheart, and it's simply too late in the game to change what we're doing."

A visible shiver rolls over her entire body, and I pull her into my arms. All of her extremities tremor with fear. I kiss the top of her head as I whisper over her, "Please believe me. It guts me to have to drag you into this. I will guard you with my life." I pull back and search her misty eyes. "Do you believe me...that I would protect you with my very life?"

I wipe away a stray tear with my thumb, her lips quivering as she replies softly, "I do believe you, Travis."

I close my eyes and savor her words. I lay my head against

her chest, pulling her into me for a tight embrace. I inhale the sweet scent of Jules into my lungs, wanting to commit everything about her to memory should this day go awry. Her trembling fingers thread through my hair as she holds me in the comfort of her bosom.

Her voice softly drifts over my head. "I'm really scared, Travis, and I don't know why, but a large part of me believes you are really trying to protect me." Her voice cracks as if she's in agony, and her fingers tighten in my hair. "I'm running on blind faith here. You can't even begin to imagine how hard this is for me. I didn't see so many things coming at me—from the kidnapping, to the car wreck, and then the invasion. The element of surprise has always been against me. I've been blindsided at every turn, and quite frankly, I'm tired of life taking *me* by the horns."

I lift my head from her chest and look into her eyes with all seriousness. "It's too dangerous for you to know anything," I stress emphatically. "You don't understand; you already know too much as it is. I can't...you can't...afford to know any more than you already do if they capture you."

"Travis, I'm already as good as dead."

My eyes bolt open wide. "No, baby, they want you alive. It's me they want dead. What you need to understand is you will pay the price for being with me. A *big* price."

"But *you* took *me*, Travis."

"That simple fact doesn't matter to them." If Nick were to get her again, she has no idea what her life would be like post-capture, and I'm on edge just thinking about it. I pray I'm wrong, but I'd fear he'd torture her, trying to extrapolate information out of her, especially if she didn't satisfy his curiosity.

"When this is over—" she starts off, but I interrupt.

"When this is over, I will tell you whatever you want to know, and some things you'll wish you never knew...if that's what you want."

"I'm just sick of being in the dark and thrown in harm's way at every turn. This is just too much."

I cup her cheeks and search her eyes. "Sweetheart, this is the last thing on Earth I want to do; believe me. They are tracking you, and they will always be tracking you, unless we put an end to it. Right now, we have serious backup. I have better protection on you than the Pope, and I promise not to leave your side for a single second. Don't you want to put an end to this chase? Put an end to the people who are after you once and for all?"

She closes her eyes and remains silent for a moment, thinking about everything I just said. "What do you want me to do then?" she asks in a voice of resignation.

"Your job is to stay within inches of me at all times. It'd be nice if you were to hang all over me too," I say with a sheepish grin. "Maybe even act like we're in love. That's all I need you to focus on. I'll handle the rest."

With her eyes downcast at the floor, she knots her hands in her lap, and mumbles, "Yes, well, that won't be so hard to do."

"What did you just say?" I ask with incredulity lining my voice as my heart hammers in my chest. I lift her chin to search her eyes for the truth. "Say it again," I softly demand.

Her eyes are rimmed in red as she stares at me dead-on, full of genuineness. "I think I *had* fallen in love with you, Travis, and I don't know whether or not it's a Stockholm thing, or if I've truly lost my mind." A couple tears of frustration spill over her cheeks as she hoarsely whispers, "How can I love and hate someone so much, all at the same time?"

"Oh, baby." I lean in and give her a gentle kiss on the lips. "I don't like to hear the past tense of *had fallen in love*, but soon, real soon, I plan on hearing nothing but the present tense. You can't hate me, Jules; you just can't. I'm not the enemy here," I whisper the last words on a plea.

"I don't know anything anymore, Travis." She sounds so downhearted and unsure of herself. I pray to God she can find it in her heart to forgive me, and truly love me one day.

"Soon, I promise you...very soon, there will be no more lies." I look at the stone in her necklace, which glistens in the morning light. As much as I want to, I can't tell her this necklace is her lifeline should our plans go south and she gets captured. I need this secret to be mine, because hell if I know where her head is right now. She's been through too much for me to be able to predict her thoughts and next moves anymore. Shit, for all I know, if she knew what was in this necklace, she could decide to ditch the medallion and take off to God knows where. Of course Nick would be the one to find her then, since he's on the other end of the GPS tracker in her hip.

These bastards need to be dealt with now while the chase is hot; otherwise, I'd take the damn tracker out myself this very minute. The device will be like drawing bees to honey, and as soon as they expose themselves, my men and I will take them out. I'm certain Jules will survive the war. It's surviving the aftermath I'm concerned about.

CHAPTER 7

~Jules~

"Relax, baby," Travis nonchalantly says, as if there's not a team of killers tracking us down, ready to pop out in front of us at any moment.

"That's easy for you to say. Not only are you a very skilled marksman, you're also used to this type of villainous lifestyle." I'm not being a smart ass. My nerves are wrecked, and he makes walking the plank look so easy.

He arches one of his brows as a half-grin easily spreads across his lips. "You're not doing so bad surviving in this lifestyle yourself. Now, do you want to start smiling, or do I need to kiss you stupid again so you can start relaxing?" he asks, then he glances to his left, noticing an alleyway. "Mmm...I wonder how many kisses it will take before you'll be willing to have me right in this alley." He looks at me out of the corner of his eye, wearing a cocky smirk.

Immediately, I blush and look the other way. A deep chuckle escapes him, and I just want to smack him for being so relaxed and carefree right now. Apparently, my non-answer is unacceptable, because when I don't respond fast enough for his liking, he makes a move. I squeal and lose sight of the sidewalk beneath my feet as he wraps his arms around my body, lifts me up off the ground, and then twirls me around.

"Travis, put me down," I giggle. The man must have a death wish. How can he look at the perils of danger and laugh in its face? He couldn't be any more unaffected by what lays around the corner. "Stop. This is not the time for playing."

He stops spinning me and slowly lets me slide down the front of his hard body as he palms the globes of my ass. I inhale a sharp breath. *He's such a bad boy. He knows exactly how to affect me.* He holds me tightly against his chest, and his eyes begin to smolder as if he's actually considering us doing it in the alleyway. He grinds his hips into me and I lose my breath. This is seriously considered indecent PDA, but somehow, he makes me not care.

He nips at my lower lip, and then huskily whispers, "I'm serious. It's either the alley, or relax." How does he do this? He's acting all horny, but able to stay all-business at the same time. He has me in a tizzy, and my panties are soaked. I wrap my hand around the back of his neck as I stand on my tiptoes so I can pull him down to kiss my lips. Oh, damn, his lips are magic, and his tongue sends butterflies flying low in my belly. The alleyway doesn't look so bad at the moment.

"How do you do this? How can you act so normal?" I whisper over his lips.

He looks down at me and gives me a cocky grin. "They don't call me Stonewall Jackson for nothing, babe."

"That's for dang sure. You couldn't have been born with a better name. It suits you perfectly." I pull away from him, and he wraps his arm around my shoulders, pulling me into his side. "At least tell me you've got nervous energy rolling through you on the inside."

"I wouldn't be human if I didn't, but I only have nervous energy for your safety, not over mine," he states seriously. He coaxes our bodies forward, and we begin walking again along the downtown streets of Raleigh. It's fairly busy for midmorning, and thankfully, it's not obnoxiously humid today.

I lean into the side of his muscled body, and he gives my shoulders a loving squeeze. This feels all too comfortable, familiar, and natural. Travis exudes a certain confidence, and it shows with every step he takes.

He looks down at me through those thick dark lashes and regards me with those sparkly green eyes. "Better?" He smiles, placing a chaste kiss on my temple. I nervously smile and slip my arm around his waist. "That's my girl. It's all going to play out fine; you'll see," he tries to reassure me.

I steal a deep breath for courage, inhaling his manly scent, and snuggle my cheek into the side of his chest. I close my eyes for a moment and soak him in, pretending none of this chaos exists. I actually ponder what it'd be like if we were actually a normal couple just going for a walk in the city on a beautiful day.

I'm sure right now, with both of us having a relaxed demeanor as we walk snuggled against each other like two lovebirds, no one would even suspect we are on the run from a bunch of kidnappers and killers. However, the stiffness of the bulletproof vest that rests against my cheek tells me otherwise. I'm thankful for the protection and for the foresight of Travis and his men to have these vests, because I feel so open and exposed being out here in broad daylight like this. I just hope if we do get shot at, it won't be in the head. What a terrible thought. A cold chill runs down my spine just thinking about it, and I cling a little tighter to Travis.

Our pace slows, and before I know it, Travis has steered us into a small cafe off the main street. I lift my head off his chest and look around, wondering what we're doing in here.

"Thought you'd enjoy a little restaurant cuisine for a change," he answers my unasked question. Then, he leans down and whispers in my ear, "Don't worry; they have gluten-free options here. I already checked it out." He pulls back and a smirk is plastered across those sexy lips of his like he's proud of himself.

Travis lets go of me, places his hand on the small of my back in a protective gesture, and guides me to a booth.

"How did you know what I was thinking?" I ask indignantly.

He chuckles at me. "Jules, I've spent the better part of a month with you, in which the last of those two weeks we've been inseparable. I know how to read people, and most especially, I know how you operate," he says as he taps the tip of my nose with his index finger.

I huff and slide into the booth while Travis snickers to himself, taking the seat across from me. "So, what are we doing here?"

"We're eating an early lunch. I believe they call it brunch," he says in a tone as if I should know.

"Well, duh. You know what I mean." I give him a stern look, but before I can dig an answer out of him, a waitress appears at our booth.

She doesn't even look my way as she asks Travis all sultry-like, "How can I help you?" *Seriously?* I wish I had on spiked high heels right now, because I'd use them to jab her in the eye. She really needs to wear a bib to catch her drool. My eyes narrow as I grow irritated, feeling an edge of jealousy coming on. I guess I haven't ever been with Travis in public to see what other women's reactions would be over his good looks and pretty-boy smile.

"Sweetheart?" Travis softly says, catching my attention while he slips his hands underneath mine. He lifts my hand with the engagement ring on it to his lips and presses a soft kiss to the back of my hand while his eyes gleam. He knows exactly what I'm thinking. *Jerk.* "Would you like something to drink?" he asks me, ignoring the waitress.

"We will both have a sweet tea, please," I sing in a love-struck voice, looking directly at Travis as he holds my stare. When she's gone, Travis arches his brow in reply to my power play, looking somewhat surprised that I've staked a claim on him. I'm somewhat surprised myself. He looks down and gazes at the ring, then gently begins rolling his thumb over the top of the sparkly diamond in quiet contemplation. The way he's possessively fondling the engagement ring on my finger sends a warm, fuzzy feeling through me, and the way he's staring at it in silence speaks volumes.

He breaks through the silence, murmuring in a low, husky voice, "You wear this well." He lifts his chin, meeting my eyes with determined resoluteness. "You will say yes. It might not be today, but you will say yes." His words make my belly flip, and he lightly squeezes my hand as if he's sealing the deal.

The silence lays heavy between us for a minute, and then he blinks his eyes, shaking his head as if he was caught in a daydream. His eyes quickly glance toward the restaurant door, and immediately, all the anxiety that lay dormant reawakens. I sit up straight, on edge, not knowing what he sees behind me. "Just relax. I've got you," he says as he softly smiles, trying to reassure me. "Nothing is going on. I just got lost for a moment." My shoulders slump in relief. "This is what you do to me, Jules. I sometimes can't think straight when I'm around you," he confesses. *Yeah, well I feel the same way.*

Nonchalantly, I scan the interior of the cafe and notice very few patrons fill the tables. I suppose it's because the lunch hour rush hasn't hit yet. Travis squeezes my hand, garnering my attention. When I look at him, he's looking at me as if he wants to tell me he loves me. I can see it in his eyes. It takes my breath away. I've seen this look before a few times, actually hoping he'd say it, but that was before. Now that I have my memory back, I remember all the lies. My heart squeezes in pain, and I need a little air to get myself back under control.

I'm not ready to hear those three little words, if that's what he's trying to tell me right now. There's simply too much chaos swirling around in my head to add another complication to whatever this is between us. Before he has a chance to say anything, I need to leave. "Travis, I'd like to use the restroom. Is that okay?" His lips thin, and he looks disappointed. The moment is lost. I can tell he's not happy, but he lets go of my hands, setting me free with a small sigh.

I quickly look around for the restroom signs, spot them, and slip out of the booth. My heart pounds in my chest with each step I take toward the bathroom. I take my sweet time in the bathroom, stalling, trying to calm my frayed nerves. Now is not the time to think about conflicting feelings and emotions over a man. I have much bigger problems to contend with than being analytical over something so shallow.

Dammit, Jules, pull yourself together. I've never been one of those wishy-washy women who let their emotions yo-yo over a man, yet it appears that way now. I have to focus on the matter at hand, which is staying alive. I'm sure a good five minutes have gone by, and I don't need Travis making a scene by busting into the ladies' room; I can see it now. I stifle a giggle. I'm sure there's not a woman on God's green Earth who wouldn't mind him tromping into the ladies' room.

I step through the bathroom door and run face-first into a solid wall of muscle, also known as Travis. He's like hitting a brick wall at top speed, and I bounce right off him. Instinctively, I grab onto both sides of his waist to keep from rebounding and falling flat on my ass. The muscles in his body are tense, and I find it odd he doesn't even turn around to see if I'm okay. Not acknowledging the fact it could be anyone who's just rammed into the backside of him, my forehead wrinkles in confusion. I lean around his waist to get a look at his face. "Travis, what's—" I stop mid-sentence, stunned frozen at the sight before me.

"Ahh, there she is—the lady of the hour," a tall brooding man sneers at me with dark menacing eyes. "You've certainly sent us on a wild goose chase, young lady." Chills of terror race through my veins. "Step away, and there won't be any problems," the man says with a contemptible smirk on his face. Scanning the length of him, I notice he has a gun pressing against Travis' ribcage, and I lose my breath.

I shake my head over and over again, my hands tightly clinging to the fabric of Travis' shirt. "No?" He shrugs. "Suit yourself. I don't have a problem shooting your lover right here where he stands."

"If you shoot, the bullet will go right through him and hit me. Is that how Nick wanted me back?" I reason with a shaky voice.

"Who said anything about shooting him in the gut. I have about ten different places I can shoot him within the blink of an eye and still miss you by a foot."

All the blood rushes from my head, making me feel dizzy. I have to do something other than let the situation control me. I'll be damned if I wind up under Nick again, let alone have this man hurt Travis.

Keeping my eyes pinned on the evil man, I slowly slide my right hand from Travis' hip until I feel the cool metal of his gun holstered at the small of his back in the waistband of his jeans. I gesture with a nod, indicating I will cooperate, playing his game to bide time. "Okay, but if I agree, you won't hurt Travis, will you?"

"I won't hurt him, unless he tries something foolish," he says with a raised brow as he glances at Travis. "Of course, once Nick gets ahold of him, I can't promise anything."

Ever so carefully, I wrap my hand around the metal grip

and slip the gun out. Since Travis is so wide and broad, there is no way this man would be able to tell what I'm about to do.

I slowly take one cautious step to the left of Travis, and the man speaks up, startling me. "That's it, Princess, nice and slow. I wouldn't want to hurt your lover-boy here."

I'm supposed to have no qualms when it comes to eliminating the enemy. That's what Travis and Stryker drilled into me. *It's either kill or be killed,* they told me. It's a lie, however; it's simply a coping mechanism. It's just not that simple. I will never be able to forget what I've already done, or what I'm about to do.

I take my second step around Travis with his gun on the ready, but before I can do anything, the man's eyes go wide and I watch in horror as he falls to the floor grabbing his right shoulder, crying out in pain. Blood spills from his arm like someone just struck oil. My hand covers my mouth reflexively as desperate terror overtakes me. My shaking hand lets go of the gun as it slips out of my grip, dropping to the floor. Travis dives over the man, pinning him down as he makes a grab for his gun. My chest is pounding with panic, and as I glance into the dining area, there are more men running our way with their weapons drawn. Without making a conscious decision, my feet take flight and I run the opposite way. Travis must have handpicked this restaurant with good reason, because there's a back entrance. Leave it to him to think of all the angles.

I push the bar inward on the steel door and break free, leaving the mayhem behind. I run like I've never ran before. I don't know where the hell I'm going, but once I can hide myself, I'll figure it out. I make it half a block before I hear heavy footsteps running up behind me. I don't look back as an adrenaline-fueled surge of panic kicks in and I pick up speed, but it's not enough.

Thick, large arms wrap around my upper body, and suddenly I'm being tackled like a linebacker. I squeeze my eyes shut, preparing for the inevitable crash against the asphalt, but it never comes. Whoever has tackled me twisted our bodies together in such a way that he takes the brunt of the fall on his back with me on top. I let out an ear-piercing scream, and I begin to buck and thrash with everything I have. Hysteria is all I feel as I try to break free.

"Jules! Calm the fuck down!" the man's voice bellows behind me. "It's me, Quinn!" he yells. My chest rises and falls as I gasp for air, my lungs burning from lack of oxygen. The crazy situation I've just lived through is too much for me to handle. My body begins to tremble, my mind becoming a scrambled mess as Quinn keeps a death grip on me. There's no digesting this. *This isn't happening.* I have the sudden urge to vomit, and I feel hot and clammy all over. Without warning, everything goes black.

I hear a deep voice fading in and out, sounding upset. "She's in shock."

"I know what the fuck she is, Stryker. I'm handling it," Travis' voice hisses over my head. I blink a few times and realize I'm being held in his arms. *Did I pass out?* As my eyes come into focus, I'm met with Travis' broad chest. I wearily lift my head up, and immediately, I'm met with stark green eyes filled with concern as he searches my face. His voice aches with pain as he asks, "Baby, are you okay?"

"No," I whisper despondently, not recognizing my own voice.

"Travis," Stryker warns, "we should've had this done by now." My brows furrow together. I've never heard Stryker use that tone with Travis before. *What's going on?*

"Fine, but I'm not leaving her side for a second," he mutters at Stryker, even though he's still holding my gaze. His lips press together in a hard line, apparently not happy about something. "Jules, we've gotta get that implant out of your hip now," he explains. "I'm sorry. I know you're out of sorts, but we have to do this, and do it quickly." *Out of sorts? What does he mean?* The confusion must be written all over my face, because he asks, "You don't remember anything, do you?"

I shake my head slowly, and then flick my gaze behind Travis, noticing we're in the back of a huge van. "Baby, you passed out after—"

"Now's not the time, Travis," Stryker interrupts with impatience. Travis flashes him a quick and dirty look. He carefully lifts me off his lap and lays me down on the floor of the van.

"What's going on?" I surprise myself by being highly

compliant, and not being the least bit interested in getting up off the floor, all while demanding answers.

Stryker comes into view and squats in front of me while he snaps on a pair of surgical gloves. "Jules, we need to get this tracker out of your hip, STAT." I tense at his terseness. He moves with quick efficiency, and then a big medical bag comes into view. Travis must feel me tensing, because he immediately lowers himself onto the floor and spoons me from behind. He slips his arm underneath my head, which acts as a pillow, and then rests his weight on his forearm as he peers over me.

He places his lips on the outer shell of my ear, giving me a light kiss. "It's okay, sweetheart. I've got you," he whispers, and I find myself relaxing at his words. Travis has always had my back from the beginning; he's proven it time and again. "Don't mind Stryker." He explains, "When he pulls out the medical bag, he gets in his zone. He's all work and no play." He pauses to look at Stryker, and then teases him, "It makes him look kinda sexy, don't you think?"

"Don't fuck with me right now, Trav," Stryker fires back, irritated as he concentrates on filling up a needled syringe. *Another needle and more drugs?* My eyes go wide. *Okay, now they've got my attention.* No longer feeling safe in Travis' arms, I begin to struggle, wanting to get up.

"Jules, dammit, hold still." Travis wraps his large thigh around my legs while his free hand wraps around my arms, trapping me tightly against his chest. I start to panic, my heart thundering in my chest. I'm feeling claustrophobic.

"Baby, relax. It's just local anesthesia. I promise, no drugs," he quickly reassures me. Then Stryker places his hand on my thigh and squeezes just enough to get my attention. My eyes are wide with anxiety as I look at him. His expression softens significantly as he finally realizes I'm not one of his hardcore men. He makes an effort to speak in a calmer voice. "Please...we're only trying to keep everyone here alive. I promise I will have this out quick, okay? I'm not going to hurt you."

My mouth suddenly turns dry, and I swallow hard. "Okay," I say with a shaky breath.

Stryker blows out a gust of air I didn't realize he was holding, and then he pats the side of my leg in a reassuring gesture. Travis relaxes his hold on me too, and I sink back into the comfort of his chest. "That's my girl. It's going to be okay," he whispers as he lets go of my arms, and begins to stroke my cheek with the back of his knuckles using a soft, feather-light touch.

I turn to look at Travis, whose eyes look almost sorrowful. "Where are the other guys?"

"They're surrounding the van, making sure we're protected while we do this."

Stryker unbuttons my jeans and pulls them down past my hips, and Travis growls.

"Whoa there, caveman," Stryker says, holding up his hands. "That's as far as I need to go. Just hold her underwear off her hip, and we're good."

"Damn straight that's as far as you go," Travis barks back in a predatory tone.

I take in a deep breath, slowly exhale, and then close my eyes. I *so* do not want to see this.

CHAPTER 8

~Nick~

"Why does it seem as if you're on a wild fucking goose chase?" I ask Justin, irritated.

"That's because we kind of are," he responds with frustration lining his voice. I sent him and a few more of my men into Raleigh after the fiasco ensued at Travis' cabin. I was down three men and pissed off beyond measure.

"Mind cluing me in?"

I hear the urgency in his voice as he ignores me, and half-yells at the driver, "Turn left! Turn left!"

"Justin, what the hell is going on?"

"Sorry, I'm a little preoccupied at the moment. We had a spray of bullets, some mass confusion, and now it appears we're chasing them down in a truck." His voice is wrought with tension and stress.

"What?"

"Look, Nick, I have to hang up. I'll call you back in a few." The phone disconnects, and I sit here stunned for a second, not believing he actually hung up on me.

The anxiety grows thick in my chest, as the chase has yet to end. I stand up and stretch, needing to rid my body of this nervous tension. I've been at this damn computer all morning, watching my monitor and tracking Julianna's whereabouts. Things were going pretty smoothly up until five minutes ago, and then it looked as if all hell broke loose.

Since my nerves are damn near shot, I decide I need a break to stretch my legs and let my men handle this. I take a walk down the different hallways of the facility, stretching my tension-filled legs while trying to clear my mind.

I have to let these men do the job I've hired them to do, but a large part of me can't help but think I need to be there physically. The team here at the facility felt it was too dangerous for me to step into the line of fire, and the program has already suffered from Travis leaving us. *The bastard.*

Travis' words echo in my mind. *You know, a real man would've come after his woman, but instead, you sent a team of dysfunctional dumbasses. What does that say about you, Nick?* I clench my fists with the need to punch something. I'm used to being the one in the fray of chaos, controlling and dictating orders. I pray to God this group of men is sufficient for the task at hand.

Just as I round a corner, I hear a scuffle behind one of the doors. I pause in front of the door to listen. It's room five. Shouting ensues, and my forehead wrinkles with growing curiosity. I hear another struggle, and I figure whatever is going on, it isn't good. I wave my hand over the sensor, and the door clicks open.

One of my new men is struggling to contain my female captive, Tara, the one who had it out for Julianna since the beginning. "That's enough," I sharply bellow. Both of them stop in their tracks and look at me in surprise and a little fear.

"I can explain," he says, breathing heavy with exertion.

I raise my brows at the new trainer. "I just bet you can." He doesn't need to explain. Since Travis has been gone, we lack having someone with his charisma. I thought his job was a cakewalk until he left. I couldn't believe all the shit he handled while keeping the peace.

I turn to Tara and eye her up and down, taking note of her disheveled appearance. "You can leave us," I tell the new trainer, not even bothering to remember his name.

He quickly leaves without a word, and not sure of what my mood is, Tara cautiously steps forward. "It feels as if I haven't seen or had you in weeks," she purrs with a pouty lower lip as she runs her long, manicured fingernail down the front of my chest. "I've missed you, Nick." I suppose she thinks the look is sexy on her, and maybe at one time I thought it was cute, but it's not any longer. I stop her hand from traveling farther south by grabbing tightly onto her wrist.

"Don't." I clench my jaw, feeling somewhat disgusted by her touch.

"Why? I don't understand," she asks confused, and if I'm not mistaken, she looks a little hurt. I used to get hard at the thought of tying her up. Now...now, the thought repulses me. Looking at her now, I don't know what I ever saw in her to begin with, with any of these women, for that matter, other than they might have filled a void for a time until I could have

Julianna.

"It's her, isn't it?" she asks in a snarly tone. "I've been yours for the better part of a year, and this...this is how you treat me?" She yanks her hand away from my hold and backs up a step, shaking her head in disbelief. "We have something, Nick," she then pleads.

"No, we never had anything. It was never permanent. You knew this. You've been promised to Rick Meyers after I'm done with you."

"You don't mean that," she softly whispers. "You can't let me go...you just can't."

"Sometimes, when we want something we don't have, it isn't everything we imagined it to be once we get it, but that wasn't the case with Jules. She is everything and more, and now that I've had a taste of her, there is no comparison, and I'm hungry for more."

She steps forward and raises her hand to slap me. I stop her by twisting her arm around behind her back, making her spin around. I lean in over her shoulder and growl into her ear, "That was a bad move on your part."

"You arrogant bastard," she hisses.

"I'd watch what you say," I calmly state. I let go of her, and at the same time, give her a slight push forward. She winds up losing her balance and falls to the floor. Unfazed by her cry of pain, whether mental or physical, I don't care. "I will deal with you later." With that statement, I turn around and leave her to herself. I have better things to be doing right now, and that is getting back to the man-chase at hand.

As the door closes behind me, I hear her let out an

anguished cry of distress, and I shake my head. She's tried to tell me she loves me on many occasions, but I wouldn't let her. I never led her on, but I guess she thought she could sway me.

One would think I had a fucked-up childhood to be this way, or to be in this sort of business, but I didn't. I had a normal childhood with normal parents.

I have found over time that there is no rhyme or reason as to what makes someone turn out for the better or the worse. I've always wanted to be king of a mountain, an entrepreneur, and on the leading edge of something big, so here I am. I've accomplished every task I've set out to do. Anything I've ever wanted, I've been able to succeed and then some.

Somewhere along the way, however, I found myself getting sidetracked, obsessed with a young woman. I never saw myself getting into this predicament with my emotions, but there you have it. Julianna owns me.

I walk into my office to see Jared sitting in one of my overstuffed chairs, reading a stack of lab reports.

"Hey," he greets, not looking up from his papers. "Thought your hands were magnetized to your keyboard. Things must be going well."

"I don't know how things are going yet. Last I heard, they were in a chase." Jared lets out a low whistle, and before he opens his mouth, I shut him down. "I don't need to hear your shit either."

"I wasn't going to say anything. I'm just damn glad you aren't destroying your office right now."

As I sit down at my desk, I reply, "I've known you too long. Every time you let out a low, long whistle, your mouth then becomes engaged with words." I key in a few numbers and pull up the tracking software program to see where my men are in the scheme of things. The small blinking light illuminates on the screen, and I feel a slight relief course through my body. As I watch the screen with intensity, one minute later, the light fades out.

"Fuck!" I blurt out, and then tap my fingers on the side of the computer screen, thinking it needs a little prompting to redisplay the little light I've been watching all day.

"What's wrong?" Jared asks, looking up from his paperwork.

"I don't know," I say with irritation, and tap a little harder this time, as the computer didn't seem to get my message. Still, no luck. "What the hell?"

Curious, Jared gets up from his chair and comes over to stand behind me. Peering over my shoulder, he leans in and clears his throat. "I don't have a good feeling about this."

"Yeah, me neither." I refresh the browser, and nothing changes. "She was all over the damn radar for the last hour, and now there's nothing." I clench my jaw in growing frustration, and then pick up my phone, getting ready to dial one of my men. My cellphone rings at that very moment, so I hang up the phone's receiver and grab my cell. It's Justin.

"What's the news?" I gruffly ask.

"I've got some bad news, boss," Justin says with hesitation, and my gut twists with dread. I stay silent for a moment, letting his words sink in.

"Looks as if they discovered the tracking device in her hip, and then removed it. After chasing down and scaring the shit out of a Coca-Cola truck driver, we searched his truck from top to bottom. Found your device pinned underneath the bumper."

There is nothing for me to say. I'm speechless. With my hands beginning to shake, I disconnect the phone call. I close my eyes as my stomach drops to the floor, and a wave of nausea washes over me.

I run my hand over my face in a show of loss and frustration, and lean back in my chair with an untold amount of tension vibrating through my veins.

"What's the verdict?" Jared asks concerned, still standing beside me.

"I've lost her, Jared. I've fucking lost her." My voice is empty and devoid of emotion as I stare up at the ceiling and shake my head in disbelief. I can't even describe the mixture of anger and loss I feel. It's causing me to have this massive pain in my chest that won't go away.

I reach out to grab my computer monitor with both hands, having every intention of smashing it to smithereens, but Jared stops me. He quickly puts his own hands on my monitor, and reassures me with conviction, "She will resurface. She has to."

"I know better. With Travis in charge, he's too smart and cunning to let her resurface. They're headed underground. I can feel it."

Jared leans down, placing his elbows on my desk, and looks at me through those thick glasses of his. "Travis may want to take her into hiding, but as we both know, if Jules doesn't want to do something, she's going to find a way around it. I have a very hard time believing she would willingly go with him and leave everything she's ever known behind. You know as well as

I do that when she gets something in her mind, she can be a hot one to handle. She's like a dog with a bone." I rub the scruff on my jawline, contemplating Jared's words. "And the man is going to run out of Blyss, if he hasn't already. That sure as heck won't help his cause."

"You may be right." But then again, he might be wrong. At this point, what choice do I have, but to keep my ear to the ground and wait?

"Do you want me to call Lance?" Jared offers.

I shake my head. "I'll let him know."

The new trainer steps into my office. "Sir, we're having trouble in room five."

"Again?" I ask, put off by the insipid intrusion.

"Sorry, sir. I didn't mean to interrupt."

"I'm not running a half-assed operation here. You either need to start learning how to handle this shit, or I need to get someone in here who knows what the fuck they're doing, and can make things start happening yesterday. Am I clear?"

"Yes, sir. Very clear." He turns on his heel and quickly leaves out my door.

This shit is not going to crumble around me, dammit. I've worked too long and hard to get this far in the game. The amount of scientific knowledge and technological security we had to put in place in the very beginning was astronomical, and I'll be damned if I let this multi-billion dollar opportunity begin to falter, all because I don't have God's gift to women here in the facility—Travis, the bastard. I have no one qualified or charismatic enough to work these women the way he did. The motherfucker. Since he's been gone, I haven't been able to replace him. Everyone is supposed to be replaceable.

I'm trying to keep a cool head and not lose my shit like last time, but it's damn hard. All I can think about is him fucking her, and I want to destroy something. Knowing how much she loves her father and Jake, I hope Jared is right. He's pretty sharp at reading people and understanding the human psyche. I have to hang on to that little bit of hope that she will surface at some point.

"I'm going to need a stiff drink, Jared."

CHAPTER 9

~Jules~

I rest my cheek against Travis' shoulder as he holds me in his lap like a child. He spreads open his legs on the bench seat of the van, and my butt slinks down onto to the soft leather cushion. I'm at the perfect height to rest my ear against his chest, and with the bulletproof vests removed, I can now hear the steady rhythm of his heart. I close my eyes, enjoying the safety of his strong arms. I'm totally spent, too tired to even ask where we're all headed.

Once the implant was taken out of my hip, Stryker immediately passed it off to Quinn, who apparently stood guard right outside of the van doors. I didn't ask what he did with it; all I could assume is that he smashed it to smithereens. Then, Stryker had to put a couple small stitches in before he bandaged me up.

All of us have been in the van for the better part of an hour now, and everyone has been quiet except for a few one-sentence comments here and there. I can assume the men don't want to say too much of anything in front of me. Either that, or they're coming off an adrenaline high and are now dealing with the aftershocks. I'm not sure who took down the man who held Travis at gunpoint, nor do I dare ask right now. Either way, it's just another nightmare for me to live with. Those images are permanently etched into my mind, and I'm not sure I'll ever be able to forget them. I snuggle farther into his broad chest, inhaling his familiar scent, trying to seek comfort for my troubled soul.

Travis slowly skates his fingertips along the length of my arm, leaving goose bumps in their wake, and then gently interlaces his fingers with mine. My belly dips in response to his light touch. I lift my chin to look at him with questioning eyes. He understands I want to whisper something to him, so he leans down and tilts his ear to my lips. "Is it all over now? Are all the bad guys gone?" He pulls away, and rests his head against the seat. A quick flash of remorse flits across his eyes before he closes his lids and softly sighs.

"No...not really, baby," he whispers back. "But they can't track us now. We're one up on them." I lay my head back down against his broad chest, and I simply want to cry. I'm so wrought with tension, and at the same time, I'm an emotional wreck. Will this never end? Am I going to have to live on the run for the rest of my life?

"Hey now." He lets go of my hand, his forefingers lifting my chin, forcing me to meet his gaze. "Don't overthink it. We're sitting pretty right now. They're not going to be able to find us, and as long as I have anything to do with it, that will be the case forever."

Forever? "Forever is a long time, Travis. Just what is that supposed to entail?" I whisper back nervously. I don't think I'm understanding the implications or magnitude of his statement.

He shakes his head and whispers in my ear, "Right now is not the time to discuss this."

I bite my lip in nervous frustration. I'm sure if we did talk about it now in front of his men, the conversation could only escalate into a major blowout, because let's face it—I can have an attitude sometimes. I have a feeling he placated me at the hotel, telling me that eventually I could call home, but somehow I don't see that coming to fruition anytime soon, if ever. *Another lie perhaps?* My thoughts are completely scattered, running from one dilemma to the next, and I can't seem to focus on any one problem at a time.

"Shh, baby," he soothingly whispers. He tries to console me by pressing my ear back over his heartbeat as he holds my head firmly against him. He begins to rock me methodically back and forth while keeping his soft lips pressed to the top of my head, whispering over me, "Shh, I'm going to take care of you. We're going to be all right."

I want to believe Travis so badly. I want to trust that everything is going to be all right. My gut instinct just knows that everything is anything but all right. The stresses of the previous two days have caught up to me, and all too soon, his rocking, tender ministrations, and the steady thrum of the van's engine has my eyes growing heavy. I'm sure with everything I've been through my body is shifting into self-preservation mode. I let my eyes flutter closed and slip into a dreamless sleep in the arms of a man I don't know if he's a good-bad guy, or a bad-bad guy.

"Wake up, baby…" I vaguely hear the words whispered over me. His warm breath fans across my ear as I hear his soothing voice speak again. "Sweetheart, it's time to get up." I don't want to wake up. I grumble unintelligible words as I ignore him and roll to my side, away from him as I pull the covers tightly around my body. He chuckles softly against my cheek before placing a light kiss there.

"C'mon, sleepyhead," he playfully whispers as he nudges me. He's making me grow grumpy. I don't want to get up, so I swat at the air behind me, but miss my target as I will him to go away.

A deep chuckle ensues, and he tears the blanket off my body in one fell swoop. All the warmth and body heat I had going on dissipates immediately. "Seriously?" I grumble irately.

His hand slips underneath my t-shirt as he places his palm on my bare skin below the crease of my breasts. I lose my breath. His touch sends a scorching fire directly to my core.

"It's time to get up, my sleeping beauty," he huskily whispers just before he softly kisses the outer shell of my ear.

"I don't wanna get up," I whine, half asleep.

"Mmm, I know what will wake you," he says as he softly

and strategically places slow and passionate kisses down the length of my neck.

"You're not playing fair," I moan. I know Travis all too well; he's going to win this one. He always wins. I give a yawn as I roll onto my back and stretch my body, placing my arms above my head while arching my back in a much-needed stretch. I know my hard nipples are protruding from the thin fabric of my t-shirt as I not-so-innocently stretch.

A low growl emits from the back of his throat, and I grin. "Talk about not playing fair." He slips a hand underneath my shirt as he cups my breast. My heart beats double-time when his thumb softly brushes across the tip of my nipple. I freeze in my stretching position, allowing him free reign over my body, and close my eyes as I bask in his tender touch. God help me, I want him.

He captures both my wrists with his free hand, and my eyes flutter open. "Travis?"

"Shh, just let me touch you." I know where he's headed with this. I know he can never stop with just one touch, and the smoldering look he's giving me is a dead giveaway. I lose my breath as he rolls my hard nipple between his thumb and forefinger. "You're wet for me already, aren't you?" His deep, husky voice adds to my wetness.

I shift my eyes away from his, blushing, and I notice we're not in a hotel room anymore. We're in somebody's bedroom. "Where are we?"

"We're at Quinn's house."

"Oh? What time is it?" My brows lift as I wonder how long I've been asleep. I don't remember anything. I thought I would've at least stirred awake with Travis having to carry me from the van. He lets out a soft sigh, removes his hand from underneath my shirt, and smooths it out before he leans over me to grab the mini alarm clock.

"It's a little after six. Are you hungry?" he replies. I shrug, not really knowing what I am at the moment. Horny or hungry, either way, it's a win-win.

"A few of the guys pitched in and cooked dinner for everyone." I slant my head to the side, studying him a moment. His hair is damp, he's in a fresh change of clothes, and he smells amazing. "C'mon, it's been a long day, and I think you need to get up and eat a little something."

Reluctantly, I sit up in bed, but apparently, I'm not moving fast enough for Travis, as he takes both my hands, pulls me out of bed, and into his arms. "You'll feel better after you eat a decent dinner, and then you can take a shower."

Travis has me holding his hand as we head downstairs. The loud, boisterous chatter of the other men's voices carries throughout the house. They're all laughing and carrying on in the kitchen, and for some reason, it relaxes me a little bit.

Someone speaks out over the voices, and says, "I don't know about you guys, but I sure as hell could use a sweet place to park my dick right about now."

"Well, Stryker, right there's the freezer," I hear Quinn respond as he begins to chuckle. "I've got a bag of frozen peas to park your dick on this time," he says, and then breaks out in laughter.

I can't help but crack a smile at whatever their inside joke is. Travis brings me to a halt in the hallway, pulling me into his side, and then whispers in my ear, "Shh, I wanna hear this one."

As we stand out of sight, I hear another voice piping in, asking, "I don't believe I've heard this story, Quinn. What crazy shit did Stryker do now?"

"Oh, my God, Chase. I never laughed so hard in my life!" Quinn exclaims.

"Quinn," Stryker warns, but Quinn simply ignores him and continues on.

"So, we had this huge party about a month ago, and Stryker's date of the week was a sexy lil' señorita who decided to make a killer salsa with jalapeño peppers."

"Oh, geez," Stryker complains, "I give up."

"After a couple hours, the party was in full swing, so nobody noticed Stryker had gone missing with his little Mexican beauty." Quinn stops to falsely clear his throat. "Thought he'd slink off for some private salsa dancing lessons." A few chuckles spill from Quinn before he can speak with any clarity.

"I don't think he was gone all that long, though. Low music was going on in the background while everyone was enjoying their own conversations, and out of freaking nowhere I hear this God-awful man-scream. I never thought I could hear a man scream like a woman until that night."

"Fuck off, dude," Stryker says irritability as the others start to chuckle.

"Anyhow, he comes busting out of the downstairs bathroom with his pants down around his ankles, running down the hall like a penguin on crack. Oh, God, that was a sight watching him stumble over himself, bare in all his glory. He made a beeline for the freezer, hollerin' out in a panic the entire time that his dick was on fire. The only thing he could find in the freezer to cool his cojones off was a carton of ice cream." The funny thing is, as animated and hilarious as Stryker is, I can totally picture everything being described.

"By this time, he must've had the attention of about twenty people, who then decided to gather around his naked ass to watch the show. For the life of me, I couldn't figure out what the hell his deal was, and when he stuck his dick into the carton of ice cream, I damn near lost it."

"Holy fuck, man!" Chase remarks as he bursts out with laughter.

"No, that wasn't a *'holy fuck'*," Stryker adds. "It was from the fiery pits of Hell. If I didn't know any better, that woman had hot embers of coal in her mouth," he jokes, but his voice is in serious distress from the graphic memory. All the men howl with laughter as Travis tries very hard to contain himself. His broad shoulders shake as he doubles over in a fit of silent laughter, grabbing his stomach. I cover my mouth, trying to stifle my giggles.

Then Quinn's deep voice booms out over the laughter as his story continues, "Yeah, but that's not all, because of the fact his dick was wet, it stuck to the ice cream. So then he had to hobble over to the kitchen sink, only to realize I didn't have a retractable water faucet." Quinn's laugh becomes so raucous it's almost hard to make out what he's saying as each syllable comes out on a cackle, "So I have to put the poor bastard out of his misery by dousing him with my cold brew, and I swear to

God, I have never seen a dick shrivel to the size of a prune before."

"And, oh, God, was that sweet relief," Stryker emphasizes. Travis can't hold out any longer as he bursts out with laughter. His entire body shakes as he leans on my shoulders, steering me into the kitchen. Everyone's in stitches, their laughter contagious, and for a brief moment, their banter makes me forget my problems.

Eventually, everyone's laughter slowly dissolves one by one, and then Stryker notices me. He clears his throat, giving his chin a quick jerk in my direction, looking somewhat sheepish. "Hope you're hungry. We have a ton of food, but you'll have to fend for yourself here," he says. "We're not used to having a woman at the table."

I meekly smile as Travis guides me by the small of my back toward the table and pulls out a chair for me. All the guys are looking at me in silence. I feel like I'm under a spotlight, and suddenly, I'm uncomfortable.

Chase speaks up, his voice laced with concern as he asks, "How are you feeling?"

I shrug as I softly respond, "I guess as good as can be expected, given the circumstances."

Travis then pulls up a chair right beside me, settling himself before he grabs a large dish of baked chicken and dishes some out onto a plate for me. One by one, the men slowly begin to make small talk as everyone eats.

Awkward doesn't even begin to describe the scene as I sit around the kitchen table with a bunch of hardcore criminals. I don't know if they're all in the same business as Travis or not, but either way, whatever they do, it can't be good. I mean, Quinn alone looks as if he could be the type of man who would handle someone else's *dirty jobs*.

One thing is blatantly obvious, however, and that is these men have each other's backs. They proved that today. How can these guys do what they did today and act so unaffected? I have a feeling I will be haunted for decades by these past two days. My appetite wanes as I think about those horrid, lifeless eyes staring right at me, and I shiver.

CHAPTER 10

The tension in my muscles has loosened, after the long, hot shower I took, and I feel more refreshed. I slip on one of Travis' t-shirts, which comes down to my knees, and notice he's laid out a new toothbrush for me beside the sink. *Thank goodness.* I hate that feeling of fuzz on my teeth.

Once I'm all cleaned up, I step out of the master bath and onto the plush carpet in the bedroom. A laundry basket is sitting on top of the bed. Someone put this in here while I was showering, and just in time too. I need a clean pair of panties. I blush at the thought of one of those men handling my underwear. It's funny how I used to have two closets full of clothing, and now I'm reduced to a couple pairs of jeans, a few t-shirts, and a sundress Quinn found hanging in his closet.

I reach in the basket, grab a shirt, and begin folding the few clothes I own, when the bedroom door opens. I look over my shoulder to see Travis slip into the room. He quietly shuts the door behind him, and then locks it. My heart begins to pound in my ears at the very sight of him, and as he walks toward me,

I can feel the sexual tension rolling off him. No matter how much I want to deny this man, my body overrides my brain every time.

I turn back around and pretend to look busy by continuing to fold. The warmth of his body comes to press against my back, causing my breathing to turn shallow. His muscular arms slip around my waist as he pulls me in tighter, pressing his erection into the cheeks of my ass.

"Mmm...you smell so good," he hums, and then flicks his tongue over my ear. He closes his lips over my lobe, sucking it into his mouth while his hot breath escapes into my ear. "What are you up to?" he murmurs, his ministrations making me shiver and my eyes flutter helplessly closed.

"Just folding some laundry," I try to reply evenly, but fail miserably.

"Sounds as if we need to make some more dirty laundry," he suggests, whispering over my sensitive skin as he kisses and nips his way down to my shoulder.

I swallow hard against my dry mouth, and whisper, "Travis, do you think maybe this isn't a good idea right now?"

"What, making more dirty laundry?" he taunts. He's doing such a good job of turning my body into a bowl of Jell-O. The man knows every underhanded trick in the book when it comes to working my body into submission.

As if they didn't get the memo, my hands still try to function and stay on their mindless task of folding. Hot, open-mouthed kisses rain down on me like April showers, and I go tingly from head to toe. I've lost my dexterity, and sloppily crumple the t-shirt up in my hands.

He notices my dilemma and chuckles, his chest vibrating against my back with that deep sexy laugh, which makes me squeeze my legs together. His hands slide beneath my shirt, and he smoothly glides them underneath the swells of my breasts. Since I have no bra on, his fingertips hone right in on my erect nipples. He begins to gently tug and twist on my hard nubs. A little moan escapes my lips.

His heated desire has turned me inside out, and I drop my head back onto his shoulder, dizzy with lust. He's not wearing any cologne, as usual, but he always emits this dangerous pheromone that makes me lose my sanity. No longer is he stirring a slow burn within me; I feel as if I've stepped into an incinerator. I'm burning up with need, consumed by his flames.

"What's not a good idea, sweetheart?" he huskily whispers. *What was the question?* I think as he breathes hot kisses along my neck while rubbing my nipples in his palms. "Oh, hell, woman. You don't have panties on," he growls.

My core begins to pulsate as he grinds himself against the bare skin of my ass in a slow serenade. He hastily shoves the laundry basket off the bed, and it falls to the floor with a thud. He removes my shirt, and then runs his hands the length of my body in a gentle and slow seductive caress. Goose bumps erupt all over my body, caused by the contrast of his heated touch against the cool of the room.

He grabs onto my hips and pulls me back into his hardness, and grinds into my ass while holding me firm and steady. He breathes in quick, hot pants at my ear, making my sex clench with need. "This...this is always a good idea," he murmurs in a low growl.

Remembering the question, I croakily whisper, protesting in vain, "But we're in someone else's bedroom." Grazing the outer lips of my sex with his fingertips, he slides a finger into me. My thoughts become a tangled mess again. I sink against his hard chest and open my legs wider for him.

"I don't give a fuck where we are. I want you."

I lick my dry lips as he dips two fingers deep inside, stretching me, filling me with need. He plunges his fingers in and out, fast and furious, his knuckles meeting resistance with each thrust, and I lose my breath.

His other hand wraps around me to squeeze the fullness of my breast in his hand. "Travis," I moan.

He trails his tongue down my neck as he whispers, "So fucking ready for me." He uses my arousal to spread over my clit, and begins massaging my hard nub with steady, firm strokes. I gasp, no longer caring we are in a house full of men. He turns me around, his eyes swirling with carnal lust, telling me he's all animal. He lifts me onto the bed and climbs on top of me. My pulse spikes as he forces himself between my thighs, spreading my legs apart.

He leans down and hovers over my lips as he uses his powerful muscles to roll his hips into mine. The thickness of his jeans presses into my core with such force I think his cock is going to rip a hole right through his pants.

How can I want something so bad, and at the same time, know it is not good for me? "Kiss me," he orders, and as he waits for me to respond, he rolls his hips into my opening again with a knowing smirk. Smug bastard knows I'll cave, because,

God...he feels so good. "Oh, God," I whimper, bucking my hips into his hardness. I lift my head and brush my lips against his. "Make me forget."

"You wanna fuck to forget, sweetheart? I can do that," he says matter-of-factly, with a bit of arrogance lining his husky voice as he runs his nose along my neck. He whispers over my fevered skin, "I'm gonna fuck you sweet, though. I want you to feel our souls connect, and then I'm gonna make you remember for the next decade what it's like when we become one." I shiver as I run my hands over the thick muscles of his arms. He pulls his mouth away, and adds with a frown, "Then maybe you'll never run from me again."

My stomach plummets, and the look on his face tells me I've hurt him. "Travis, I'm so sorry."

"Shh...I get it." He kisses my lips. "You were scared," he softly reassures me with another kiss, "but that was also a dangerous thing for you to do." I know it was a dangerous move, and it could've been the wrong man waiting outside that restaurant door instead of Quinn, but I wasn't thinking and I ran scared. He pulls back, regarding me with solemn eyes. "Promise me you won't run again, not unless I tell you to, okay?"

"Okay," I softly reply. I'm just glad he's handling this subject in a calm manner. "I promise."

Satisfied with my answer, his lips softly caress mine. "I couldn't bear it if anything were to happen to you." He runs his tongue over my lips, and I open to him.

With the silky feel of his warm, wet tongue on mine, my lower belly flutters and a rush of wetness pools at my opening.

Our tongues slide over and around each other's in a fevered fury of passion. I thread my fingers through his short hair and tug at his roots. He breaks away, breathing heavily, and then sits back to unfasten his jeans. Never once removing his heated gaze from mine, he slides them off his toned body as his chest rises and falls silently with excitement.

He lays back down over me half-naked, his tight black t-shirt outlining and hugging all of his upper body's muscles. He snakes his arm underneath my waist, pulling my body into his, my hands grasping onto his biceps. His tongue flicks back and forth over both breasts before he settles on a nipple, and then he takes it into the warmth of his mouth, sucking hard. I arch my back and hiss when he gently bites. My core clenches with need. My fingertips find the hem of his shirt, and I struggle to inch it up his body, but I can't.

Filled with a dizzy lust, I whisper, "Travis, you forgot to take your shirt off." I want to feel the warmth of his skin on mine. He lets go of my nipple and immediately moves to the other one, attacking it fast and hard. "Travis," I breathe out.

He looks at me from underneath those long eyelashes of his while he runs his tongue around my erect nipple in a lazy circle. "No," he says, and then before I know it, he's fully on top of me, claiming my mouth in an all-consuming kiss.

Shirt forgotten, I'm too full of desire to care. I spread my legs open wider, my throbbing pussy screaming for a release. I suck in a sharp breath of air when he breaches the opening of my sex with one thrust of his hips. He settles himself balls-deep inside me, swallowing every last needy whimper from my lungs.

I run my fingers underneath the back of his shirt and graze his skin with my fingernails. His arms squeeze tight around me as he pumps himself into me using a slow, rhythmic pace. I meet his thrusts, and grind my hips into his with all my might as we taste each other with out-of-control, sloppy yet passionate kisses.

When I wrap my legs around his waist, I'm immediately forced to let go as he rolls our bodies over. I'm now sitting on top of him, still impaled on his hard length. He grabs my hips, digging his fingers into my flesh as I place my palms over his chiseled chest for stability. I look to him for direction, and he doesn't hesitate to take over. His roped forearms flex with movement as he guides my hips up and down while he thrusts himself inside me, making for double the pleasure. We both groan together, filling the space of the bedroom with noises of our lust and heavy panting.

He spreads his legs open wide, and then guides my legs between his which forces my legs closed. The lips of my pussy are compressed tightly around his thick length. My hands fall to either sides of his shoulders, propping myself up on the soft mattress.

"Now you're gonna feel what it's like when *I* make love to you," he promises on a whisper. With fire in his eyes, his fingers tighten around my hips. New sensations I've never felt before have me squeezing my inner muscles around him as he guides me back and forth over his slick cock. The sensualism is to die for.

"Oh, my God," I breathe out shakily. It feels like I'm the one making love to *him*. It's such an erotic feeling that my brows pinch together in ecstasy. My eyes burn, and they squeeze shut on their own accord, the exquisite intensity being too much.

"Look at me, Jules," he hoarsely whispers. I force my eyes open and a heat flare goes off, spreading an inferno of fire through my body. The look on his face is one of love and adoration, and I lose my breath. A large part of me is hoping he'll say those three words.

Breathing heavily, sweat appears on his brows as his eyes beg me to feel the connection. "Do you feel my soul, Jules?"

"I do. I feel you, Travis," I freely admit, gasping for air. The feelings that are passing through us are too overwhelming to deny. He narrows his eyes with determination and compresses my thighs even tighter as he thrusts himself up and into me, except it feels like I'm the one pumping into him.

"Don't you dare ever forget that our souls belong together. We're one, Jules. One."

It's indescribable how incredibly good this feels. My channel is squeezed tight as he fills me. He thrusts himself in and out of me, generating a heated friction within that special erogenous zone deep inside me. My clit is being simultaneously stimulated as I move over him. I'm thankful he's guiding my movements with his strength, because right now, I feel myself becoming erratic in motion as I climb to the edge of a hellacious orgasm.

His beautiful eyes swirl with unspoken love, and then the silent soul connection becomes blurry as my eyes water, but I don't dare close them. My orgasm rips through me, and my mouth gapes open as I let out a cry of intense pleasure. My body shakes and trembles as Travis keeps up the rhythm, thrusting himself in and out of my slick pussy.

"I'm gonna come, baby," he groans as his forehead wrinkles and his lips twitch. "You're so beautiful, inside and out," he whispers in a pained voice. My inner walls are so compressed around his thickness that I can feel the second he releases his essence as his cock pulsates deep inside me. His thrusts become more inconsistent and shallow as our souls meld together as one. I squeeze my core muscles, heated fervor flows through my veins, and my oversensitive clit spurs me on and into another orgasm, keeping in tandem with Travis'.

Breathing heavily, I shake my head as I stare down at this beautiful man in wonder. Euphoria like I've never experienced before with him brings a tear of joy to my eye. I continue to thrust my hips slowly over his shaft, and then grind down to roll my hips over him despite the fact we've both taken our pleasure. This feeling is too good to ever stop.

"Baby, c'mere," Travis whispers. My heart still pounds hard against my breastbone as I lay my overheated body on top of his. Coming to rest my cheek against his broad chest, I close my eyes as I breathe in his musky scent, savoring the moment. His strong arms wrap around me, making me feel loved, cherished, and adored. He softly strokes my hair lovingly, and I feel complete inside. His strong heartbeat thrums in my ear, and his deep voice rumbles through his chest. "Did you feel that, Jules?"

"Yeah," I reply in a sated voice. He holds me tighter against his body, and then presses his lips to the top of my head.

"Don't ever forget it."

"I won't." I breathe a soft sigh over his chest, agreeing with him, even though I'm left more confused than when we first started making love. I hate my inner thoughts sometimes, because I have to ask myself, *What the hell am I doing?* I'm taken back to the reason why we shouldn't have had sex in the first place. This perplexing connection we have can only lead to no good.

He knows what he's been doing all along as he continually succeeds to manipulate every square inch of my body and mind. He had strung me along in the dark, taking full advantage of my memory loss, and then made me fall for him. I don't even know what his plans are for me. We've been under so much pressure, and being constantly on the run, we haven't had time to address the bigger picture. I don't know what he wants from me.

CHAPTER 11

"You're being awfully quiet there, sweetheart," Travis softly notes. "What's going through that pretty little head of yours, hmm?"

Now that my lusty haze has cleared, reality has set back in. There's too much going on in my brain, and I can't make heads or tails of it all. My emotions are being pulled every which way, and I feel as if I'm ruthlessly being ripped in two. I go from feeling uncontrollable lust with one man, to feeling guilt over another, and it's not right.

I am having *consensual* sex with a criminal, and isn't that, like...oh, I don't know...a mix of cheating on Adam and Stockholm Syndrome? What the hell am I'm doing? I'm not being true to Adam, Travis, or myself.

"Jules?" Travis prods.

"I'm okay." I hide my shame by snuggling further into his neck.

"No, I don't think you are." He disengages our bodies and sits up to look at me. Immediately, I stretch to my feet and grab the blanket to pull it up around me. He then rolls me onto my back, forcing me to meet his gaze as he lifts a questioning brow. "Are you cold?" he asks in a concerned voice.

"Maybe a little bit," I lie.

His lips thin in thought as he rubs the sides of my arms with his hands, heating my skin. "You don't feel cold. In fact," he adds with a little smirk, "I had you pretty heated up." I feel even more shame with him voicing what we just did, so I avert my eyes from him. "Hey, what's going on?" he asks, and then gently guides my chin with his fingers as I'm met with a set of narrowed, quizzical eyes.

I steal a deep breath and decide to clear the air. "I think I need to talk to Adam. I think I deserve that much," I blurt out quickly before I lose my nerve. For some odd reason, a part of me feels as if the request is betraying Travis.

"What the fuck, Jules!" he exclaims, his body vibrating with immediate anger. "You *think* you need to talk to him?"

I shrink back into the pillows as he gets up off the bed in a rush. He finds his jeans on the floor and hastily puts them back on, and suddenly, I feel very cheap. Hostility is evident in his short, abrupt movements, making the hairs on the back of my neck prickle in alarm.

Zipping up his pants, he turns around with a snarl and shakes his head at me, waving his hand back and forth between us. "What we just did...my God, Jules...did it even remotely mean a damn thing to you?" he bellows, his tone full of incredulous disbelief. The muscles in his jaw visibly clench as he places his hands on his hips, and then his voice hardens to stone. "No, you can't get in touch with him."

My mouth drops open in surprise, and both of my brows lift high. "No?" My voice comes out high-pitched. "You decided just like that?" I shoot back as I snap my fingers together.

"Oh, I'm sorry. Let me rephrase that for you so you can better understand," he says in a sardonic tone. "Not *no*, but fuck no!" he yells. "There. Is that better? Did I speak a language you could comprehend?"

My heart pounds loudly in my ears. I swallow hard and damn near choke on the lump in my throat. Nervously, I twist the sheets in my hands and pull them up to my chin. I can't cope when he gets enraged like this. I remember *this* Travis from when he took my medallion at the facility.

I have a right to be upset, don't I? "I don't understand, Travis. It's a simple request," I softly plead. "Can't you understand—"

He cuts me off mid-sentence, "He was in your life, once upon a time. It's past tense, and your past is behind you now; that chapter is closed."

"I don't remember closing any chapters in my life," I whisper, narrowing my eyes, "and my past just doesn't go away because you tell it to. You said at the hotel that I could eventually call home. When will the right time be, Travis? You keep leading me on."

"Calling home is a far cry from wanting to call Adam," he bites back.

"Adam was my home too," I whisper, defeated, and drop my chin to my chest. "You're never going to let me go...are you?"

"Look, this discussion is over." Exasperated, he grits out, "I don't keep your past lover's contact information, and even if I wanted to, I wouldn't even know where to begin looking."

My head jerks up as I pin him down with a hateful glare. "Oh, bullshit," I spit out, pissed off over the fact he can blatantly lie without blinking an eye. "Don't you dare try to lie to me anymore with your bullshit lines, Travis Jackson." I point my finger at him with renewed determination. "That's a load of crap and you know it! You've got enough equipment and intel at your fingertips for an army." I lean forward, my icy eyes drilling a hole into his as I become determined to win this one.

"At least he never lied to me. You seem to have a pathological habit of it. If you ever, and I emphasize the word *ever*, want me to start trusting in you, then stop. Lying. To. Me!" I shout, pointing at my chest. "I only trust you to protect me, but when it comes to my heart..." I pause to steal a breath while shaking my head. "I don't trust you as far as I can throw you. I want to talk to him."

"Don't make me be a bigger dick than I have to be," he growls in a low timbre. "Don't push me; you won't win this one, not by a long shot."

"You're never going to let me talk to anyone from my past ever again." My heart sinks and my hands begin to shake. One would think I'd get it through my thick skull that I'm going to be his prisoner until he decides to release me, if that day ever comes. "My past is all that I have," I whisper as my voice trails off.

"No. No, it's not. You have me now."

"No, I have nothing right now." I shake my head, my lips

slipping into a solemn frown. "I have nothing except for secrets and lies."

The bed dips as he sits down beside me, firmly grasping me by the shoulders, vexed I would even say such a thing. "You have *me*, dammit! I'm busting my balls here to keep you safe... keep *us* safe. After all this time, after everything we've been through together...and this...this is what you think of me?"

I scoff in his face. "Tell me, just what am I supposed to think of you? You've lied so much you probably wouldn't even know the truth if it hit you in the face." I grit my teeth. "I need some time to think things over, Travis. I haven't had any time to process anything. It's like the minute I got my memory back, all hell broke loose, literally."

"Baby, there's nothing to think over," he says as if I'm being ridiculous.

"Maybe for you there isn't. Don't you get it? I don't know who you are."

"Yes. Yes, you do know me. You've seen the real me. You've *had* the real me, and I know you feel this powerful thing between us."

"Whether I feel this *thing* between us or not is inconsequential." My eyes widen, the emotional turmoil pouring out of my mouth. "My God! I killed a live human being just one day ago! I can't process that. I'm not a killer!" My eyes narrow on his with stark realization. "But you are, aren't you?" I whisper. My hand covers my mouth as I acknowledge the horror as it sinks in. "Your job is to drug women with Blyss, and then sell them," I whisper the horrendous words behind my fingertips. I've become so familiar with him that I've justified my captivity for a relationship in order to cope. A strangled cry emits from the back of my throat and my stomach lurches.

My God, he's a sex trafficker! His touch on my shoulders becomes too much. I jerk myself away from his hold and scoot back in the bed until my back hits the headboard. Panic stricken, I need to get away from him. Travis reaches out for me, and I hold my hands out to stop him. "Don't...don't touch me. I can't...I can't do this right now." My heart hammers in my chest. Pain...I feel so much pain.

"You're not thinking straight right now, baby." The look on his face turns worried, his voice tender and soft. "I think it's time we discuss the big elephant in the room."

"Which elephant, Travis? Are you referring to my state of captivity, or the fact I had to shoot and kill a human being in the last forty-eight hours?" I bite out.

His lips thin and he ignores the captive remark. He takes a deep breath before letting out a dramatic sigh, as if the world is weighing heavy on his shoulders. His eyes plead with mine. "I need you to trust me. There are things I want to tell you, but I can't right now." He waves his hand between our bodies as he continues his petition. "We need to get our relationship back on track."

"Relationship? Are you delusional?" I bark. "All I've done is take leaps of faith with you, trust you, but each leap is lined with deception, and each lie is delivered with a stone wall face. I can never tell what's real with you. What are you trying to say, Travis? Because there is no black or white with you. You only live in shades of grey."

His eyes close briefly in defeat before he answers me. "I can't expect you to understand any of this, Julianna." He reaches out and gently places his hand over my chest, supporting the weight of my medallion in his hand. His green eyes bore into mine, piercing me deep within my soul. "I'm begging you to keep trusting in me, because the less you know, the more preserved your life will be. I swear to you, I have your best interests at heart. What we have, Jules, it's real."

I shake my head. "You're trying to confuse me. You're so good at manipulation I don't know which end is up."

"Tell me something." He pauses to study me. "In our most intimate moments, tell me you didn't feel the same spark of soul-connecting electricity as me. Tell me you felt the very same connection with Adam. I want to hear you say he made your heart race ten times more when he kissed you. I want you to tell me you wished he were your next breath to breathe at the mere sight of him. Tell me I'm lying about that, Jules."

It's a sight to watch this grown man soften his felonious eyes as he pleads with me. He's twisting my heart all around, making an unsolvable puzzle in his wake. When I don't answer, he leans in nose-to-nose, daring me to deny his claims as he hisses through clenched teeth, "Tell me, dammit! Tell me I'm wrong."

I'm taken aback by the ferocity in his voice, and my stomach twists with angst. "I can't do this. I just can't. I can't just jump in with both feet, Travis," I hoarsely whisper as a lone teardrop leaks out of the corner of my eye. "I don't know what awaits in your murky pool of lies, and I can't see through the hordes of piranhas swimming around you, ready to eat me alive." Another teardrop slips, and my eyes become blurry. "I had a life, you know," I cry through clenched teeth. "I had a fiancé, and God knows what he's going through right now. You just can't erase my past like this, and then expect me to fall in line with a compliant smile on my face."

I suck in a ragged breath, tears clogging my throat, both pain and frustration taking over my emotions. "You're telling me my previous life as I once knew it is now over. You're saying I have to stay with you, because you're *protecting me,* but yet you won't tell me why. You're sugarcoating reality, and the actual reality is you're holding me captive." A pained cry leaves my lungs as I pound on his chest with my fists. "Everything is wrong with this picture, Travis! Everything."

I slide my body to the side of his, trying to get away from him. I need some breathing room. He grabs my elbow to stop me, but I yank my arm out of his grasp and glare at him through watery eyes. "Don't," I hoarsely warn. The crushing weight of the combined stressors is too much to for me to handle. Anger and pain are thick inside my chest like the viscosity of saltwater taffy, causing me to gasp for air. "Just let me be."

His eyes convey hurt, but I refuse to look at him anymore and have him affect me. I quickly slip off the bed and stop to grab a few clothes from the tipped over laundry basket. With my hands full, I make my way to the bathroom, and then lock the door behind me. I grab onto the sink's countertop and close my eyes, stealing a deep, shaky breath. I notice my hands are trembling. I think I'm on the verge of a nervous breakdown. For all I know, maybe I'm having one now. A few more silent tears spill over my cheeks. My insides are torn to shreds.

Insanity hangs in the balance by a mere thread. The only thing keeping me from entering no man's land is a tiny glimmer of hope. I have to keep the faith I will see my dad and Jake again, the only family and unconditional love I have left. I quickly slip on a t-shirt and panties. A firm knock sounds on the wooden door and it startles me. There is nothing he can do or say to ease my pain.

"Jules, open the door. You're in distress, and I can't have you shutting down on me," he orders with a stern voice. "The things you've been through over the last forty-eight hours," he pauses, and then softens his voice, "well...you really shouldn't be alone and upset like this. I'm concerned, baby."

Concerned? If he were concerned for me, he'd let me call home. Anger bubbles up from the pit of my stomach, and I'm glad for it. I'd rather pour my energy into anger than spend the time in a mess of self-pity, so I snap.

My lungs explode with vehement sarcasm, "What's the matter, Travis? Did you run out of Blyss, or do you have a dose waiting for me if I open the door?"

A loud boom crashes into the wall on the other side of the door, and I jump back. Startled, my heart leaps into my throat. By the sound of it, Travis has punched a hole in the wall. I know what I said was a low blow, but I don't care; he asked for it.

"Open the goddamn door, now!" he roars as he pounds on the door with a heavy fist. My eyes bolt open wide in alarm. He's so enraged his voice and actions scare me. I back up a few feet, wondering if he's going to bust down the door. *Has he gone crazy?* Why would I want to open the door to a raging lunatic who's seeing nothing but red?

It sounds as if a herd of cattle are barreling into the bedroom, and then the next thing I hear is Stryker's voice bellowing out, "What the fuck, man?"

"Get the fuck out, Stryker. This isn't your battle," Travis yells back.

Then I hear Quinn jump into the mix with his deep baritone voice. "You need to back off a minute and chill."

"You don't tell me what to do..." His voice is cut off as I hear a rustle ensue outside the door. Then Quinn's voice emits an ominous tone full of such vexation it scares the crap out of me. "I said to back the fuck off, Travis. If you don't, I'll throw you in a set of handcuffs 'til you settle your ass down."

I press the palm of my hand against my pounding heart. Quinn's threatening tone would have me opening the door if he told me to, because I'd hate to know what he'd do if I didn't. Thank God he's on my side right now, providing me with a little distance from Travis.

Some very colorful words are exchanged, but the end result is a tremendously mad Travis slamming the bedroom door behind him, and then I'm left in ear-ringing silence. *Well, that was exciting.* I slide my body down to the floor, the cold tiles giving me a slight chill. I rest my head against the wall and close my eyes.

It's times like this I wish I had some music to escape into. I would especially love a set of noise-canceling headphones right now. There is only one band in particular that can always be counted upon to soothe my soul, no matter the mood or circumstance I find myself in. I know Def Leppard doesn't sound soothing or consoling to many people, especially in this type of adversity, but their music has always been able to reach me, providing an inner clarity like no other.

I close my eyes and imagine the band on stage, with the bright lights shining overhead as the crowd roars for another song. The music starts, and I hum along with the tune. I have every single beat memorized in my head, both forward and backward to my favorite song, "Hysteria".

I'm imagining I'm the set of drums...no, not the drummer, but the drums themselves. I'm the Tom-Toms, the snare, the bass, and the cymbals all in one as I feel every beat of percussion vibrate through me. Totally immersed now, the calm beat and cadence envelops me, and I can breathe a little easier now. The feeling I get with music has to be equivalent to an alcoholic getting his first drink of the day; it's indescribable.

Travis' loud, thunderous voice suddenly erupts through every wall in the house as he yells at the top of his lungs, and then another door slams with a thunderous crash. My eyes pop open with alarm, and the trance I put myself in is gone.

His rage echoes through the bathroom, bouncing off the walls, and I can't take it. I press my fingers into my ears, trying to drown out the shouting. I begin to hum again while methodically rocking back and forth, trying to calm my frayed nerves.

After a few minutes, I remove my fingers and find all is quiet and calm for the moment. Knowing the bedroom is empty, curiosity gets the better of me. I soundlessly open the bathroom door and hear Travis' deep voice filtering through the wall of the next room. Carefully, I creep to the other side of the room that's adjacent to mine and press my ear to the cool drywall to eavesdrop.

"Give her some breathing room, Trav," Stryker tries to reason. It's amazing to me how many hats Stryker wears as he seamlessly and effortlessly adapts to each situation he finds himself in. He goes from a hard-ass gun-toter, psychologist, happy-go-lucky surfer dude, to an all-business, hard-edged medic on the front lines.

"She's in a fuckload of emotional distress right now," he calmly states, and then suddenly raises his voice, startling me. "Back the fuck off. She just got her memory back, killed a man, watched a couple more drop before her very eyes, and she's still in your possession—by force, I might add. How the hell is she supposed to digest all that in two days?"

"She should know..."

Stryker interrupts him with a loud scoff. "You're such a self-centered dick sometimes, Travis. Can't you push aside your needs for one minute, and put yourself in her shoes?" His voice goes from displeasure to heated hostility. "Did you even stop to think how you've not only put her in eminent danger, but all of us too by letting your foolish heart get in the way? You decided what was best for you. You didn't even consider us. You're in the fucking slave trade business for God's sake!" he roars. "And you're not helping matters by scaring the shit out of her and punching holes in the wall."

I surmised they all knew what Travis did, but to hear Stryker verbally confirm it has me going numb on the inside. It leads me to believe they all support his lifestyle then. Maybe

Stryker and the others are involved too. A cold shiver runs down my spine. Who knows? They could've been the actual men who took me that fateful night. Everything was such a blur, it was dark to boot, and then they promptly knocked me out.

Travis' voice lowers to a mumble, and I can't make out what he's saying. I give up pressing my ear to the wall and lower my head into my hands. I have no one to turn to at this point, and I really need someone to talk to. Better yet, I should find a way to escape, and for some stupid reason, a large part of me doesn't want to. The thought of leaving Travis twists my heart like a wrung out rag. I shake my head at myself. I'm sure I have Stockholm Syndrome now, and I seriously think I need professional help.

My mind is like a piece of unclaimed luggage, thoughts endlessly cycling the same route on a conveyor belt, taking the same path over and over again. I have never in all my life been faced with such an odd internal struggle of this magnitude before.

I'm sure if I could separate myself from this entire situation, I could process and sort my mind out. The thought of being in my dad's and Jake's arms again makes my heart speed up with anticipation. It's been too long. I miss my family, my home, and my simple little life. If I can get out of here, I know they can protect me from Nick and his men. I'm more than certain once I'm surrounded by my dad's army of men I'll be guarded better than the Queen of England, and then I can call Adam once I know I'm safe. The prospect of being able to obtain my freedom gives me a sense of renewed hope.

CHAPTER 12

Morning sunlight streams into the room, and judging from the brightness, I'm guessing it's close to ten in the morning. I glance at the alarm clock on the nightstand, and sure enough, it's a little after ten. I must've slept hard last night, because the last thing I remember was being curled up in the fetal position crying my eyes out; the emotional exhaustion wiped me out.

Loneliness fills me up inside seeing his empty side of the bed. I had locked Travis out of the bedroom for the entire night, and he wasn't happy about it. I wasn't happy about it either, but I felt like I needed the space. Unfortunately, I'm left just as confused this morning about my feelings as I was last night.

My stomach grumbles, reminding me I didn't really eat a decent dinner last night, and now it's past breakfast time. I roll out of bed, use the bathroom, and then find an elastic hairband to put my hair up into a ponytail. I throw on a pair of Travis' gym shorts, which are way too big, and roll the waistband over a few times until they stay put. I then find one of his t-shirts and slip it over my head. His cotton t-shirts are extra comfy, and I tell myself that's the real reason why I'm wearing it, not because I can smell his scent still lingering in the fabric, or the fact wearing his clothes makes me feel closer to him somehow. I don't bother with putting on socks and shoes. I already know I'm not going anywhere today.

I make my way downstairs, and as I round the banister on the last step, I hear the voices of the men carrying on. They're having multiple conversations at once, one talking over the other. I'm not sure I'm ready to see Travis yet. As I approach the kitchen, I linger in the entryway.

All of the guys are sitting around the large kitchen table with a spread of both pistols and assault rifles, all disassembled. Tiny square cleaning cloths and other paraphernalia clutter the table. I watch as Chase picks up a can of some sort of gun cleaning solvent and sprays it onto a bristly brush. Instantly, I catch a whiff of the unique scent.

The sight of them cleaning their weapons turns my stomach. If I don't see another gun for the rest of my life, it will be a minute too soon. Everyone looks up at the same time, except for Travis, whose back is facing me. The other guys fall silent, Travis being oblivious to my presence as he continues to ramble on about something, sounding upbeat and jovial.

I must be really sick in the head, because he's a sight for sore eyes, and my body aches to be wrapped in his arms. Quinn clears his throat, interrupting Travis, and when he looks up at Quinn in question, Quinn nods in my direction.

When Travis turns his head, his genial mood is immediately wiped off his face as he shuts down, giving me that damn stone-walled expression. I die a little on the inside knowing it's me who put the cold glare in his eyes. He has all his walls back up, and his fortress is locked down tight as he continues to penetrate me with his hard scowl. He then scoots back his chair in a dramatic fashion, making a loud scraping sound against the tiled floor as he stands to his full height.

"I'm out of here, guys," he says heatedly, and with that, I feel like I've just been punched in the gut. His curtness and coldness has me feeling embarrassed, and I feel the heat of my humiliation turning the tips of my ears red.

"Where you going, man?" Stryker questions with a confused look on his face.

"Out. I'll be back later." As if he's speaking to me personally, he continues, "If she tries to escape, tie her up, and lock her in the basement." I choke on the air in my lungs, my hand pressing against my racing heart.

Chase speaks over the collective, shocked stares of everyone in the room, "Dude, I don't think that's necessary."

Travis whips his head around, and the tone of his voice sends a chill down my spine. "Perhaps you didn't hear me correctly, so let me rephrase. If she tries to cut loose and isn't properly restrained for when I get back, someone's head is gonna roll for it. You wanna oppose me now, let me know," he snarls as his fists ball up, readying for a fight.

"Whoa," Chase leans back in his chair and raises his hands high in the air in mock surrender, "I got your back, man. I'm on board."

With those last words, Travis turns away from Chase and looks to Stryker. "Just leave my handgun alone. I'll finish it when I get back." He grabs his keys off the kitchen counter and doesn't even brush past me to leave out the front door. Instead, he leaves out the set of French doors just off to the side of the kitchen, where the den is. I jump back, startled when he slams the door behind him.

The room goes completely quiet as I just stand here awkwardly, feeling more stupid by the second for wearing his clothes. As I look around the room, all the guys stare at me in silence with a bit of sympathy.

I bite my bottom lip out of nervousness, and I wonder if they're all upset and blaming me for Travis' bad mood. I'm seconds away from doing an about-face and running back to the bedroom to drown myself in self-pity and tears, but Quinn catches my attention. He shoves his seat back and gets up, quickly making his way toward me in a determined manner.

When he reaches me, he holds out his hand for me to take in a silent gesture of amity. "You hungry?" he gently asks. Looking like a lost kitten, I nod, not saying a word. He gestures with his outstretched hand again, softening his eyes as he wills me to accept his hand in an act of kindness as he prods, "C'mon, I'll find you something you can eat. We have a little bit of everything here."

I tentatively slip my hand into his and he pulls me into his side, wrapping his arm around me in a comforting hug. His warm embrace settles me, reminding me of the brotherly love only Jake could provide. God knows it feels good to have someone show some empathy. I have to admit; I didn't expect Quinn, of all people, to show any compassion. His exterior is always so Rambo-like, but come to think of it, so is Jake's.

With his arm around me, he guides me to the refrigerator,

and as he opens the door, he leans down to whisper in my ear, "Don't take it personally. He didn't get his beauty sleep last night. Had to sleep on the sofa with Ranger, who snored in his ear all night." He tilts his head down to meet my eyes with a silly grin playing on his lips, looking to get a reaction from me. "Sometimes his hormones go all dysfunctional, and when they do, he's worse than a houseful of women PMSing with no chocolate."

Stryker overhears the conversation, and mumbles under his breath, "You fuckin' got that right." My lips curve into a small smile. I can't help it, and Quinn's goofy grin is a bit comical, along with Stryker's comment. His bright, blue eyes twinkle with satisfaction when I return his smile, and he gives me an extra squeeze in what only feels like a brotherly hug.

"He'll blow off some steam and get over it." Quinn reassures me, and then gives me a playful wink. "Okay?" Still feeling shy, I nod my head once again.

"All right," he says loudly, changing the subject with renewed determination to make light of a strained atmosphere, "how about a country style brunch? I've got bacon, eggs, and grits." Another smile tugs at the corners of my lips. This is exactly like something Jake would do to put me in a better mood. Growing up, Jake would always distract me when I was having a bad day by making me something yummy in the kitchen.

"Ahhh, I can see I'm on to something here. Is that your morning poison?"

My lips twitch with a grin, and he raises his brow in question. "Cat got your tongue? Gotta tell me how you want this combo to go," he cheerfully says as he lets go of me, grabbing the carton of eggs from the shelf. "Let me guess; a gluten-free, lactose intolerant southern girl like you takes eggs over easy with a slice of veggie cheese, and then mixes it all together in a bowl. Am I right?"

I will never know how he nailed that one. I'm simply amazed. "I'm impressed. You got it right."

He stops to regard me with mock offense, his hands full of bacon and eggs. "Sweetheart, I'm never wrong. And as long as you can get that bit of trivia through your pretty little head, you might learn a thing or two."

Unintentionally, a loud snigger bursts forth, and my hand flies to my mouth to cover the blunder. His eyes narrow on mine, but they're full of mirth, and his lips twitch in amusement.

"Dude, make me some too while you're at it," Stryker pipes in.

"Then get your lazy ass up here and help. This ain't a bed and breakfast."

After breakfast, I decided to stay busy and clean up the kitchen. The guys have made a serious mess in here, as dirty dishes are stacked high in the sink and the countertops are cluttered from last night's dinner. I have nothing better to do anyway. As I load the dishwasher and wash the pots and pans, the guys continue to banter back and forth with each other while they finish cleaning their guns. It's kind of funny to listen to them rib each other. I can tell just from this little bit of time I've spent with them that they have a camaraderie that's unbreakable.

When I'm finished in the kitchen, I glance at the clock on the wall, and it reads almost noon. I look around, wondering what to do next to keep my mind busy. It's bad enough all I can think about is Travis and how he left pissed off. My stomach twists into a knot thinking about it. I know with idle time on my hands I'll just further confuse myself with my conflicted feelings. I turn around and notice Quinn is the only one left in the room with me. He most likely stayed behind on purpose to make sure I wouldn't run. *Probably a smart thing to do.*

Travis still hasn't returned to the house as far as I can tell. Quinn gestures for me to have a seat at the table across from him, and I hesitate. His look is serious, and I'm not sure I want to hear what he has to say.

"C'mon and have a seat," he says as he pats the wooden table with the palm of his hand. "I want to talk to you for a bit."

I slip into the chair across from Quinn and sit down with nervousness. Not knowing what to say or do, I drop my chin to my chest and twist my fingers nervously.

"Hey, look at me," he softly requests, and when I do, I'm met with the most brilliant hue of blue. His lips have turned down in a frown, and my heart skips a beat. I don't like the sudden shift of mood, and it puts me on edge.

"I'm not one to babble on with bullshit, so I'll just cut to the chase here." Dread fills me from head to toe as I hold my breath, preparing for the worse. He lets out a loud sigh, and the next thing he says stops my heartbeat in its tracks. "Do you want to know about Adam?" he asks me point blank.

What's the catch? I glance to all four corners of the room, expecting...what, I don't know. He's acting covert, and it's throwing me off. "Why?" I ask in a disbelieving whisper.

He leans forward in his chair as if he has some big secret to tell me. "I asked you a yes or no question," he says bluntly, and lifts a brow as he waits for my response.

I swallow hard. The man knows how to play hardball, and hell yes I want to know about Adam. "You'll let me call him?"

He shakes his head. "No, but I'll show you."

My brows lift high, taken aback with confusion. "Show me? I don't understand." Will he take me to him?

He stands up, walks over to my side of the table, and then gently takes me by the hand. "Come on. I just think you need to know."

I let him hold my hand as he takes me down the hallway. With each step, my heart pounds loudly in my ears, and I don't get a good feeling about this.

Still downstairs, we come to a stop at a set of closed doors, and I notice a small keypad affixed to the wall. Quinn punches in a sequence of numbers, and then turns the knob, opening the door to a huge computer room.

Holy shit! Who are these people? Is this an extension of the facility in Atlanta? They're equipped with state of the art electronics and gadgets I've never seen before. I can't quite seem to soak in my surroundings. I'm too stunned to move, so he tugs at my hand, pulling me into the room. He guides me to a black computer chair and takes a seat beside me as he turns on one of the many computer monitors.

It seems like forever since I last looked at a computer screen. I turn to face Quinn, who isn't paying me a bit of attention. Instead, he's focused on entering things on the keyboard, shifting his gaze back and forth from it to the monitor. His brows furrow as he works on the task at hand, acting all businesslike.

He lifts his chin in a quick jerk, indicating I'm to look at something on the screen, and as I do, I see Adam's name on a file. Quinn clicks on the blue folder to open it up, and suddenly a slew of pictures stream across the screen as he slowly clicks through them in a slideshow fashion.

My hand covers my mouth as my pulse spikes at the sight of Adam's picture. My God, it's really him. The familiarity of his personality and looks washes over me, causing my eyes to water. It feels like forever since I've seen him, a sight for sore eyes. The next picture that opens up confuses me, and instinctively, without realizing it, I place my hand over Quinn's to stop him from clicking to the next picture.

Adam's in this picture with another woman. A real woman...a beautiful one. *What the hell?* "What is this?" I whisper to no one.

"This," Quinn says matter-of-factly, "is Mr. And Mrs. Adam Taylor." My head goes all tingly, and I let go of Quinn's hand. I couldn't have heard him correctly.

"What did you say?" I hoarsely whisper as my world shifts, turns on its axis, and spins the other way.

He ignores my question and clicks to the next photo, one that speaks well over a thousand words. She's in a wedding gown, and Adam's in a tux. Thankful I'm sitting down, I begin to feel queasy. I thought I knew how deep his love for me went. "He's...he's married?!" I declare in disbelief. I lean in to get a closer look at the screen, not wanting to believe my eyes.

Quinn turns to face me, giving nothing away until he sees the shocked looked on my face. His eyes turn to concern for me, and then his features soften as if he's remorseful. Quinn reaches out with his hand, pausing and unsure, but then decides to place it on my shoulder.

"It looks like a shotgun wedding," I express with incredulity. It's breaking my heart, and I feel a tremendous sense of loss wash over me, one that I can't explain. I feel the air go still around me as my blood freezes, giving me a horrid chill. My extremities begin to shake, so I wrap my arms tightly around myself as I squeeze my midsection.

"I can't believe he moved on like that...like I was nothing," I numbly whisper while staring blankly at the computer screen. Seeing Adam smiling and utterly happy with another is a hundred megawatt shock to my heart.

"No, you've got it all wrong," Quinn's voice breaks through the conversation I'm having with myself. "You don't understand; he was forced to move on. He had to do this."

No. No, he didn't *have* to do this. I shake my head. No matter how you slice it, there is no excuse for him to have moved on like this, not in this short amount of time. There is no digesting this information. It sits on my stomach like a sushi plate gone rancid. My stomach lurches and flips over. I cover my mouth with my hand as I try to keep my brunch down.

"I think I'm going to be sick," I whisper through my fingers. In a flash, Quinn has hoisted me up out of the chair, and in the blink of an eye, I find myself in the bathroom face-to-face with the porcelain God as I lose my food.

CHAPTER 13

"Oh, my God!" I cry out in a pained wail as I hover over the commode. I wrap my arms around my waist as I dry heave, the acid burning from my gut to my esophagus.

"Shit," Quinn mumbles. He has my hair gathered at the back of my neck with one hand while he rubs my back with the other. When I think I've expelled every last drop of fluid from my body, Quinn flushes, and then guides me on shaky legs to the sink. He lifts me, having me sit on the bathroom counter. I watch as he makes fast work of setting out mouth rinse for me, and then wets a rag with cold water.

My hands tremble as I bring the mouthwash to my lips. I feel so empty inside, both literally and figuratively. When I'm finished rinsing, he steps between my legs to place the cool rag at the base of my neck.

Why did he show me Adam? Why did he give me news that would further turn my life upside-down? I shake my head, refusing to believe what I just saw. "It's a lie. He wouldn't do that," I hiss out in denial. *It has to be a lie.*

Quinn drops the rag on the counter and steadies me by holding onto my shoulders. "It's true. It was all right there in black and white."

Love is blind, isn't it? And I begin to wonder if he really ever loved me to begin with. Then another thought crosses my mind, one in which I don't like at all. What if he had been cheating on me the entire time we were together, and kept that woman on the side? He had ample opportunity to live a double life since I was attending college, and living in a dorm. I cover my mouth with my hand, feeling my stomach lurch, and I gag.

Quinn cups my cheeks, searching my eyes. "I know what you're thinking."

I look at him, astounded, through my blurry eyes as I wipe a tear off my cheek. Anger builds, and my breathing quickens. How dare he try to assume what's going on in my mind. "How could you even begin to understand what I'm thinking?" I hiss.

I try to push against his broad chest to get down, but he doesn't budge. He's determined to have his say. "It's my job to read people, and women are not as complicated as the world seems to think," he says adamantly. "It's easy to tap into the female psyche. Right now, you're probably asking yourself why he didn't fight for you, or maybe you're thinking you must not have meant that much to him in the first place if he could've up and married someone else so quickly. Maybe he had someone on the side...because, let's face it. How can someone who was engaged one minute, turn around and marry someone else in such a short period of time, especially when you were head-over-heels in love?"

My upper lip curls into a snarl. It makes me even madder

he thinks he knows it all. "Why keep tabs on Adam at all then? What's the point?" I cry out.

"It's our job to keep tabs on everything concerning you."

"Whose job?" I ask, incensed. "Who besides Nick just has to know in finite detail every aspect of my life?" I spit out with full-on anger, beginning to hyperventilate. Never before have I felt so violated in my personal life by so many people all at once.

"Calm down, blue eyes," he says placidly, as if I'm getting myself all in a tizzy over nothing. The strength of his character emits a certain confidence, combined with an arrogant pompousness, as he purposely doesn't answer my question.

"You're not going to tell me, are you?" I bark angrily, challenging him.

He gives a slight shake of his head. "Nope." Then he smacks his lips together in a matter-of-fact, haughty manner.

"My God! Who are you people? Part of the mafia?" I spit out venomously. They must be, because how else can they get all of this information? A new horror of knowledge washes over me, and I forget about Adam for a brief second as I think about who these men are actually associated with. "No wonder you guys have a bunker."

Quinn throws his head back and laughs, finding both my questions of alarm and statement amusing. I seriously don't find my questions funny, not at all, and it pisses me off all the more that he has the audacity to find humor at a time like this.

"We've been known to associate with them a time or two," he says, half-chuckling. I'm flabbergasted, and when he sees my mouth gaping open in shock, he adds, "Now c'mon, having a bunker is actually the norm nowadays. You'd be surprised how many preppers are out there who do that shit, but those who are military, especially those who served in Special Forces and saw action...now they come back from overseas all bat-shit-crazy."

"Is that what you guys were...Special Forces?" I ask, hoping they're associated with anything but the mafia.

"No...no, we're not. We really don't have any excuses, other than we're just crazy as shit." He pauses to regard me, contemplating something in his mind for a few beats before he adds, "Shit, do you always ask so many questions?"

I'm taken aback for a split second. "You insensitive, arrogant pig; yes, as a matter of fact I do ask a lot of questions," I say pointing toward myself. "This happens to be my life we're talking about."

Before I can continue on my rant, he cuts me off.

"Calm down, sweet cheeks. Don't get your feathers in a ruffle. I'm just asking questions too. No offense was meant. Don't make me your punching bag."

Perhaps I am looking for reasons to get angry and lash out.

My state of mind can't seem to grab onto one emotion and keep it there. My mind wanders all over the place as I grow quiet, thinking of Adam getting on with his life, the reality of Adam no longer being mine, and the fact he didn't wait for me...he was my life, my everything. We had three strong years of history together, and he just turned his back on me and walked away.

"Why didn't Travis tell me?" I close my eyes, whispering to myself. The familiar sting of tears begins to brew behind my eyelids as I face the cold, hard truth.

Quinn grabs my hand, squeezes it, and then steps back and grabs a box of tissues from the other side of the counter, offering me some.

I grab a handful of tissues from the box and wipe my nose. I look at him with pained eyes, and whisper, "Thank you."

He purses his lips together, looking torn, as if he wants to say something else, but he keeps quiet. He reaches out, gently tucking a few strands of my hair behind my ear. The loving gesture just makes me want to cry all the more. My heart feels as if someone punctured my chest cavity, pulled out my heart, and then stomped on it. Before I know it, I've leaned my forehead against his broad shoulder and begin to bawl my eyes out.

"He has his own reasons for not wanting you to know," Quinn says in a soft voice.

I lift my head off Quinn's shoulder and come face-to-face with his bold cerulean eyes. Their sparkle is both calming and mesmerizing at the same time.

"What are his reasons?" I softly demand. "If you've showed me the worst, surely you can tell me at minimum why Travis hid this from me."

Quinn doesn't hesitate in his reply, "He didn't want to see any more pain or hurt on your face, especially as your heart broke for another man. He didn't want to know how you would react. I think he was hoping for indifference, because he wants to be your end-all, be-all."

My eyes narrow as a tear slips out from the corner of one eye. "Years of a loving history with one's fiancé aren't just forgotten in the blink of an eye, Quinn."

He briefly closes his eyes, and lets out a heavy sigh. "That's part of the problem. A few of us here know that feeling all too well, and he didn't want to believe it would've existed for you."

"Then why...why did you tell me?" I choke out.

"Because you needed to know. No matter what happens between you and Travis, you needed to know the truth."

I begin gasping for breath. The simple act of breathing becoming a laborious chore, and then I grow dizzy. Quinn lifts me off the counter and carries me upstairs to his bedroom, shutting the door behind us with the heel of his foot.

"Breathe, little one. Take a deep breath," he gently commands. I try to steal a deep breath, but I can only manage short, fragmented gasps. Once I get enough oxygen in reserves, I let it all back out with one long, loud pained cry.

Quinn holds me tight in his arms as he sits down on his bed, positioning himself so he's resting his back against the headboard. I curl myself onto his lap as he presses the side of my head against his chest. He whispers over my head as I continue to cry for all I'm worth, "That's it; let it all out."

With Quinn reminding me so much of Jake, I pretend he actually is Jake as I take comfort in the illusion. I bury my face in his shoulder as uncontrollable sobs wrack my body. I don't hear when Travis enters the room, but I feel him. His presence always fills a room. I've become attuned to his distinct aura, and my body always hums when he enters. It's like a sixth sense.

"Jules," Travis whispers at my back, and then places his hand on my shoulder. Reflexively, I arch my back, trying to escape his touch. It burns through me, and I can't handle him right now.

Confusion begins to war with my mind as part of me aches to feel his soft, loving touch, and the other part of me wants to be miles away from the traitorous, lying bastard. I'm not ready to face him. I begin to struggle in Quinn's hold, shaking my head profusely, crying out in distress. "No...no...no..." I howl over and over again. Quinn holds me tighter against his hard body, not letting me escape.

I feel claustrophobic and begin to panic. I clutch at the fabric of Quinn's shirt in total anguish. God, please make the pain in my heart stop, please.

Quinn's deep, gravelly voice sounds out over my wails as I hear him telling Travis to back off. "Trav, she's not ready to see you. You need to go, man."

Travis stands over me, resolved to win this as he always is. He's determined to never lose. "She needs me," he states firmly. "I can't leave her like this."

I shake my head, burrowing my eyes into the front of Quinn's shirt. Travis removes his hand, but leans over me, bringing his mouth close to my ear. Travis' voice sounds choked as he pleads, "Sweetheart, you're killing me here. Let me take care of you."

I twist at Quinn's shirt with a death grip, refusing to look at him. Quinn cuts in, effectively shutting Travis down once and for all. "Travis, you need to get the fuck out...now."

Travis lets out a resigned sigh. "Come get me if she changes her mind."

"You got it," Quinn calmly replies. I'm amazed how Quinn can always get Travis to listen to him.

Out of the corner of my eye, I watch as Travis leaves the room, and then I slump back into the arms of another criminal, searching for a solace that doesn't exist. I don't know how much time has gone by before I realize the tears have dried out and the only sound in the room is my breath hitching. Quinn continues to make soothing sounds while stroking the length of my back in a calming manner.

"Quinn?" I whisper with a hoarse, scratchy voice.

"Yeah?"

I incline my head back, gazing into his crystal blue eyes. "Why didn't Travis tell me, again?"

"For several reasons." He pauses as his hand brushes back a lock of hair from my neck. "He didn't want your heart to shatter like it is right now. The second being he wanted you to choose him over Adam before you found out."

"So why did you go against him then, and wind up telling me?"

"Because I already know where you belong, and I think you do too. I didn't want you looking back, wondering about what-ifs, and then it ends up messing with your relationship with Travis. Most importantly, I didn't want you to feel any guilt over your choices."

"But I can't keep living in lies, or in captivity. The constant threat of danger lurks around every corner. It's just...wrong and inhumane to keep another human like this." Why am I trying to convince another criminal to suddenly think about getting a set of morals, and make him realize that stealing another human is wrong? There is no convincing men like them. They're in this business for a reason.

"Well, you are definitely in an unusual set of circumstances, that's for sure," he says, staring at me in all seriousness. "However, it's Nick who has, and continues to create the perilous dangers, and if I remember correctly, he's the one who had taken you from your life," Quinn points out as we both fall silent for a few minutes with me digesting his words.

I find myself suddenly chewing on my thumbnail, a very old, nervous habit, one I had when I first left home, going off to boarding school. Stress and insecurity are the culprits, and it pisses me off, because it took me a long time to lose the habit. Quinn's stare is intense, and I can't take the heat from it any longer, so I shift my gaze to his chest. He pries my finger away from my mouth, and keeps hold of my hand as he breaks the silence.

"Even if you were to be set free this very second, you know you could never go back. You do know that, right?" The tenacity of his gaze bores a hole straight through me, and I swallow hard.

Confused, I ask him to elaborate. "I don't understand."

"Let's say if Nick wasn't even part of the equation anymore; the bottom line is you've been through too much to go back to what it was you had before. If you went back to your old life, you wouldn't survive it. Things would never be the same. You've acquired too much new history."

"New history?" My brows furrow in confusion as I study his face and soak in his every word.

"Think about it for a moment. One of the reasons why we're such a tight knit group is because at one time or another, all of us have killed. Nobody in your old life will be able to relate to what you've been through...or what you're about to go through. They won't know how to handle you, and you won't know how to cope." He pauses and gently runs his thumb over my cheekbone in a soothing gesture. "But Travis can relate." I bite the inside of my cheek as he speaks with keen perception. "Not only will he help you, but he loves you...you know?"

I shake my head as I whisper, "He's never said so."

He takes a deep breath, and then lets out a long and controlled exhale through his pursed lips. He nods as if he's agreeing with himself, and then softly speaks, "Travis is the type of guy who's more about letting his actions speak louder than words, you know? He's got a few skeletons in his closet, and he has a hard time opening that door of vulnerability." Then he eyes me cautiously. "Do you love him?"

The question catches me off guard, and I find myself nervously looking away. He lets go of my hand and captures my chin in a light grasp, reestablishing eye contact. No matter how personal a question, I can tell he's not going to let me get out of this one. He raises a brow in question when I hesitate.

"I believe I fell in love with another man, Quinn. One who doesn't really exist."

His lips thin as he shakes his head at me. "No, you didn't. Travis is the same man as he was yesterday, that he is today, and will be tomorrow."

"I don't think that's true," I whisper. "He's left me confused as to who the real Travis is. Every time I turn around, I catch him in a web of lies."

"Don't judge him so harshly, Jules," he states pointedly. "Everything he's done has been to protect you, and I might add, he still is."

I can't seem to argue with that particular fact, other than there might be an ulterior motive I'm not privy to. A large part of me wishes I never got my memory back and we were still at the cabin, continuing to fall in love. A headache has developed behind my eyes, and it's getting worse, most likely from all the crying and stress. Without thinking, I start massaging my temple.

"You're getting a headache, aren't you?" he asks, narrowing his eyes in concern. I look away, and he quickly steers my chin back toward him. His beautiful eyes flick back and forth over mine as he asses me. "I'll get up in a second and get you some Tylenol and water," he says in a soft, low voice, being mindful of my headache.

"Thank you."

"For what?"

"For taking care of me, and for telling me the truth."

"Jules," he starts off speaking emphatically, "you've got to know you're everything to Travis, and because of that, you've become part of our family here. We take care of each other."

I lay my head back down against his big, burly chest in resignation as I snuggle against his warmth and let out a loud sigh. I'm literally exhausted. The crazy roller coaster of emotions I've been on over the past few days is pulling my sanity's strings. I just want to crawl in a hole somewhere and sleep for a week. I close my eyes and pretend he's Jake with his big, brotherly, protective arms wrapped around me.

"Since you guys know so much about my previous life, can you tell me if you know anything about my dad and Jake? How have they been, and are they still looking for me?" I ask as my voice fades along with my hope.

"Babe, I don't know about any of that. I'm sorry. I was just told to investigate Adam, and make sure…" He trails off, not finishing his sentence.

I open my eyes. "Make sure of what?"

"Nothing…sorry."

I bite my lower lip hard, forcing myself to be quiet. I know he's hiding confidential stuff I'm not supposed to know, and maybe at this point it's best I don't know. What I do know is these guys are not a dog and pony show. They've done some homework, and I'm sure someone knows something about my dad and Jake. I know Quinn wouldn't tell me anyway; he's the kind of guy who only tells people things on a need-to-know basis. Every single one of these men are a vault with their secrets, and they must have a mass collection of them running ten-miles deep.

CHAPTER 14

~Travis~

I'm sitting outside on the front porch swing in the cool of the evening with a tall glass of ice tea as I talk to Stryker. I'd prefer to be nursing something stronger in my glass, but I promised myself I wouldn't drink myself into a stupor like I did last night.

"She's in a high level of shock, and you won't be doing her any favors if you step in and force yourself on her," Stryker warns. I lay my head back, resting it against the swing, and close my eyes as Stryker continues drilling into me all of his psychobabble bullshit of why I should do things his way in regards to getting Jules to come around.

"I feel like I'm in a no-win situation here, and it's driving me nuts. If I give her space to breathe, Stryker, I just know she's going to run the other way."

"Do you hold that little amount of faith for what the two of you built at the cabin? I've seen the looks she gives you when you're not looking. It's evident she's fallen for you."

"She doesn't take being lied to very well, and I can hardly blame her. If she can't feel she can trust me, we have nothing. I've told her some pretty big doozies, and I've run out of excuses and white lies to placate her." I rub the back of my neck and sigh in defeat. "She's at her breaking point; I can feel it, and I can't give her the answers she wants right now, especially when I don't have most of them myself."

"Her head may be telling her to leave, but her heart can't let you go," Stryker insists. "She's confused, and you have to understand both the mental and physical traumas she's incurred, and how they relate to her psychological state. She's highly fragile, Trav, and I'd venture to say she's damn near psychopathic. I'm sure I don't have to remind you what it was like when you had your first kill, do I?"

"Oh, I remember it, but I didn't make myself an island, shutting everyone out."

Stryker scoffs aloud, and I pull my gaze away from the edge of the darkened property line to look at him with narrowed eyes. "Mind telling me what you find so funny?"

"You've got one thick head, buddy. Look over your hard-headedness for a minute, will you? Not everyone can bounce back from traumatic shit like you, and not everyone handles stress in the same manner as you do. You keep forgetting there are multiple factors at play here." He shakes his head at me, irritated he has to lay it out for me as his voice rises in frustration. "Besides the fact she's a female, her brain isn't operating on all four cylinders. Do I really have to reiterate everything Grant told you in regards to her head trauma?"

He leans forward in his chair, resting his elbows on his

thighs, locking his eyes with mine as he tries to drive home his point with a heated tone. "All the behavioral fluctuations she's been experiencing is to be expected, Travis. It's not like she has control over this...control over the speed of her mental and physical healing. You know damn well there are medically proven negative side effects related to what she's been through that can lead to a psychosis in the blink of an eye."

"No, I don't need a recap," I gruffly state, "nor do I need you giving me a lecture on all this shit."

"Apparently you need some sort of reminder, Trav, because you're acting like a lovesick fool. I never really understood that term before, until now," he says, shaking his head as he leans back in his chair. "I think you've lost more than your sanity when you decided to fall head-over-heels for this girl. I believe you lost a chunk of your brain in the process."

"Fuck you."

Stryker half-laughs at me. "I have *never* seen you this tied up in a knot over a woman since Clarissa. You went off half-cocked, running wild with your emotions on this one, and that is not the Travis I know. Hell, I didn't think Stonewall had any emotions left.

"Fuck off, Stryker," I warn. "I've got my shit together, and I'm in control of myself. I know what I'm doing."

Stryker breaks out in a set of deep, low-sounding chuckles. "You *think* you're in control. This girl has you all fucked up, which surprises the hell out of me, because even when you had Clarissa, you were in control of your emotions. You were still the notoriously badass Stonewall Jackson everyone knew you to be, but this," he shakes his head, "this takes the cake, and I don't need to remind you what happens when you let your emotions take the driver's seat."

"I'm still the same calculating and measured man who can think five steps ahead of everyone else." I glare at Stryker, ready for him to get off my case. "Contrary to popular belief, I have thought of every angle possible and then some for my decisions. Granted, I did most of this last minute, flying by the seat of my pants, but I still had a formulated plan. I'm sure right now it looks as if I'm coming off as the lovesick fool you say I am, but all I'm trying to do here is help ease her pain."

"Nothing is gonna ease her pain, buddy." Stryker begins ticking off all the crazy shit that's happened to Jules while being under my care. "She's had head trauma, wound up with amnesia, and then she killed another human being, was kidnapped twice by sex traffickers, and in her mind, she's *your* captive this go 'round. Of course it doesn't help matters when she finds out the love of her life up and remarried within a month of her disappearance." His eyes narrow on mine as he lowers his voice, "That is one motherfucker of a pill to swallow."

My nostrils flare in anger as I growl at him through clenched teeth, "Don't you think I know she's going to be haunted for the rest of her life? I'm the love of her life, dammit! She needs *me*; I can help heal her."

Stryker bursts out in sardonic laughter. "It's not about you! You impulsive jackass, none of this is about you. Are you that fucking dense? We just went over all this shit yesterday, and nothing has sunk in."

My hands ball into fists, and I'm seconds away from

jumping up off this porch swing to pummel his face into the wooden deck. Stryker raises his hand in defense, probably hoping to God I don't punch the shit out of him, because he knows I can deliver a blow that will knock him out for the rest of the night.

"You're a trained killer, Trav; all of us here are. It's our second nature to kill and not look back. Even though we did train her, it was quick and dirty, and you know it. She wasn't mentally strong then, and she's not now. She shouldn't be making any decisions right now, and the least you can do is give her the space she needs to breathe. She needs space."

I spread my fingers wide and shake out my hands, trying to calm down. "I comprehend and recognize her situations for what they are, but I know her, goddammit. I know how she operates. If she gets too much quiet time on her hands, she might have the penchant to stew on it and begin to develop a mental illness. Depression sucks, man. That shit runs deep, and it not only steals your optimism, but it fucking obliterates it. It will drive a knife into my gut if I see that happen to her."

"I get it. I know where you're coming from," Stryker agrees, "and I know you don't want history to repeat itself, and neither do I. She's not Clarissa, and I think she's stronger than that. None of us here want to see her spiral down into the abyss of a depressive episode, but I think because you're hypersensitive to her situation, you're being too overbearing."

He's most likely right. Surprisingly, she's taken to Quinn, and truth be told, I was shocked to see it. I don't think I've ever seen a soft side to that man, but I think he's helped calm her quite a bit. He told me earlier he felt like he got through to her some, talking a bit of sense into her. God, I hope so. I don't know what I'd do if she were to go off the deep end.

Stryker and I fall silent as I digest our conversation and think about the love of my life. Sometimes, in my head, I can still see her acting out with her quirky antics, and I laugh to myself when I think of all those crazy things that transpired at the cabin. I think about the palmetto bug episode, to the gluten-free catastrophes I barely evaded. I'm trying my damnedest to understand her, but I'm failing miserably.

The screen door squeaks out in protest, breaking our silence. Both Stryker and I turn our heads simultaneously to see who's stepped out onto the porch. I guess Stryker was right after all. He said she'd eventually come around, and here she is.

I school my features, however, wanting to act unaffected by the last twenty-four hours. As I eye her with caution, her lightweight sundress catches my eye. She must've pilfered through Quinn's walk of shame closet. Damn, she looks fine. She's barefoot, and her long hair is lying around her shoulders, and I can't help but think what she would look like pregnant with my child.

I hate that I'm going to have to uproot her yet again, but that's the way it has to be. For her safety and sanity, we're going to have to disappear. If she can just get through this last leg of stress without breaking, we'll be home free. She will adapt; I know she has it in her to do so. Once I help her get through her psychological turmoil, she'll be back to her old happy and optimistic self.

Silently, she makes her way over and stops in front of me. Her eyes are still rimmed with a tinge of red, but at least the puffiness has calmed down. I get why she shunned me this afternoon. Not only was I an asshole to her this morning in the kitchen, but I wasn't going to let her know about Adam, and she knows it. She's been through enough shit. I wanted Adam's marriage to not matter to her.

Stryker clears his throat, and moves to get up out of his chair, taking Jules entry as his cue to leave. "Later, man." The screen door slams shut behind him, and I half-grin when he shuts the front door too.

I turn my attention back to this blue-eyed angel, who stands in front of me twisting her fingers in a knot. I itch to pull her onto my lap and squeeze her tight, but I don't. I can see the conflicting emotions running across her face and it kills me. As much as I want to break the tense silence, I wait for her to speak first.

"You knew all along, didn't you?" she nervously asks.

My lips thin, making a hard line. I don't want to elaborate on her question. Opening my mouth can only lead to another fight, so all I do is nod in agreement.

"Why didn't you tell me?" Her voice squeaks, sounding pained.

I let out a long-winded sigh and briefly close my eyes. I should've known she would pick this apart. "Ohh, my curious little Jules. Would it have made a difference?" I eye her skeptically as she soaks in my question. "Honestly, sweetheart, because I'm tired of you hurting. I'm tired of being the bearer of bad news. I just wanted to be able to spare you from living in any more pain for once."

"I don't understand. I'm already in pain. I've been in pain

since the day I was ruthlessly ripped from my home." She frowns and turns her head to look off into the darkness. "I've asked myself a hundred times already if he even loved me to begin with, you know?"

"Oh, on the contrary," I interject, not wanting to see her put herself down. I reach out, taking hold of both her hands, hoping to provide her some form of comfort. "From what I heard, the poor guy had a major breakdown after your disappearance." Her head whips around with speed, her hair flying in her face as she searches my eyes, seeking the truth.

"Then why didn't he wait for me?" she asks, her voice hoarse. Her question kind of pisses me off. She shouldn't care that he's not available anymore. My forehead wrinkles, and my eyes narrow with irritation.

"Wait for what, Jules?" I ask, highly annoyed. "Nick doesn't play games, and he made damn sure that chapter in your life was closed. Adam had to marry, because if he didn't, Nick would've ended his life." She gasps, and then her features turn distraught as she tries to pull out of my hands. "Shit, baby, I'm sorry." I squeeze her hands, not letting her go. I pull her toward me, placing her between my legs. I mentally berate myself for snapping.

"Come and sit with me?" I ask hopefully, changing my voice to a softer tone. Her face turns sad and she drops her chin in defeat. "I don't want to fight, Jules. I just want to go back to what we had. Please, come sit down beside me."

I let go of her hands, and lean over the side of the swing, picking up my glass of iced tea off the porch floor. I take a sip of the cool, sweet concoction, then lean back against the wooden slats on the swing, patting the empty space.

I watch her closely as she slides in beside me, curling her legs underneath her sexy little sundress, and I wrap my arm around her shoulders, pulling her in close to my side. "I'm sorry about this morning," I admit. I use my feet to push off the floor of the porch, giving us a little swing. "You want a drink?" I offer her the glass of tea.

Her eyes never leave mine as she takes the glass and then takes a small sip. Seeing her plump lips wrap around the rim of my glass makes me want them wrapped around my cock. I miss her, and yet she's right here. Apparently I have no shame, because as I take the glass from her hand, and with a shot of courage, I lean in to brush my lips against hers. When she doesn't pull away, slap me, or tell me to go to hell, I figure I have her approval, so I swipe my tongue over her soft lips. All I want to do is go slowly and savor the tender feel and taste of her.

I groan when she opens her mouth willingly to me, and then she darts her tongue out to touch mine. Not hesitating, I take without apology and slip my tongue past her lips. When our tongues collide, the coolness of the iced tea she has on her tongue and the warmth of her mouth makes for an erotic contrast.

"I think my favorite kind of kisses are make-up kisses now," I mumble, grinning over her lips.

"How do you do that?" she whispers, panting over my lips.

"Do what, darlin'?" My lips twitch with a knowing smirk as I bend over and place the glass of tea on the floor. I love how my kisses always affect her reasoning abilities.

"Make my belly flip and dip every time you touch me?" An unsuppressed laugh escapes me, and she takes a playful swat at my chest. "Well, it does. Every time we touch, I seem to lose my self-control. It's like you've got this voodoo magic thing going on every time I get within five feet of you."

A sly grin spreads across my lips. "So is that the secret? Keep a five-foot rope around you?" She takes another swat at me, and I grab her wrist, pulling her into me. "Hey, now. I'm not doing anything we haven't done before. Your body already knows what it likes. It's your mind who's fighting you," I counter with an intense stare. "Kiss me again, and then deny me. Tell me no; I dare you." With those last words, I make my move and assault her with a scorching kiss, tasting her in such a way she can do nothing but take what I dish out. I pull her body flush against mine, and she moans. Her pert breasts rub against my chest. I use my free hand to cradle her cheek, tilting her head to the side so I can delve deeper into her mouth.

I will never be able to get enough of her. Talk about a landslide of love—I'm in an avalanche. I pull away just enough to tease her with my tongue, making her dizzy with desire as I whisper a seductive challenge over her lips. "Tell me you're not on fire for more. Deny me now, and tell me we aren't meant to be together."

"I can't," she whimpers as she opens her mouth wider, searching for me, but I continue to hold back.

"Damn right you can't. You may not know where you belong, but I do. I never had a moment's doubt." I give her everything I have as I unabashedly drive my tongue into her mouth, thrusting in and out of her warmth as our tongues tangle with heated passion. I grab her by the back of the neck, forcing her body to meld with mine as I fuck her mouth with my tongue.

My hand leaves her cheek to slowly peruse a trail over the soft, supple skin of her neck. Her pulse is racing beneath my fingertips. My hard-on is killing me. I want so badly to slide into her tight pussy and experience the euphoria of coming deep inside her. I then cup the swell of her breast in my hand and pinch her hard nipple. She whimpers in my mouth, my name a whispered prayer. "Travis."

I soothe the injury, rubbing gentle circles over her breast. Her hips move in time with my tongue, and I know her little pussy is on fire. I blindly find the hem of her dress and slip my hand underneath the material. I trail my fingers along the inside of her thigh, and I groan when she spreads her legs apart, giving me free access. My fingertips slip past the elastic band at her sex, and I dip two fingers past her folds. She's so wet I slip all the way in to my knuckles. "You're so damn sexy." I take pride knowing I got her juices flowing faster than the speed of light. She helplessly whimpers in soft little pants, moving her hips against my fingers as she tries to get more penetration, but I back off.

"What do you want, Jules?" I gruffly whisper between kisses.

"I want you, Travis." Her breathing is erratic, and her kisses grow sloppy. It's sexy as hell to watch her lose all inhibitions. She fists my shirt material in her hands, breathing hot and heavy when I let her come up for air. "Please fill me."

I smother her with hot passion and give her what she

wants. Torturously slow, I pump my fingers in and out of her wetness, stretching her silky walls. Oh, God, I think I'm gonna love make-up sex. Everything feels new, raw, and fervent. I pull my fingers out of her heat and wipe her juices over her clit, rubbing back and forth over her firm nub. She turns her head to the side, gasping for air, trying to stifle a moan. I dip three fingers in this time, and grin when her lungs deflate with a loud, "Ohhh, my God."

"You like feeling that fullness, sweetheart? You're pussy has soaked my hand. Let's see if I can make it sing." I work all three fingers against her g-spot while using my thumb to slide over her wet clit. I pull her lips back to mine and swallow her moans and whimpers.

I can tell when the sensations start to become too much for her to bear, because she tries to pull away from our kiss, and at the same time, her legs want to clamp down, shutting me out. I'm not having it. My grip tightens around her neck, making her take the over-stimulated pleasure. The heat between us is so extreme, it's off the charts.

Using more pressure, I circle her hard nub faster and faster, and drive my fingers in long and deep. I make her pussy take everything I have. She can't hold still; she's writhing all over my fingers as I hold her lips to mine. I'm thoroughly enjoying her fucking my fist, and after a few more minutes of torturing her, I let her have her release. I curl my fingers inside her tight walls, pumping inside her over and over as my thumb relentlessly works to stimulate her to orgasm.

When she detonates, she spasms around my fingers. Her legs shake uncontrollably, and she goes slack in my arms. As her orgasm rips through her body, I continue my assault until I feel she's spent every last ounce of her pleasure. When her tremors settle down around my fingers, I slowly bring them to a halt, leaving them deep inside her.

When I pull back to look in her eyes, I can feel her restrained love for me. Her blue eyes are so intense. The way she's looking at me, it's palpable. I will never let her go, not as long as I see this. It's on the tip of my tongue to tell her I love her, but I hold back. Maybe because I want to make sure I'm not rebound material. Fuck, I don't know. It's torture not knowing where her head is. I know she's in her own living hell right now too.

"I need inside you now, baby," I rasp. I need to be one with her. "That was sexy as fuck." I slide my fingers from her wet heat, latch onto the crotch of her panties, and tug.

"Travis," she whisper-squeals, suddenly aware of what we just did.

"Don't go shy on me now, baby. Thinking you're gonna get caught is half the fun."

Her breathing quickens again, as does mine when she lifts her hips, allowing me to slide her panties off. As she turns to plant a hand on either side of my chest to straddle me, I quickly peel off my gym shorts. No sooner does my rock-hard cock spring free does she take pause, and then quickly decides to drop to her knees in front of me. "Oh, hell," I groan. She's wearing a devilish grin as she peers up at me.

"Deny that you don't want this," she taunts, using my own words against me.

"Don't be a damn cock tease, woman. You know I want

your sexy lips wrapped around my dick."

"Language," she scolds playfully.

"I've got your language, baby..." Before I can say anything else, the words get caught in my throat as she leans forward and licks the tip of my dick. "Fuck," I groan. I watch her mouth as my length slowly disappears past her lips and deep into her warm, inviting mouth. As she pulls back, her tongue rolls over the tip, and I'm going to explode watching her do this to me.

She takes me all the way in this time, and I fist my hands at my sides, hissing through clenched teeth. She's warm and wet, and a shiver rolls through me as she bobs her head over my hard length.

She switches her technique, applying suction as she sucks me in deeper. Holy hell. My chest rises and falls with quick pants, and then she undoes me. She uses her tongue to lick and caress a sensual trail along the underside of my dick as her little hands come up to cup my balls. She rolls them in her hands, fondling me as she takes me all the way in. I feel her lips hit the base of my cock, her throat opening fully as I slip in a little deeper, and I'm done for.

"Whoa, whoa, whoa." I'm two seconds away from exploding, and I want to make this last. I lean forward and lift her up onto my lap, and her legs automatically spread open, straddling me. "You're going to be the death of me, woman," I breathe heavily, trying to get myself back under control.

Her eyes glisten and dance with satisfaction that she can undo me at the drop a hat. "Pretty proud of yourself, aren't you?" I ask wryly, arching a brow.

"As a matter of fact, I am," she whispers with a smirk as she hikes up her dress, and then she settles her opening over the tip of my head, taking control of the situation again. I grab her hips to slow her down before she can slide down over my length, but I'm too late. She impales herself fully in one quick stroke, and I lose my breath.

"Oh, God, woman." She grinds herself down and around to the base, seeking friction against her clit. Damn, she's a little minx. Her sex squeezes me tight, making me see stars. I have to slow her down. I use all my strength to hold her hips still as I stay nestled deep inside her. "Slow down, baby," I plead with labored breath. I lean forward and take her lips in a gentle, endearing kiss.

Once I have my dick back under control, I use my upper body strength to guide her hips up and down at my pace. I pull out just until her pussy holds the tip of my cock in her, and then I control the movement of her hips, gyrating her pussy over me in small tight circles. "Feel good, baby?" I whisper, but before she can answer, without warning, I slam her hips down over my length while thrusting myself upward in one hard, deep thrust.

She cries out into the night. I grind her clit over my pelvis, and then lift her hips up again to repeat the sweet torture. "Fuck, you feel so good," I groan. The sensation of our hips moving in tandem with each other, stretching and circling into her with my thickness, has me close to the edge. I take her nipple into my mouth, and suck hard at her breast through the thin fabric.

"Oh, God, Travis," she cries, holding onto the wooden slats behind me for stability.

I repeat the process of lifting her off me and swirling her hips as I tease her with the tip of my dick. Each time I slam her pussy down over my length, she groans, and it feels as if I'm entering her tight pussy for the first time, every time. I loosen my grip, letting her work me the way she wants while I gently rock her back and forth.

"Please, don't stop...I'm coming," she breathes out on a frantic whisper. Her head falls back as her eyes squeeze shut, and I pick up the pace, digging into her hips as I thrust in and out of her. Her entire body quivers with euphoria, milking my shaft, and I can't hold out any longer. I let the sensations take over, and lose myself in the depths of this beautiful woman, growling out my release.

After we both come down from our high, I wrap her tightly in my arms. She snuggles her nose into my neck, and sighs. I run my hands underneath her dress, and up the length of her back, needing to feel her soft, supple skin. I softly caress her with the pads of my fingertips. I don't want to lose this connection we have. Lately, it seems after our blind passion fades away and we separate, there's always something that causes friction. I'm sick of us both driving wedges. I'd sleep on this porch swing all night if it meant she'd fall asleep with me still inside her. I've never been superstitious, but damn if it hasn't crossed my mind.

I continue to swing us back and forth at an easy pace, allowing the crisp country air to cool us off.

"Travis?" she mumbles into my neck.

"Hmm?" I respond, lost in thought.

"I have a question."

I can't stifle my laugh; it comes unhindered. "Of course you do, Jules."

She sits up, and looks at me with false irritation.

"Okay, fine. I'll give you that one, but I do have a concern," she says as she twists her body and places her fingers along the incision mark Stryker had to make to get her tracker out. "I feel a small knot here where that tracker was taken out." She looks from her hip back to me with troubled eyes. My brows furrow at her comment as I brush her fingers away and feel for myself.

"I feel what you're talking about, but I think that's normal healing." My lips thin as I concentrate, carefully palpitating the tender area. "It doesn't feel or look swollen, and it's not warm to the touch, so I don't think it's infected. In all seriousness, I think you're fine. It's probably just a little scar tissue. I think it'll smooth out in a week or two."

With my diagnosis given, she relaxes back into me, laying her head back on my chest. I kiss the top of her head and breathe her in. I don't want to think what life would be like without my Jules. I hug her a little tighter, thankful I have her in my arms tonight.

CHAPTER 15

~Jules~

I jolt awake, my heart pounding in my throat. I've broken out in a cold sweat, and my body is trembling. I was living in a nightmare; it felt so real. I was shooting at people and watching them fall to the ground, saw them writhing in pain as they bled to death. I press my hand to my heart and feel it wildly beating out of control. My gosh, that was absolutely horrid. Is this what it's going to be like every night when I close my eyes and go to sleep? Will I have to relive nightmares about killing people, seeing blood, and have massive adrenaline surges that wake me up out of a dead sleep only to find myself soaked in sweat, and distraught?

It would be really nice to have Travis comfort me right now and softly stroke my hair while whispering in my ear, telling me everything is going to be fine. I roll my head to the side and see he is out like a light and softly snoring. I close my eyes and sigh. I really don't want to wake him. He has gotten next to zero sleep to speak of for the past forty-eight hours. I think he's been running on solid adrenaline. He's always been a light sleeper, waking up anytime I would stir, but right now, he's sleeping deeper than I've ever seen.

I roll over, look at the clock on the nightstand, and sigh. It's four o'clock in the morning. I get up on my shaky limbs and shed my soaked clothes. Cold chills race down my arms and over my bare body, making me shiver. The air conditioning wreaking havoc on my clammy skin.

Not wanting to disturb Travis by rummaging around, I slip on the first thing I can see in the dimly lit room. My jeans and a clean t-shirt it is. Of course, call me a weirdo, but I can't put on a tight fitting t-shirt without my bra. I can't stand my nipples poking out against the thin fabric.

I curl myself up on the overstuffed chair in the corner of the room and pull a blanket around me, trying to get warm again. The last thing I want to do is climb back into a cold, damp bed with wet sheets, so I sit here wide-awake and begin to think about things I probably shouldn't be thinking about.

Gazing upon his sleeping form, he looks so tranquil as his chest rises and falls in an easy, peaceful rhythm. He's so damn handsome. Well...let me rephrase; he's so damn *hot*. Things between us couldn't be any more messed up right now, and one question in particular that sticks out like a sore thumb is, *Why hasn't he ever told me he loves me?*

This relationship I've found myself in, if you can call it that, has been built on nothing but lies. I mean, the sex is absolutely phenomenal, but once we calm down from our passion, what's left? All of the things Quinn told me about them working with the mafia, and the way they all run around with guns and killing…I'm not comfortable being a part of that lifestyle.

I close my eyes and rest my forehead in my hands. I'm so confused. I miss my dad, and I miss Jake. I know between Jake and my dad, they can help me sort through all the rubble in my head. They can help me see things from a different perspective. My fear is that I have Stockholm Syndrome.

I need time to clear my head and think straight, something I haven't been able to do since I regained my memory. Yes, if I were able to take a step back and get away, I believe I could objectively reevaluate my circumstances, and decompress from all of the shock and mayhem. If Travis and I are truly meant to be, it'll still be there once I figure myself out.

My heart thrums with anxiety from the mere thought of making an attempt to escape. I sit here and consider my options if I were to try. Thinking of simply walking out the front door, even at this hour, I wouldn't make it two feet off the porch. Quinn is sleeping on the pullout sofa in the living room, which is basically at the bottom of the steps. My only other option would be the windows. I cringe; there's no way I'd jump down two stories. I'd break my neck.

I leave the blanket behind as I get up to check what lies on the other side of the window in our room. Moonlight creeps in through the slats of the mini-blinds as I slowly inch them open just enough to peer out. I'm surprised to see I have a three-foot ledge only two feet down. My forehead wrinkles as I think about this puzzle. The ledge below is still too high for me to jump to the ground, but I wonder what would happen if I could manage to get to the A-frame of the roof, and walk around to the back side of the house. I remember seeing the screened-in porch from the kitchen window when I was doing dishes. I noticed it had a flat ceiling and thought it odd, because I've never seen one like that. I can only presume the roof is flat too. It must have been an addition the guys built onto the back of the house.

I look back over my shoulder to see Travis lying flat on his stomach facing the other way. I bite my lower lip out of nervousness. *I can't believe I'm about to attempt this. What's the worst that could happen?* I guess the worst that could happen is I'd get caught, then maybe tied up, and then afterwards, I'd get a good yelling at. All those things are punishments I can handle.

Shoes...shit. Where are they? I look around in the dark, finally spotting them. My tennis shoes are underneath the edge of the bed. I tiptoe slowly to retrieve them and slip them on with no socks. I can't be choosy, now can I? I pause for a moment and decide it best to leave his engagement ring behind. I place it carefully on top of the nightstand and silently back away.

If I'm going to do this I can't think about this beautiful man sleeping only a few feet away from me. One who has spent every waking breath trying to protect me. Every cell in my body is screaming at me to get back in bed and cuddle up to him. Go back to sleep and forget this ever crossed my mind. I shake my head free of the conflict, and suppress thoughts of everything Travis—his masculine smell, the way he makes love, the way he looks at me with such endearing love, but has yet to say the words. Not only am I a victim of Stockholm and captivity, but I'm a victim of love.

My heart begins to race as fear bubbles up from the pit of my stomach when I creep back toward the window. My palms are slick with sweat, and I rub my hands against my jeans to rid myself of the moisture before I attempt to raise the window. I pray it's not screwed shut, or worse yet, one of those windows that squeak in their tracks upon opening. The fact that these windows are not wooden, but newer-looking, might be in my favor.

Through the moonlight shining in, I spot the lock and slowly flip it to the left, disengaging it. I wiggle my fingers to release the growing tension for the agile task at hand. I brace myself for the worst as my fingertips find the lip at the bottom portion of the pane, and slowly, inch-by-inch, I begin to raise it. Once I get it halfway up without a sound, the night's warm air wafts in, and I look back over my shoulder to see Travis hasn't budged an inch. If anything were to wake him right now, it would be the sound of my pounding heart.

Holy crap, this is anxiety city. I look long and hard at him one last time before I shimmy myself out the window. Since there's no drop, I'm able to shut the window except for the last inch or so. I don't want to push my luck, especially at this point. What could I say if I was caught? *Oh, gee, I thought I'd just open the window and get some fresh air, you know?* Yeah, right.

Wasting no time, I carefully walk on eggshells as I follow the roofline in the moonlight above. Once I reach the end of the house, I thank God it's a three-tiered house. The roof continues on in such a way I'm able to take a large step over to the second half of the house. I've never considered a fear of heights before, and if I did, the thought would be greatly overshadowed by the exhilarating sense of freedom, which is beginning to wash over me. I feel a little more in control of my future suddenly, and it's a giddy feeling.

I reach the peak of the roof, and then begin to descend toward the back of the house. The closer I get to the back porch, the faster my pulse races. I let out a breathy sigh of relief when I see that the screened-in porch roof is indeed flat. I'm down to a twelve-foot drop now, which is still too high for my liking. After a few seconds of thinking this through, I lay down on the scratchy shingles, perpendicular with the edge of the roof. My heart is literally pounding, and I swear it's going to explode.

I take a deep breath, begging myself not to screw this up. Slowly, I edge myself backward until both my legs dangle from the roof's ledge, my stomach pressing into the edge of the roof's shingles. My fingers find their place along the border of the roof as I scoot my body back a little bit more, praying I don't sway too far one way or the other and lose my grip. A soft grunt escapes me as I slip off the edge. I've successfully maneuvered myself to hang from the edge of the roof top. I figure what was once a twelve-foot drop should now only be between a four and five-foot drop with my arms extended. *I can do this.*

I let go and land on my feet, then promptly fall back on my ass. I've hurt nothing from the short drop. I take stock of myself; I feel good. I look around first to make sure I've not been spotted, but the house is pitch black. I stand up and carefully begin to slink my way around the front of the house before I make a break for it. As I do so, a motion detector light clicks on, and every organ I own is lodged in my throat. I'm standing in the middle of the yard like a deer caught in the headlights of a moving vehicle. Panic-stricken, I know how they feel now.

My feet start moving before I realize what I'm even doing, my legs pumping as I sprint across the soft grass. The further I get away from the house, the faster I run. This is the first taste of freedom I've had since this entire fiasco unfolded and I was captured. It feels fucking liberating, the feeling causing a spike of adrenaline to surge through my bloodstream, allowing me to run faster and longer until my heart feels like it will explode. My sneakers hit the asphalt in a rhythm all their own. My lungs start burning, but I savor the pain and the pleasure all at once.

The further I run away from the house, the more guilty I feel for leaving Travis behind, but I know this is the right thing to do. None of this capturing and owning another human being shit is right. There's nothing honorable, ethical, or moral about it. It's wicked and it's wrong.

So why does it feel like I'm losing a piece of my heart the further away I run? It's like my head knows what's right, but my heart wants me to turn around—being a human captive be damned. *Stupid, Jules, just stupid. You can sort out your feelings later.* I haven't seen my father and Jake in over a month, and right now, it feels like years.

As I am running away, it's odd I even notice there are fewer stars in the sky as opposed to the night sky at the cabin. Memories taunt me as I remember warm nights out on the front porch of the cabin. Travis and I would talk about the stars and how much brighter they were out in the country. *Why am*

I thinking of stars at a time like this? All of it was a fairytale. A lie.

My legs start to give out and I stumble. I'm forced to slow down my stride and focus on my breathing. I'm growing tired, but I refuse to give up, so I force myself to push on as I half-stagger and half-jog. I let the thoughts of having my entire life ripped out from under me fuel my anger, which in turn feeds my energy to keep moving forward. I've lost so much of my future, the most important thing being Adam.

My vexation has me pumping my legs faster and harder. I feel beads of sweat beginning to trickle down the side of my face, and the cool early morning air feels good against my overheated skin. The only thing I can hear is the rhythmic pounding of my feet on the asphalt and my hard breathing. My lungs continue to constrict as they fight for air.

My mind is willing my body to go the distance, all the way to Atlanta, but my body has other ideas. Against my will, the muscles in my legs, combined with the lack of oxygen in my lungs, have my body coming to a screeching halt. *Dammit.* I can't push myself any farther, and I bend over, grasping my knees with my hands as my chest heaves like a seventy-year-old chain-smoker. I turn around and glance back, and see nothing but a bright-lit moon against a clear, dark sky. I don't know how far I've run, but it feels like a couple of miles at least. I look around and notice the sky is changing to a lighter gray. I haven't seen one single car since being on these back roads at this hour, and to me, that's a good thing.

Placing my hands on my hips at the small of my back I lean back and stretch out, taking another deep breath to fill my lungs. Then I start to walk out my fatigued and tired muscles.

I have to keep moving, especially if I'm going to make it. I've resorted to power walking now, knowing it's better than just walking, but not as tiring as running. It feels as if another half-hour has gone by.

When the guys drove here, I knew we were out of the city limits, but my gosh, these roads are just going on forever.

Since I fell asleep on the way here, I have no idea if I'm headed in the right direction or not. All I know is I'm still on a two-lane country road, and hopefully making my way toward the city of Raleigh. I have no idea what I'm going to do when I get there either, other than try to find a way to phone home.

The quiet morning I've been used to hearing for the past hour is interrupted by the sound of what could only be a diesel truck. It's coming from behind me, and I immediately tense up.

These are the moments I wish I had a gun to defend myself if I needed to. Unfortunately, the guys have them under lock and key, or they're kept on their own body. There would be no way any one of them would let me have a firearm either.

I quickly turn around and see a large red Ford pick-up truck. It looks very used and abused, and at the sight of it, I slightly relax, knowing it's not Travis. However, I swallow hard against the lump in my throat when the truck doesn't drive by. It slows down, and then comes to a full stop a few feet away from me. I'm about to find my second wind and run, but before I do, I catch a glimpse of the driver. He's a good-looking guy; I guess you could call him a redneck, but he's a handsome-looking redneck.

He leans his head out the window, giving me a friendly

smile, and I minutely relax.

"You lost, darlin'?" he calls out with a rich southern drawl.

I quickly shake my head. "I'm fine, thank you."

He eyes me up-and-down then pitches his head to the side, a lock of blond hair spilling over his forehead while he watches me warily.

"You don't look fine. In fact, I'm a little concerned for you. Don't find many women walkin' along a dark country road, 'specially at 5:30 in the morning. Not unless you're doin' a serious walk of shame with nothing but the shirt on your back."

I don't know how to respond to that comment, but at least he's nice enough to say I don't look like a hooker. Even though it's 5:30 in the morning, and I've cooled off from my long run, the hot and humid air has started to seep into my skin, rendering me parched and fatigued.

"Why don't I give you a lift into town?" he offers. "Is that where you're headed?"

Shifting my feet, I don't answer. I'm wary as hell going anywhere with strangers. For obvious reasons. As if he could read my mind, he holds his hand out of the truck window with his palm facing me in a friendly gesture to show me he's harmless. "I'm just a country boy showin' a little southern hospitality. I just want to help a lady who looks to be in distress." His southern accent, charm, and the twinkle in his eyes have him looking so sincere. Trying to ascertain his intentions, all I can come up with is he truly wants to be a Good Samaritan. I decide to take a chance. "C'mon, what do you say? It's a long hike into Raleigh from here."

"Okay," I meekly reply, biting my lower lip with worry.

I'm tired, and it would be best if I get off the road and out of plain sight, especially with daylight breaking. I'm sure the guys will be freaking out the second they find me gone. I make my way to the passenger side of the truck and open the door. When I step up on the running board, I glance into the back seat and suppress a grin. This is definitely a man's truck. It's filthy, full of trash, with old crumpled paper bags of fast food and empty water bottles strewn across the entire cab.

"Sorry about the mess. This is my work truck. If I'd known I was going to be picking up a pretty little lady this mornin', I would've brought my brand new GMC Sierra Denali 2500, v8 engine with 420 horsepower and 460lb-ft of torque," he says as if he is *Tim the Tool Man*, and then his lips twitch before he breaks out into a beautiful smile. His grin and silliness is infectious, and I giggle, returning his smile.

"Well, damsels in distress can't be choosy now, can they?"

His smile dissipates, and his expression grows serious as he looks at me with concern. "Are you...a damsel in distress?" I pause, hesitating to step fully into the truck. He must see the conflicting emotions running across my face, because he tries to reassure me.

"It's okay, sweetheart. I'm not going to hurt you. I'm happy to help. It's what real gentlemen do here in the south." Oh, if he only knew what other gentlemen do here in the south, he wouldn't be saying that.

I take a moment to study him before climbing in. He has a strong build, and a very nice tan, as if he works under the sun, on a farm maybe. The color of his striking blond hair is one that even I'm jealous of. He can't be much older than me.

He pats the empty seat beside him, garnering my attention. "C'mon," he encourages with a smile, "I don't bite." I go ahead and hoist myself up into the front seat and close the truck door.

Judging from his helpful and sweet personality, I could see where he wouldn't have the first clue about what debauchery goes on in the business sector of the south. This handsome young man is what the real south was made of. I have to remind myself not everyone is out to hunt me down. I let out a breath I didn't realize I was holding as I let the tension leave my taught shoulders, and then I sit back to relax.

He puts the truck back in gear, glances behind him, and then gets back on the road. We ride in silence for about a minute before he takes his eyes off the road for a quick second as he looks at me with a flash of worry.

"I don't know what you're going through, but whatever it is, you can trust me. I can get you the help you need."

"What I really need is a phone," I mumble, not expecting him to produce one.

"Well, why didn't you say so?" My eyes open wide with disbelief as he reaches into his back pocket and pulls out an iPhone. Judging from his attire and the condition of his truck, I wouldn't have thought he would own such an expensive phone. My face must be all-telling, because he lets out a hearty laugh. I pull my gaze away from the phone cradled in his hand and look at him with confusion.

His lip twitches with mirth as he speaks, "Don't let the looks fool you, sweetheart. I'm in construction, and I make damn good money. I don't dress nice onsite, and by the end of the day, not only have I been rough on my truck, but *I'm* dirty."

His lips spread into a beautiful white smile with perfectly straight teeth, and two of the sexiest dimples appear in his cheeks. "I wasn't kidding when I said I have a nice truck. I've got a lot of other nice things too," he says as he holds out his hand, offering me his cell.

I just bet he does have a lot of other nice things. I grin at his innocent comment and take the phone from his hand. I turn it over in my hands a few times, realization dawning that I haven't had a communication device in over a month. It's a precious piece of technology I'd always taken for granted. I don't know what to think it feels so weird.

"Do you need some help turning it on?" he asks, breaking into my thoughts.

Still staring at the phone, I answer him, "I've never seen such a thin plastic protective case before is all." Which is a lie.

"It's one of the best covers money can buy. It's waterproof too," he explains.

"Mm," is all I say as I press the button to turn on the phone, and then swipe across the screen to access the keypad. With shaky fingers, I type in the numbers nice and slow, trying not to dial the wrong number from over-excitement. The time on the phone says it's a little after 5:30 in the morning, and I'm positive my dad won't care if I wake him up at this hour. Knowing he keeps his cellphone by his side at all hours, I know it is right beside his bed. Heck, he even takes it into the bathroom with him when he showers in the morning. He's that busy.

The phone rings three times before he picks up, his voice groggy from sleep. "Hello?"

"Daddy?" I breathe in a relieved gasp as I close my eyes, thankful to hear his familiar voice.

"Oh, my God! Princess!" he shouts, immediately awake. "Where are you? Are you okay? I've been looking for you everywhere. I've turned every corner of the world upside-down trying to find you." His words rush out in a panic.

"Daddy, I'm okay," I reassure him. "I'm in Raleigh, North Carolina right now. I need you to help me find a way home. I don't have any money or ID on me, so I'm in a big bind."

As I explain to him I'm in a stranger's truck heading toward Raleigh, he asks to speak with the young man. I hand the phone back over to the stranger, and I find out through their conversation that his name is Heath. I guess it's pretty rude of me that I didn't even find out his name, and he's rescued me off the side of the road. I hear him exchange personal information with my dad as they talk for a few minutes longer, and then he ends the call.

Why did they hang up? I wasn't done talking to my dad. Before I can utter my question, Heath cocks his head to the side, looking at me with raised brows, and lets out a low whistle. "You must be somebody very, very important, young lady. Your father wants me to take you to the airport and have you fly out on a private jet. He hung up so he could go ahead and make arrangements stat. He also asked me to personally see to it that you get on that jet safely." He pauses, giving his full attention back to the road, and then changes lanes. "It's not every day someone offers you twenty grand to ditch half the workday and see to it that someone's daughter gets on a plane headed home." He shakes his head with incredulous disbelief.

"Honestly, I told your dad that wasn't necessary, but he sounds as if he's the kind of man you don't say no to."

A genuine laugh escapes past my lips. "Oh, you couldn't be any closer to the truth." I'm so happy and overjoyed right now, I'm sitting on the edge of my seat. No cost is too much for my dad to have his little girl back, and nothing is spared to see it through. I let out a huge sigh of relief as a big smile paints my face.

"Sounds like you're more than just a damsel in distress," Heath says, eyeing me cautiously. "You must really be going through something epic to be two states up from Georgia, and stuck in the middle of nowhere with nothing on you."

"You have no idea." I don't elaborate on that statement, and he doesn't ask. As we get closer to the Raleigh belt-line, we start passing fast food places and he looks to me. "Would you like some coffee or breakfast on the way to the airport?"

"That sounds awesome. Thank you. There's just one slight problem though, and I'm not being picky, but can we stop at a Harris Teeter that has a Starbucks inside? I'm sorry I don't have any money, but my dad will pay you back," I reassure him.

He bursts out with genuine laughter, and then he runs a hand through his thick blond hair. "Are you kidding me, darlin'? I think I can afford whatever it is you need, especially after your dad just wired twenty grand to my account."

Wow, there are no words, I think as I slump back into the cushioned seat of Heath's truck in relief and briefly close my eyes. Resting my head back against the headrest, I gaze out the window, watching the morning sunrise come up over the interstate as it casts a bright light on a new day full of hope. Elation fills me as rays of sunshine filter through the clouds above, emitting a lighthearted spiritual feel. It feels odd how everyone is rushing around, each in their own little world as they get ready to start their daily grind. I wonder how many of these people take their life and freedom for granted.

CHAPTER 16

~Travis~

I roll over in bed with the intention of wrapping my arms around Jules and having a morning rendezvous, but quickly realize her side of the bed is empty. I'm always the first one awake in the morning, so this surprises me.

Maybe she's in the bathroom. "Jules?" I call out, but I'm met with silence. I get out of bed and throw on a pair of jeans. "Jules?" I call out again as I look into the bathroom. Being a light sleeper, I have never had her be able to slip out of bed in the morning without me knowing about it. I make my way downstairs, looking into each room as I make my way to the kitchen. Quinn and Stryker are drinking coffee at the table.

"Guys, has Jules been down here?"

They both shake their heads. "Stryker and I have been the only ones up for the past half-hour, Trav. What's up?" Quinn asks concerned.

"Jules isn't upstairs, and I can't find her."

"She's gotta be upstairs. You're the first one I've seen

surface from the bedrooms."

I shake my head. "No, man. I already checked." I don't like the bad feeling creeping into my gut, and the guys can see what I'm thinking.

"Travis, she's here. I sleep for shit on the sofa; I'd know it if she came down those stairs at any point," Quinn tries to reassure me, but it's not working.

I turn around on my heel and head back up the stairs, taking three at a time with the guys following fast behind me.

"Jules!" I yell out, panic lining my voice. I give hand signals for the other guys to check the other rooms one-by-one as I head back to our bedroom, looking for clues. As the guys call her name, I scan over the bedroom, scrutinizing every inch of the place. The light streaming in through the window catches my attention, and that's when I notice the window is an inch ajar. "Fucking hell!"

I lift the blinds all the way up and open the window to look out. "Travis! What did you find?" Stryker asks from behind me.

I turn around with a grim feeling. "I think she took off out the window."

Stryker shakes his head. "Nah, man...there's no way."

I lift a brow. "Really? If you wanted out bad enough, how would you get out?" Stryker rubs the back of his neck in a nervous gesture. He knows I'm right. "Shoes. Where are her shoes?" I skirt around Stryker, looking for them.

"Umm...Travis," Stryker says warily. I turn around and receive a sucker punch to my gut. Stryker stands beside the bed, holding up her engagement ring.

"*Sonofabitch*," I snarl. "How the fuck could this have

happened?" Immediately, I go into combat mode and begin barking orders. Everyone disperses with a task as I quickly get dressed. Every minute that ticks by with no sign of Jules is a minute in Hell.

Everyone scrambled to get their shit and gear into the van. Stryker is the last one in the van, and he slams the side door closed. As soon as Chase turns the ignition key, I'm on Quinn. "When will we be able to get her voice signal?" I ask as Quinn starts setting up the electronics.

"Calm down, Trav. Trust me, you'll be the first to know. You need to sit the fuck down and let us do our jobs," he says with irritation lining his voice as he continues to work on his laptop. He's the kind of guy who can play a game of chess, figure coordinates on a map, and fly an airplane, all at the same time, and yet be fully engaged in a conversation. I will never understand how the hell he does it. The man is a genius. "I'm pulling up her tracking signal right now."

I move in behind Quinn, looking over his shoulder at the laptop screen. He points his finger at the bleeping dot on the screen and explains, "She should be showing up in this area here, but she's not." He turns to look over his shoulder at me, his eyes wide. "I think she's in the fucking air."

"Holy. Fucking. Shit. Are you sure?"

Stryker looks over at me and nods. "He's right, man."

"She had no I.D., no money, nothing."

"Yes, but there is nothing her daddy can't handle, right?" Quinn asks.

I close my eyes and grit my teeth. "Fuck. I can't believe this is happening." I steel a deep breath and face reality. "All right. Georgia it is. If that's the best educated guess we can come up with, and if we just sit here, waiting for her to touch ground, we will be losing valuable time."

"Are you all on board with this?" Quinn asks everyone.

"You know we are," Stryker says.

It's at least a six-hour drive to Atlanta. I would love to fly, but I think TSS would frown at the amount of weaponry we would be toting along.

Two hours into the trip, and I'm about to crawl out of my skin when Quinn announces Jules has hit ground. I sit on the edge of my seat, greedy for intel, but Quinn says nothing more. "Well, dude...where the fuck is she?!"

"I'm getting there! Hang on to your panties, woman," Quinn replies while staring intently at the computer screen.

"Chase, I need you to make some phone calls. I have a feeling it's time to pull in some back-up," I order.

Chase glances back from the driver's seat, giving me a quick nod in the rear-view mirror.

"Yep, just what we thought. She's in Georgia. Private landing strip, no doubt owned by her daddy," Quinn utters.

"Can you get a voice on her, yet?" I ask.

"Already on it. Might take a little time; we're a little out of range, but I'll work something out."

"Shit, that's not good enough," I bite out. I'm so damn wired my gut feels as if it's churning battery acid.

Stryker, the ever-knowing psychologist, leans in to whisper, "You're not going to do her any good, not this way. Not to mention, you're more apt to make mistakes, and one of us could wind up dead over it."

I take a deep breath and lean away from him before I coldcock him. He's right, but I'm not in the mood to hear his shit. I stare out the window, growing more anxious as I watch each mile go by in what feels like slow motion.

"Trav," Stryker cautiously starts off. He can't help himself. He always has to give his two cents even though I know he's only trying to help. "She's not Clarissa. This is a different set of circumstances."

"Is it really, Stryker?" I look at him out of the corner of my eye. "A marred soul is a marred soul, no matter how you slice it. Who's to say what one person goes through is less significant than another? All because you evaluated and measured this shit out on the Stryker tipping scale?"

"Fair enough. I guess what I'm trying to say is maybe she's a fighter to the bitter end. I don't see her giving in."

And that right there is my fear—Jules throwing in the towel, giving up on life.

I lean my head back against the car seat and close my eyes. Every single scene, every finite detail of my past, comes rushing in like a tidal wave to the forefront of my mind. There is no tamping down the raw emotions that have washed over me.

Clarissa was the love of my life. Her family moved in across the street from Grant when I was in the fifth grade. Grant's wife babysat for them a lot, and the little squirt grew on me. Every spare second of her life, she was constantly spending it in my space. By the time I left for the military, she was starting her freshman year of high school. She didn't know it then, but I knew I was going to marry her.

By the beginning of her senior year of high school, things were happening fast between us. We were getting serious about each other. I wanted to be there for her when she graduated, but I couldn't. I was doing a tour overseas.

As a graduation gift, I wanted to fly her overseas to meet me in Europe, and I knew her parents would flip their lids, so I offered for her older brother to come along too. I smile at the memory. She was excited as shit when her folks said yes.

The guys and I had our R&R scheduled and her tickets were bought. I had no idea. She was too young, too innocent, and far too pretty.

I thought she'd be safe traveling with her older brother. *The stupid bastard.*

They had arrived a few days early to do some sightseeing in Europe, because I sure as hell wasn't interested in being a tourist. The only sight my eyes were going to be on was her in my bed for three days. I don't know how the hell Stryker did it, but he managed to sweet-talk our commander into letting us take off a day early.

When I got to the hotel to surprise her, she had left. Cellphone service was not the best back then. So my buddies and I took off to the bar down the street. I'll never forget that night. As fate would have it, I ran into her piece-of-shit brother at the bar. I remember being out-of-my-skin ecstatic, expecting to finally see my girl. I glanced around, and not seeing her in the crowded little bar, I asked her brother where she was. He said Clarissa had taken off for the bathroom, but that had been a while ago. Instead of investigating, he brushed it off, thinking she had decided to dance or some shit.

Immediately, I started searching for her, and then panic began to envelop me when no one could find her. Quinn, with his *Rambo* ways, was able to gather some information from a patron. Apparently he had found someone who had some intel for a price. I would've handed my whole life savings over if need be. It was an organized setup, and apparently there were a few guys who regularly *worked* the local bars, looking for pretty young women. They managed somehow to drug her drink, and when she went to the ladies' room, that's when they made their move.

Motherfucking human traffickers had make their move. Stole her, robbing her of her dignity and soul.

Yeah, little did I know the sex industry was legalized there, which opened the doors for forced prostitution and trafficking, and the fuckers in power wonder why sexual exploitation is out of control. They rolled out the red carpet to the Transnational Criminal Network. You can't tell me those corrupt officials don't know what the fuck they're doing. They helped facilitate the lucrative business. Of course, prostitution is legal, but to purchase said prostitution is a crime. Go figure.

The slick bastards are so sophisticated and multifaceted; I found out later they've acquired close to five million women over time. Law enforcement could barely skim the top of that shit. Needless to say, it was up to me and my men to get her back, and I couldn't have done it without them. They laid their careers and lives on the line for me. Yeah, my men and I went rogue. That's a whole 'nother story.

When we found her, with what little clothing remained on her body, she was strung out on coke and huddled in a corner with five other women who looked the same as her. I will never forget those eyes. Those eyes were fucking hollow, far away, empty, and despondent. I was surprised we were able to find her. Lucky for us, we had finally caught up to the bastards two days later, and had we been one hour later in finding her, she would've been gone forever on a boat to God knows where.

Unfortunately, it was already too late for Clarissa. They gang raped her, and that's all I could get out of her. We spent the next two days holed up in a hotel room together, trying to help her cope. I know they did more, but she couldn't bring herself to talk about it, not when it was too fresh and raw. I'd like to think between Stryker and me that we had her mind set in the right direction. I tried to get more time off, but my CO was not having it. I had to send her back home with her worthless brother. Why I didn't go ahead and kill him, I don't know.

I found out she had to go into counseling within days of her getting back home. I barely got to talk to her, being overseas, and it gutted me. Two weeks later, her parents sent word she had committed suicide. Didn't I feel responsible as fuck for that?

From that day forward, I lived in vengeance. Transnational

Criminal Network was on my list as soon as my military term was up. Granted, the difference I've made has been but a faint echo, but I feel as if I'm doing my part. I know when I'd take out one outfit, another two would spring up somewhere else.

I didn't like my hands being tied to rules and regulations that come with a badge. I figure criminals don't have rights, and they lost their rights the second they took another. My men and I decided to be independent contractors. When the CIA got wind of a developing drug that would alter perceptions and act as an ecstasy drug, I didn't blink twice to sign up.

I let out a heavy sigh, I've never felt so overwhelmingly helpless as I do right now, and I pray to God history is not repeating itself.

Quinn claps his hands loudly, startling me. "Hot damn!" he shouts. "I've got voice transmission."

CHAPTER 17

~Jules~

Making my way off the airplane, I take the last step off the stairs and onto the tarmac. Immediately, I recognize the private landing strip, and an indescribable elation fills me. I spot one of Dad's many black limos already here and waiting for me. My heart skips a beat, knowing I'll see Jake too. I'm almost to the vehicle when the driver's side door opens, and a big burly man steps out. My step falters, and the look on my face can only be one of disappointment.

"Where's Jake?" I ask disconcerted, halting in my steps. Jake is always the one to come get me, unless, of course, he's out of town.

This man is scary big, and I haven't seen him before. I back up a few steps, and the man immediately throws his hands up in surrender. "Trust me, he wanted to be the one to pick you up. He told me to tell you personally he cut his business trip short, and he's enroute as we speak," he explains. He regards me with what looks to be empathy and compassion as he continues, "Your dad chose me for the job, because I'm the best in the business, and I don't have to tell you twice how dangerous the real world is."

Touche, Mr. Big Man, I think to myself. I open the car door for myself, and as I slide into the back seat, I'm immediately hit with the fresh smell of leather. I feel safe on one hand, but highly disappointed on the other. Why didn't my dad come out here to greet me if Jake couldn't? I mean, he never has come to greet me any other time, but this situation is entirely different.

I'm so lost in thought I don't even realize the car is pulling off the airstrip until the driver clears his throat to speak. "I'm Alex, by the way." I half ignore him as I look out the car window, excited to be home. "Your dad wanted to come, but I decided against it." I whip my head around to give Alex my full attention as he continues, "I told him due to the given situation, it would be easier for me to protect one person instead of two. There was no reason to put extra people at risk being out in the open."

I suppose that's true. I didn't think about that; not to mention, he spent a vast amount of money to get me home the safest and fastest way possible. "I'm sure everything is going to be fine, but one can never be too careful, can they?"

I shake my head, speaking softly, "No, definitely not."

We ride in silence back to my house, which is a very short distance, and the closer I get, the more anxious I become. It seemed as though I would never see my home again. Pulling into the long drive, tears of joy spring forth, and a large lump forms in my throat. I try clearing my throat, but it doesn't work.

As soon as Alex puts the car in park, I've already opened the back car door and have bolted out. An indescribable exhilaration fills me as I spring up the all too familiar brick steps leading to the front entryway. The doors are unlocked, and as I step into the foyer, all the familiar scents accost me. I take in a deep breath, inhaling every good memory this house gave me.

"Daddy!" I yell out with enthusiasm as I run down the hallway to his office. "Daddy!"

"Princess," he calls out as I round the corner of his office door. "Oh, my God, you're home. I can't believe it," he cries with joy as his arms spread open wide. I bury my face into his shoulder, and a long, suppressed sob escapes my lungs. "Shh... you're safe now." There is no way in hell I will ever be able to talk to him about what went on inside the facility, or what I was put through. A shiver skates down my body, and my limbs tremble at the thought of being a sex slave.

"You're shaking, Princess," my dad whispers over my head, his voice full of concern as he squeezes me tightly. "Are you okay?"

"I don't know, Daddy," I weep. "I just don't know." I melt into his embrace. There's a small gap of silence as he holds me tightly, and I let out a huge sigh of relief, thankful to be in his arms.

Someone clears their throat behind me, and it echoes throughout the room. Maybe it's one of the bodyguards garnering for my dad's attention, but my dad doesn't say anything. Clearing their throat again, the sound is louder this time, and my forehead wrinkles. *Maybe it's Jake,* I think with anticipation, and with that thought, I turn around to see.

As I twist around, I feel as if I've been hit by a Mack truck. My heart comes to a standstill as I'm confronted with the man who started all my nightmares. He's casually sitting down in a calm fashion with his arms stretched out along the back of the love seat, and his ankle crossed over his knee. "Nick," I breathe his name on a whispered breath, taken aback. I shrink back into my father's chest and visibly shiver. The memory of everything Nick did to me comes rushing back like a tsunami.

"You remember me, Princess?" he purrs, exuding a superior arrogance, which has my heart leaping out of my chest.

"You..." I scowl, pointing at him with a shaky hand. My voice fails me as he gets up from the sofa, approaching me with a haughty grin. If it's even possible, I sink farther back into the protectiveness of my father's embrace as my pulse thunders through my veins.

Every instinct I have says to run, get out, but my feet won't move. I glance at the door, wondering if I could even make it at this point, but I don't think I can. As he nears, I shake my head, willing him to go away, but no words come out. This can't be happening. When he stops directly in front of me, I finally find my voice. "Oh, my God, Dad! He's...he's the one who took me!" I croakily whisper in fear.

Nick's lips twist in a smug smile as he slightly tilts his head, raising a questioning brow. "What are you talking about, Julianna? Your father called me the minute he heard the exciting news that you'd been found and were coming home."

My father steps back out of the way as Nick steps forward,

and immediately, I feel as if I'm a sitting duck. "We've been looking day and night for you." The longing in Nick's voice as he reaches out to clasp my hand turns my stomach. "Is this how you welcome the one who did everything in his power to get you back safely?"

My father steps to the side of me, and when I turn my head to look at him, he adds, "I believe you two have met, no?" Then he has the audacity to chuckle. *He actually fucking chuckles.*

My eyes go wide as I shake my head in disbelief. How am I supposed to process this? My fight-or-flight responses can't decide what to do, because, hello...I'm in the safety of my home now. This isn't supposed to be happening.

"Dad?" I whisper-cry for help in one word.

Nick grasps both my arms and pulls me into his body. I'm so dumbstruck I'm rendered speechless; even my own limbs betray me. Then Nick leans forward to run his nose along my jawline, breathing softly over my skin as he whispers in my ear, "I've missed you so much, sweetheart." He pulls me in tight until our chests touch like two long-lost lovers, and then he wraps his arms around me.

"I think now would be a good time to tell her the good news, wouldn't you say, Lance?" Nick's deep voice floats over my head, and then drizzles down my body, sending chills to my very core.

I turn my head as I nervously peer at my father. "Daddy?" The pitch of my disconcerted voice quavers. "Tell me what news."

"Nick has informed me you two are getting married next week." He then narrows his eyes at Nick with an unnerving glare, arching a brow. "That is, unless you think you can't hold onto her this time."

Not believing my own ears, an audible gasp escapes me. Nick leans down, guiding my panic stricken gaze to meet his confident one. "Oh, I'm positive." Shivers wrack my body, and I try to squirm out of his hold, but he's too strong. "How about we sit down so we can talk, sweetheart?"

Pulling myself out of my shocked stupor, I hiss, "Let me go!" I turn toward my dad with pleading eyes. "Help me. You don't understand." *Why is he just standing there?* "Dad?" I repeat, as I twist around, pulling away from Nick, but his grip tightens to the point of pain and I wince.

I shoot my dad a quizzical look, one of pure distress, and watch in horror as he nonchalantly turns his back on me, walking to his desk to pull out a cigar from his humidor. "What the hell is going on?" I yell in anger, suddenly forgetting my fears.

"Ahh, inquisitive as ever I see, aren't you, Julianna?" my father starts off in a calm voice. He seems more intent and focused on his precious cigar than the matter at hand. "You see, Nick and I are business partners." He pauses to place the unlit cigar underneath his nose and inhales, closing his eyes. "I'm a silent partner, if you will, a money-backer to Project Blyss," he states simply.

I feel the second my heart stops beating, and I go numb and tingly on the inside. I get the distinct impression that this isn't the end of his story. A bigger bomb is about to drop and detonate as I realize my entire life is exploding into smithereens before me.

"You what?" I hiss incredulously. I want to claw his fucking eyeballs out. I elbow Nick in his gut to get away.

"Whoa there, Princess." Nick stifles a grunt while he gets a better grip on me, preventing me from cutting loose.

"That's right, you heard correctly. Just so happens Nick here, came along at the most opportune time with an offer I couldn't refuse."

"You sold me! Your own daughter?!" Anger like never before consumes me. I yank hard on my arm to free myself, and almost succeed, but Nick is prepared this time. He's too strong and quick. "You are sick. You are twistedly psycho, and you need help!" I spew.

My dad eyes me down, regarding me for a silent moment. An eerie stillness settles over him. "You know, I did the right thing. Your behavior patterns mimic your mother's more and more every day. I knew...I just knew you were inherently born to be on their side," he sneers.

My voice is a dubious whisper, "What? What are you talking about?"

"It's the same thing she said. Said I was sick, except I'm not. She was constantly trying to drug me." He narrows his eyes on mine as he comes to a conclusion. "I can tell it'd only be a matter of time before you'd want to do the same. Slip psychosomatic drugs in me where and when you could. Yet another reason why you need to be under lock and key, and controlled with drugs."

"What? Where's this coming from?"

An angered huff of air leaves his lungs, as if I've offended his intelligence. "That's what I'd like to know. I've been nothing but good to you, thinking I could trust you all this time, but I can't. You are one hundred percent your mother." He pauses to put his cigar down, placing his hands on the desk as he leans in with a glare. "She continually tried to poison me, you know. It got to the point where I saw her sneaking it into my food and drink, and one of those times, she outsmarted me. She damn near left me to die."

As if I was just sucker-punched, a burst of air leaves my lungs in a whoosh. *He's making no sense.* I blink several times and sway, thankful now that Nick is holding me. "What are you saying?"

He waggles his finger at me. "Oh, I think you know. Everyone always acts innocent, but it always turns out to be a front. She forced my hand; I had to take action against her."

Everything turns into slow motion. I feel prickly tingles from the roots of my hair to the tips of my toes as he moves to the front of his desk to stand before me. "I don't understand," I barely whisper. "You killed my mother?"

"Oh, for Christ's sakes, Julianna, can't you read between the lines?" he sneers, highly agitated. "Yes, she was not on my side. She was against me from the beginning." He then gives me an evil look, challenging me. "Don't you deny it either. You might come off all innocent, just like your mother did at first, but I can read right through you."

The hairs on the back of my neck prickle as an ominous dark cloud hovers over the room. The gloomy atmosphere seeps into my bones, and it should make me want to run, scream, fight...something, other than just stand here thunderstruck with my mouth agape as this possessed demon paces back and forth in front of me.

"You see, your grandparents were on my side after I had to take action against your mother. The way they took over and helped cover up the *mishap*," he says, using air quotes. "They helped to make it look like an accident to protect me, but soon, I found out they too had ulterior motives. It didn't take long before I was onto them too, and they knew it."

My upper body sways, and Nick holds me tighter against his chest. I can't seem to process his words. "Your grandparents...they could see their demise coming a mile away, and I have to give them credit; they played it smart. They tied you to an insurance policy, one so intertwined—well, it pissed me the fuck off. Once you turned twenty-one, you were to inherit Oakley Global Enterprises, and if anything were to happen to you at any given time, all Oakley holdings would go directly to charity. I couldn't let that happen, now could I? When you turned twenty-one, you were to inherit all of the wealth." He stops pacing the floor and locks his gaze with mine, sending a cold chill down my spine. "The bottom line is I couldn't allow you to get the upper hand on me. I had to find a way to get you to sign all holdings over to me once you turned of age."

"Holy fuck," Nick whispers in disbelief beside my ear.

"So, you see, I was in a bit of a quandary, but Nick here came along at the right time and I found the perfect solution. Nick said this drug, Blyss, which I've invested in, would be the drug of the century. He went on to explain about his high-end operation, and how not only being a captive, but also a subservient one, would have these women obeying their master's every command. So I'm sure you could see I found the perfect solution to my dilemma."

All I can do is shake my head in dazed shock and utter, "No."

My dad stops his pacing to smile at me. "You'll soon realize this is a win-win for all of us. I could've done something far worse to you," he says, giving a quick jerk of his chin toward Nick behind me, "but I'd say he's a pretty fine catch. Wouldn't you?"

"What the fuck is going on here?" a deep voice bellows from behind. *It's Jake.* All of us turn to see Jake, whose nostrils are flaring. He stalks into the room, his biceps stretching the confines of his dress shirt as his hands clench into tight fists, ready to strike at any moment. I tug to break away from Nick, but he's not letting me go.

"Jake, help me," I cry out, "please..."

Nick holds me tighter as Jake heatedly flicks his eyes between both my dad and Nick, assessing and digesting the scene. It's then I notice Jake stalking in with a limp, and my heart squeezes. He took a bullet trying to protect me. My dad holds out his hand in a halting motion, as if that's going to keep Jake from advancing, limp or not. "Stop right there, Jake. This doesn't concern you."

Jake stops within a couple feet of all of us, his upper lip twitching with intense hostility. "The fuck it's not my business. Julianna has always been my business. You said your delusional shit was under control. What'd you do, Lance, pay off your fucking psychologist?! I can't believe you went batshit-crazy within your own delusions!" Jake bellows.

A pained whimper escapes me, and my chest constricts. I can barely breathe the words, "You...you knew?"

Jakes shifts his gaze to mine and shakes his head, remotely softening his eyes. "I didn't know this, Jules, I promise. I only knew of his paranoid schizophrenia. His parents hired me when you were just a little thing to watch over you, and to keep tabs on Lance." He turns, eyeing my father up and down with passionate enmity. "He had to go through a series of medical treatments a good while back. It was one of the reasons why I had to send you away to boarding school while he was going through therapy. It was for your own protection."

"That's enough!" my dad barks.

"What's the matter, Lance? You worried your daughter will think less of you for having a severe mental disease?" His voice drips with a loathsome rage. "Afraid you would appear less of a father if she knew? Well, I think you've just topped yourself." He takes a step closer to my dad, pointing a finger in his face. "You fucking promised you'd tell me if you got those feelings again, and it's been what? Almost six years since your last episode?" He shakes his head in disdain, acute revulsion radiating off his entire body. "All this time, I thought you had your shit under control. Turns out you were only lying dormant as you had this shit planned out for years. No wonder you've been acting so normal all this time; you thought you had the ace in the hole."

"Correction, I hold the ace," Nick arrogantly chimes in.

Jake whips around to face Nick with bared teeth.

"And you...you sick motherfucker," he grits out, his voice filled with rage, "you can let her the fuck loose, right the fuck now. There is no fucking deal."

Nick's body stays eerily relaxed behind me, and then he chuckles. I can see through my peripheral vision him giving a quick jerk of his head toward the door as both Jake and I take a look. I swallow against a thick lump in my throat as a sick sense of déjà vu washes over me. Those are the men who took me the last time, and the three of them are heavily armed.

"I don't think you want a repeat of last time, Jake," Nick reminds him with an authoritarian voice. "How's that leg healing?" he taunts.

Jake's chest heaves with fury. "This isn't over, not by a long shot."

"Oh, but it is," Nick smoothly states. "Everything has been signed, sealed, and delivered. No returns, no exchanges, all sales final. I suggest you think of that, should you try something stupid."

So this is it? My life has been bargained away because of a deeply disturbed, paranoid, schizophrenic man? Everyone's words are becoming muffled, and I can't make out anything past the fact that somehow at some point, I signed important papers that I don't remember. Either that or they forged my name, which wouldn't be hard to do. Combine that with all their criminal contacts, anything is possible.

I feel like I'm in a jousting tournament and I just lost. I lost big time. My lungs constrict as I feel the sharp lance piercing my chest, spearing through my heart as it exits out my backside. A very sick feeling falls over me, making my face turn hot and flushed. I feel clammy and dizzy as I grab onto my medallion, clutching it with the palm of my hand, grasping for something familiar to give me comfort.

"That's another thing I'll be glad to be rid of," my dad says as he steps forward to unclasp the necklace from around my neck. Both Jake and I just stand here frozen, unable to do anything as I try to get a grip on my physical and mental being, but nothing is cooperating.

He tosses my medallion in the air and catches it with an evil smirk. "Do you know how sick I was of seeing you wear this every damn day? I'll be glad to be rid of it once and for all. It was a constant reminder of how traitorous both your grandmother and mother were...and now you."

His words and actions paralyze me. Beads of sweat have gathered along my upper lip. I feel nauseous, and my vision sort of pixelates from the edges. My inner balance is so screwed up that all I can think about is how I'm going to fall flat on my face. The last thing I remember as my knees give way is not hitting the floor.

I slowly rouse from a deep sleep, still too tired to open my eyes. I realize my head is lying on a hard, muscled thigh acting as a pillow. Must be Travis' lap I'm lying across. My mind is hazy from sleep, but I can't remember the dream. The sound of a highway surrounds me, and I know then I'm in a moving vehicle.

I smell leather, a lot of leather, and I wonder what Travis is up to. I'm sprawled out on a very comfortable, roomy backseat of a car with the warmth of a blanket laid over top of me. My hair is being played with, and on occasion, softly stroked in a loving manner. I start to wriggle awake, and am met with a deep, soft voice that doesn't belong to Travis.

"You're awake." My eyes flutter open, confusion swirling around me. My pulse spikes, and I try to sit up. I'm in a panic-induced haze as memories begin to pound me like a tidal wave. Nick gently nudges my head back down on his lap, encouraging me to stay put. "Easy there, Princess," he says soothingly. "You've been out for a good while. Just relax."

I roll my head back slightly to peer up at him, and he looks down at me with tender, sympathetic eyes, which display nothing but warmth. His fingers are caringly stroking the side of my cheek, and as I look at him in my disoriented state, I notice how exhausted he looks.

"Where am I?"

"I'm taking you home with me," he softly replies as he runs his fingers through my hair.

I swallow hard against the sick feeling brewing in my stomach. "Back to the facility?"

His lips form a thin line as he shakes his head. "No, baby. I'm taking you to a place where we both can call home."

"Home?" I ask even more confused. I have no home. I have no life. I have nothing.

Nick reaches over me for a second, and when he leans back

against his seat, he has a bottle of water in his hand. "You need to stay hydrated," he says, ignoring my question. "Let me help you sit up." Apparently, his definition of me sitting up is sitting in his lap, because when I begin to move, his free hand slips underneath my armpit as he lifts me onto his lap.

I'm not ready to be face-to-face with Nick, so I rest my cheek against his shoulder and stare at the blanket draped over me. I feel the muscles in his chest move as he unscrews the cap on the water bottle.

Bringing the opening rim of the bottle to my lips, he tilts it, forcing me to take a sip. "C'mon, sweetheart. Take some tiny sips for me." I have no choice but to comply. When he pulls the bottle away, he kisses the top of my head, and I hear him inhale my scent. "I've missed you so much," he whispers forlornly. "I've been worried sick about you."

"I'm fine," I quietly assure him. He leans forward to put the water in a cup holder to free his hand, and then he runs his fingers through the back of my hair, massaging my neck as he holds me tightly.

"I wasn't fine. I was miserable without you. I'm just glad you're in one piece." He pauses to kiss the top of my head again before he continues, "I don't want you anywhere near the facility, or any place other than home, for that matter. I just want it to be you and me, with no outside interferences as we build our relationship."

I have nothing to say to his remark. I think my heart turned to ashes the moment I found out my dad was a murderous psycho. I'm fairly certain I'm still in shock. I'm beginning to recognize the symptoms of shock now, and unfortunately, I'm learning to roll with it.

Nick continues, his baritone voice mingling with the sound of the tires on the road. "You will love it there, I promise," he assures me. "You will have anything and everything you could ever want or need, including all the love you could ever hope to have in a lifetime."

I'm hollow inside as his words bounce around the now empty chambers of my heart. He lifts my chin to meet his gaze, his eyes gleaming a pretty sable as he searches my face. "You believe me, don't you?"

"I do," I whisper in response. His eyes narrow on mine as he works something out in his head.

"You belong to me, Julianna. We belong together...you know that, right?"

I'm exhausted, and honestly, I don't know what the hell he wants from me, other than a fairytale ending. "Yes," I whisper in defeat, my somber face acknowledging him.

He scrutinizes my lack of excitement for being his captive, yet again. "You don't seem like you want this, Julianna."

Oh, my God. He can't be for real right now. What the hell does he expect me to say at a time like this? *Yes, thank you for making a deal with the devil and rescuing me from the fiery pits of one hell, just to go into another?*

His emotions flip in the blink of an eye, and the growing annoyance radiates off him from my lack of response. "Do you miss him, Julianna?" he asks through gritted teeth in a contemptuously low tone. He doesn't give me time to process his question before his voice turns into untamed, outrage. "Did you enjoy fucking him?"

What the fuck? I jolt backward as if I've been bitch-slapped in the face. He painfully grips my cheeks, his upper lip twitching as he grates out, "I asked...did you enjoy *fucking* him?" he repeats.

My heart takes off like a jackhammer gone crazy. How the hell do I even begin to answer a question like that? And I'm fairly certain he knows the answer. Is he looking for another reason to be angry with me so he can whip me on his cross again? When I don't respond fast enough, he barks loudly, "Well, did you?" I flinch, my eyes wide with shock and dismay.

His eyes have gone wild, and I'm frightened of his volatile and unpredictable mood swing. He nods as if he's figured out the answer for himself. "I thought so," he concludes, disdain dripping like thick syrup from his voice.

He roughly releases my cheeks, and I don't know how to handle him. With his anger barely contained, and knowing what he's capable of when he's pissed, especially where his jealousy of Travis is concerned, my brain scrambles to try and think of something to say to calm him down.

My hands start trembling with the memories of what happened the last time I purposely made him jealous. Survival mode kicks in as I hear myself blurt out, "It didn't mean anything."

He cups my right cheek, scrutinizing my every feature up close and personal as he looks for deception. Nick's unspoken rage fills the silence in the limo with such thickness it makes it hard for me to breathe. His eyes tell me he wants so badly to believe me, so I put forth my best effort to quell his skepticism.

"He stole me, Nick. I didn't have a choice. I was deliriously drugged by the time he got to me, and I was in such pain when he abducted me I couldn't fight back, even if I wanted to," I reason.

His eyes quickly flash with remorse. The muscles in his jaw visibly clench, and I hope he's internally berating himself for whipping the shit out of me. Then he surprises me with what he says next, "I'm sorry. I lost sight of your punishment. I didn't mean to take it that far."

Tentatively, I cup his face, feeling a week's worth of scruff bristling against the palm of my hand as I look into his eyes. "I forgive you, Nick," I shakily whisper. "It wasn't right what I said to you that night. I'm sorry too," I softly confess, showing true remorse in my eyes.

"What happened when he took you? I need to know."

I carefully explain to him everything, from the car accident to the memory loss that followed. I recapped the last few weeks for him, all the way up until the invasion happened. I don't want to discuss the atrocities of me having to kill anyone, and I hope I never have to talk about it. I want to erase it, forget it ever happened.

Nick listened intently, not once interrupting me as he soaked in every word. After I finished explaining, I notice he's calmed significantly, and his breathing has evened out. "Once I got my memory back, Travis still had every intention to hold me hostage, but the first chance I got, I escaped."

"You ran home, though. You didn't run to me," he says like a petulant child.

"I didn't know where you live, Nick. I had no numbers, nothing. If I was against you, wouldn't I have called the police the first chance I got?"

Nick half-laughs. "I fucking own half the police, but yes; I'll give you that. You didn't run to the authorities when you had the chance."

Silence grows between us for a brief moment as he studies me. He glances at my lips as if he wants to lean in for a kiss, and I'm not ready for that, so I begin to talk out of nervousness to keep a conversation going.

"He drugged me with Blyss the entire time, told me so many lies while manipulating me at every possible turn. He's been using me, Nick." Damn, Travis sounds really bad when I paint him in that light.

Nick's eyes soften. "Yes, I know he drugged you. He stole a shitload of Blyss when he took you." My heart begins to settle down now that I think Nick is less maniacal, and I let out a sigh. Then his lips turn down in a frown as deep regret fills his eyes. "I should have never left your side that night," he confesses.

Reassuring him, I gently place two fingers over his lips, shushing him. "You didn't know. It's not your fault."

He wraps his arms around me, pulling me into him for a tight embrace. "Nevertheless, you are my responsibility and I let you down."

Silence settles between us as he guides my head back to his chest. My left hand settles over his heart as I take in a breath, inhaling his all too familiar cologne. You would think I'd hate the smell, because of the association it represents, but I don't. He smells incredibly delicious. His fingertips massage my scalp, and I close my eyes as I listen to the thrum of his heartbeat. I realize by the beat of his heart, he's still wired, even though he appears calm, gentle, and caring on the outside. He then whispers over my head, "Did my men shoot at you?" A tinge of rage is evident in his question.

"Yes," I tell him. The memory so fresh, I grasp onto his dress shirt, clenching his fabric with my fist. "Bullets whizzed by my head, they were so close I could hear them whistling through the air."

All his muscles tense as he holds me tightly. His lips rest against the top of my head as he mumbles, "I'm so sorry." I want to say it's not his fault, but it is. All of my predicaments trace back to Nick as being the root of all my turmoil. I have no idea where this home of his is, and right now, I don't care. A wave of exhaustion suddenly overcomes me, and I do the only thing I know to do anymore to escape the mental pain, and that is to fall asleep.

CHAPTER 18

"Wake up, sweetheart," Nick whispers in my ear before his soft lips press against my cheek. I stir and stretch out my limbs, and notice immediately my legs don't fall off the edge of the limo's back seat. In fact, I feel like I've been sleeping on a cloud. I peel my eyes open, and I'm met with Nick's beautiful smile.

"Where am I?" I ask, confused.

He kisses my nose first, and then answers me, "You're home, sweetheart." I roll my head to the side and realize I'm in his master bedroom, on his king-sized bed, and tucked under a thick, soft comforter.

"I don't remember you carrying me in."

His smile grows wider as he rubs his nose with mine in a gesture of familiarity.

"Your body apparently needed the rest. You've been sleeping for several hours now. It's dinnertime. You have to be hungry by now, no?"

I'm too sleepy to be able to discern as to whether or not I'm hungry, so I shrug my shoulders.

"Mmm," he murmurs, "maybe you'll feel like eating after a nice, hot shower." A hot shower does sound wonderful. Being that I've been up since before the crack of dawn, and then ran a marathon, I feel sticky, grimy and somewhat chilled. I nod in reply.

"C'mon then, let's get you up." And with those words, he peels back the blanket and I shiver, suddenly cold with the need to have scalding hot water warm my bones. He gets off the mattress and holds his hand out for me.

I take his hand and scoot out of bed as a chill runs through me. I quickly glance around at my surroundings, and as I take in his décor, I'm somewhat surprised. His tastes are not what I would've expected them to be. I pegged him as clinical and modern, but as I look around the room, it's full of ornate and eclectic décor, with splashes of color everywhere.

"Do you like it?" I pull my gaze away from the grandeur of the room and sheepishly smile at him. "I've done my own homework too," he says, grabbing me by the waist and pulling me into him. "I've come to know your tastes for unique pieces of art and composition. I put most of this together myself, but I've left many open spaces on the walls so you can display your own masterpieces as you accomplish them."

He leans back, looking at me as his thumb rubs between my brows, smoothing out the wrinkles. His lips lift in a sly grin. "What? Don't look so surprised. How could you not think I wouldn't want pieces of your work spread throughout our home?"

I'm speechless. What am I supposed to say? Nick looks jovial and happy, and I'd prefer this over maniacal Nick any day. I decide to return a small smile, one that I don't feel, in order to keep the peace. He leans in and quickly brushes his lips against mine, and I close my eyes.

"Let me show you to the master bath." He guides me into the bathroom, and my eyes go wide. It's freaking huge. It's as big as one of the bedrooms back at the cabin. Pointing toward the earth-toned marble shower, he states, "The towels are already warm for you." I spy two thick, plush towels draped over a towel warmer, and I can't wait to feel the soft warmth on my skin after I clean up. I hug myself out of awkwardness, not knowing what to do with myself.

Nick then steps forward and opens the large shower door, turning the water on for me. "It's a little tricky to figure this system out for the first time," he says as he focuses on the feel of the water streaming out. When he's satisfied, he steps back and wipes his arm dry as he turns to look at me.

"Go ahead and shower up. I'll go downstairs and see how much longer it will be before dinner will be ready." Nick leans in, and gives me a chaste kiss on my cheek before he leaves.

Suddenly, I feel all alone in this big bathroom. I feel cold and empty, both inside and out as I quickly get undressed and step into the shower. "Ohh..." Goose bumps erupt all over my body as the hot water hits and cascades over my chilled skin.

I close my eyes and lean into the spray, allowing the water to rush over my face, and I begin to think about the past twenty-four hours. I've stayed strong for far too long, and held back tears one too many times, all in the name of hope. I scoff aloud.

Hope. What a joke.

The memories come charging at me like a hurricane with gale force winds, knocking me off my feet, and before I know it, I've fallen to my hands and knees in wretched despair. My crazy, dysfunctional, and fractured life is just too much for me to bear. My heart and soul have been destroyed, blown into subatomic particles, which can never be pieced back together again.

Looking back, it all makes sense now. The year I was sent to boarding school was when my dad was extra moody. I remember Jake toted him around an unusual amount of times, but they passed it off as being extra busy with his business. This must be why Jake never had a life and could never get married. My dad kept him busy around the clock with his psychosis issues, and at the same time, he had to watch over my safety.

I thought the reason for my dad's distance was business-related stress, but in all reality, he was having paranoia episodes and untold doctor appointments, all because I was looking and acting more and more like my mother with each passing day.

Oh, my God. My mother! How could he? He stole my entire life from me! My brain feels like it has just been dipped in batter and deep fried in the devil's kitchen, searing my consciousness to a crisp, marring and scarring what little bit of inner spirit I had left.

As the water rushes over my head, I grab fistfuls of hair and tug hard at the roots. My heart has been ruthlessly ripped out of my chest and bled dry. I wish I could just simply die at this very moment in time. My mouth gapes open as I try for a shrill cry of pain, but no sound comes out. My chest constricts in agony.

My lungs burn, scream, and claw for oxygen, but I can't inhale. *Good, maybe I will die.*

At some point, my body finally catches up with my emotions, and I let out a long-winded wail. A torrent of tears follows close behind as I grieve for everything I never had, and nothing I will ever obtain.

I've lived in an endless cycle of constant insanity, and an unhealthy psychosis is knocking on my door. The decision is made; I unlock the deadbolt and answer by opening the door wide open with welcoming arms.

A set of strong, muscular arms slide around my waist and pull me up off the shower floor. When it becomes apparent I can't stand on my own two feet, Nick sits down on the shower floor and pulls me onto his lap. He's still fully clothed, and how I even noticed is beyond me. He tries to disengage the death grip I have on my hair, but I won't let go; I'm a mortal mess.

"Let go of your hair, baby," he softly demands. His hands thread themselves over mine in another attempt to loosen my grip. "Please, let go," he pleads.

I'm cataplectic, unable to move, but somehow he loosens my fingers, and the second he frees my grip, my hands promptly search frantically for something else to grab onto. Nick's shirt is the next closest thing I find. I fist his shirt and twist it as pure turmoil rolls through me.

"Oh, God, take it away, Nick," I cry out in distress. "Take the pain away...please," I beg imploringly between sobs. He firmly holds my head by cupping my cheeks, forcing me to see him through my blanket of tears. His eyes unexpectedly look tortured, full of empathy and somberness as I wail in his arms.

"I'm right here, baby," he chokes out as if he feels my pain. The water streams over his face, but he doesn't blink an eye as his stare penetrates mine, "I promise you, no one will ever hurt you again."

I wrap my arms around his neck and bury my head into his chest, sobbing until I have nothing left. I don't know how long I lay over Nick like this, but he holds me without complaint, continually consoling me. Once I've cried myself out and my breathing has evened out, I come to rest my head on his shoulder. The same familiar smell of his spicy cologne still clings to his skin, and as I breathe in his sultry scent, the desire to lick and swirl my tongue over the muscular ridge of his neck overcomes me.

What the hell? And then it quickly dawns on me that I know this feeling. I know it all too well. He must have drugged me with Blyss at some point while I slept. I should be livid, but for some odd reason, one that I can't explain, I just accept it. In fact, it's probably a blessing in disguise. Lately, I've found that sex and orgasms can be a potent distraction to escape the pains and realities of a fucked-up life.

He whispers sweet nothings over my head as he rubs my back, rocking me back and forth in a soothing motion. Once he feels that I've settled down enough, he gently slips out from underneath me and stands up. His clothes are stuck to every inch of him, outlining every taut muscle he owns. He looks like he's been caught out in a heavy downpour.

I'm feeling very naked and exposed, so I curl up in a ball and wrap my arms around myself. Nick doesn't pause to ogle or make me feel uncomfortable. He stays focused as every move is made with purpose and intent, as his face is full of nothing but concern. I watch him as he reaches for a loofa and pours soap on it. Even his fancy dress pants are clinging to his taut, muscular ass, hugging every perfect curve. When he turns around to face me, my lips twitch.

"What's so funny?" he asks as he squats down in front of me.

"You look like a drowned rat." Then I realize I've ruined his expensive clothing, and my smile fades. "I'm so sorry."

"Shh...don't you dare be sorry for anything." I reach out to take the sponge from him, and he pulls it back out of my reach. "Uh-uh. Let me take care of you." I drop my hand, conceding to his wish. As he lifts my arm to begin washing me, I suddenly become shy of my nakedness, and I look away. We both stay silent as he makes quick work of washing my entire body, and then he gently coaxes me to stand up under the spray to rinse out my hair.

I swear he must have his own hot water tower in his backyard, because I know we've been in here for what feels like an hour. When he's done, he shuts off the water and reaches outside the shower door to retrieve a warm towel. Dry warmth from Heaven wraps around my shoulders, and I shiver with goose bumps it feels so good.

"Let's step on out. I have a terrycloth bathrobe in another warmer for you." I step out of the shower and stand on the bathmat as he continues his task of drying me off while he works in his sopping wet clothes, trailing puddles of water everywhere he steps. The bathroom is nothing but clouds of white steam, with condensation dripping from the walls. Once Nick wraps me up within the warm bathrobe, he bends down and scoops me up into his strong arms.

"Nick," I whisper shyly, "thank you, for taking care of me."

"No need to thank me," he tells me as he carries me back to the bed, and then gently lays me down on top of the soft comforter. He leans over me, his hair dripping water on me as he steals a chaste kiss from my cheek. "That's all I've ever wanted to do is take care of you."

He stands back up and rubs the back of his neck, regarding me. "We can eat up here in our room tonight, okay?" I roll onto my side as I face him. I watch him with curiosity as he quickly peels off his soaked clothes, throwing them into the bathroom as they make a loud, sopping splash onto the tiled floor.

Stark naked, the man has no modesty issues as he walks around the room with confidence, and I can't help but rake my gaze over the flexing muscles of his upper body and thighs as he moves. The man screams masculinity and sexiness from his head to his toes. He glances at me out of the corner of his eye as he dries off, and I see a smirk playing on his lips. I think he's going to out me for ogling, but he doesn't say a word.

He then throws on a pair of boxer briefs and a pair of dark sweat pants that ride low on his hips. His hair is tousled from his hasty towel drying, and it makes him look all the more sexy. He rounds the bed, climbing in behind me, and pulls me into him while wrapping his arms around me.

Once he's settled, my voice comes out hoarse as I ask, "Why?"

"Why what, baby?" Nick softly replies in my ear.

"Why did Lance have to kill my mother in cold blood?" I can feel his body stiffen behind me, but the pain is so great I have to talk to someone. "I've been cheated, Nick, and in the worst possible way, and then some. Every time I think I don't have any more tears left to cry, more find a way to surface."

Nick kisses the top of my head, remorse lining his deep voice, "I don't think now is the time to discuss this."

"I need to know. I need to know what happened. There never will be a good time to discuss this."

He lets out a soft sigh in response. "True. There never will be a good time to know the truth, but honestly, I don't know what his paranoia is about. I don't understand the medical implications of schizophrenia or how it affects people's brains. I'm sure Jared would be able to explain it. I honestly didn't know about your mother or grandparents until the moment you yourself found out. After you passed out and I made sure you were stable, God, I was furious. Lance took things too far. When I asked why the hell he had to crush your spirit like that and tell you those things, he said it was time you knew."

Nick pauses and squeezes me tightly, and I know there's more, but he doesn't want to say.

"Please tell me."

"As you know, Jake was not a happy camper, and he tried to convince me to let you go. He tried to reason with me, but when he finally realized there was nothing he could say or do..."

Twisting around in his arms, my eyes panic-stricken, I interrupt him, "Please tell me you didn't hurt Jake. Please…"

He lets out a deep sigh, and then rests his forehead against mine in hopes of comforting me. "I wanted to; believe me, I wanted to, but I know how much he means to you. Plus, he had been protecting you all these years in ways I didn't even know about, which earned him some respect from me." He shakes his head. "No, Jake is fine, but he's been warned."

"I will do whatever you want, just please promise me you won't ever hurt him," I beg, gazing into his chocolaty eyes.

"I wouldn't worry about him. I believe he got the message loud and clear. He won't interfere." He tilts his head back so he can look directly into my eyes as his thumb gently wipes away a stray tear. "I hope you realize how much I love you. You're about to witness the great lengths I'm willing to go to in order to make you happy. Believe it or not, when you hurt, so do I." He kisses my cheek slow and tender before he whispers in my ear, "I'm willing to go so far as to exact revenge on your behalf, if that is your wish."

I lose my breath from his confession. Stunned disbelief doesn't describe what I feel. This has to be a set-up. There is no way two birds of a feather who flock together would ever destroy each other. There is too much business to be had, too much money to be made.

As if he's reading my very thoughts, he clarifies, "I'm not owned by anyone, Julianna, not even your father. The only thing I've ever needed or wanted in this life is you."

I swallow the lump in my throat as I contemplate his words, and decide even if he is telling the truth, I can't believe him. I no longer trust anyone in this life except me, myself, and I from now on. I do the only thing I know to do anymore, and that is to lie. "I'm tired of all the killing and backstabbing, Nick, you know?" I close my eyes and a shiver runs through me. I spook myself as I feel a ravenous hunger stirring within, desiring to be the one shedding blood and acquiring the satisfaction of doling out vengeance for myself.

"We will get through this. You'll see." The back of his knuckles softly stroke my cheek as he continues, "You will smile again. Once you see how much love I have for you, you'll be able to heal." A salty tear escapes from the corner of my eye, already knowing that I will never be able to rebound from this.

"Shh, baby...don't cry." He takes hold of my hand and twines his fingers in between mine. "I told you from the beginning I take care of what's mine. You have my word I will work day and night to mend your broken soul." I study his features, mainly honing in on his stark jawline. His scruff is new to me, evidence of his worry.

Without thinking, my fingers tenderly stroke his cheek, fascinated by the new stubble, and he closes his eyes, leaning into my soft touch as he tells me, "You have no idea how much I worried about you, or how much sleep I lost wondering how you were, or if you were treated right." The strain in his voice thickens. "I wasn't sure what Travis' game was. At first, I thought he wanted a ransom of some sort, but when I never heard from him, I knew he wanted you for himself."

His grip tightens around my hand, worry evident in his questioning eyes. "Did he hurt you at all?"

I shake my head in response as I turn my head and stare off

into space. "No, he was good to me," I whisper into thin air. I don't want to think about Travis right now. I don't want to think about what games he had been playing all along, or how he broke my heart, or what I could've possibly thrown away. My future holds nothing for me now but darkness anyway, so it doesn't matter. No one in their right mind would ever want me after this. I'm a fragmented mess with a black and hollow soul.

Nick pulls me from my thoughts as he starts to set warm kisses along my jawline. "I've missed you so damn much," he murmurs into my neck, breathing softly over my skin.

A faint knock sounds at the door, and Nick lifts his head, speaking in the direction of the sound. "Yes."

"I have your dinners ready, sir," a meek older lady's voice sifts in through the closed door.

"We'll be eating up here this evening, please."

"Very well, sir." And with that, the voice disappears.

Nick turns back to me and places a kiss on my forehead. "I want to feed you dinner in my bed tonight, and then I just want to hold you all night long."

"I don't think I can eat, Nick."

He looks down at me with irritation. "You haven't eaten all day, and you already look as if you've lost some weight. I know you're working through a shitload of shock, but you have to keep up your strength."

I stay quiet just for the sake of not arguing. I really don't want to eat, and I know he will personally feed me if I shuffle my food around. All I want to do is find a dark corner somewhere and die.

CHAPTER 19

~Nick~

I've waited so long to wake up beside my girl every day, and the icing on the cake is I don't think she's bullshitting me. I think she actually wants to be here. Only a few days have passed since I brought her here to my house, and she's been very clingy the entire time, not wanting to leave my side for a second. She has been quiet, and that's to be expected with the blow she took from her dad. I showed her the art studio I had made especially for her in hopes to lift her spirits, but she displayed indifference, and that concerned me. But even with all the stresses she's had in the past and at the facility, she was still enthralled with art, but that doesn't seem to be the case anymore.

She rolls over and looks at me with those sleepy bedroom eyes, and flashes me a small grin. All I want to do is crawl back in bed and hold her close to me. I tighten the knot on my tie a little too tight, reminding myself to keep my shit in check. I want her. I want her real bad, but I'm not taking her until she approaches me and begs for it. I'm trying something different this go 'round. Maybe it's a little bit of reverse psychology, mixed with me wanting her to make the first move.

I had Jared work with her morning dosage of Blyss by adding in something for depression, and then tweaking her evening dose with a sleeping pill to help her get a good night's rest. I'd like to think she's slowly coming around.

"Good morning, baby," I say with a warm smile.

She stretches out like an alley cat, and my dick twitches in response. Her hard nipples protrude through her thin negligee as her back arches in a long, drawn out stretch. "Hey," she softly whispers.

I purposefully remove my gaze, turning around to run some gel through my hair, fighting myself tooth and nail from taking her. The woman looks perfect in my bed.

"How'd you sleep last night?" I try in vain to keep the conversation moving.

"I slept pretty good. I'm actually surprised I haven't had any nightmares since I've been here." I spin around, and she immediately covers her mouth as if what she said was a spilt secret.

"What was that?" My eyebrows pinch together as I stride to the side of the bed and sit down beside her.

She sits up against the headboard, pulling the sheets up over her chest, looking shy. "Um…I guess I've had a nightmare or two, but it's nothing to worry about."

My lips thin. I'm not happy this is the first I've heard of it. "Is this something to worry about? What are your dreams about?"

She worries her thumbnail between her front teeth, and I pull her hand away to get an answer. "Julianna?" My stern voice tells her I want an answer.

"Sometimes, I wake up in the middle of the night dreaming about all the shooting and stuff from when those men invaded the cabin." She tries to play it off as no big deal, but I know better. I've been held at gunpoint before, and I remember the first time seeing someone drop to their demise.

With the news of her father, it didn't even dawn on me she'd be dealing with that post-traumatic shit too.

"Fuck," I blurt out and grind my teeth. My idiot men...and God only knows what's happened to them. I'm sure they're all six feet under by now, including Mitchell. I haven't heard back from them, and I want like hell to ask, but she's in too fragile a state to interrogate. I don't need her reliving yet another nightmare, when she just had the mother of bombs dropped on her. Soon, though, real soon, I'm going to need her to tell me about everything Travis Jackson, so I can pin the bastard down.

She sinks back into the pillows and shirks away from me, my outburst startling her. I let out a deep sigh and shake my head. "Baby, I'm not upset with you. I'm so sorry you're having nightmares." I reach out and cup her cheek, softening my eyes. "Promise me if you have one, you'll wake me up, yeah?"

She nods and solemnly looks away. "Come here, sweetheart," I gently instruct, opening my arms to her. She scoots to the edge of the bed and snuggles into me. *Note to self: continue adding sleep medicine to her Blyss. I don't want her having to deal with nightmares.*

"Why are you all dressed up?" she asks, just now realizing that I'm wearing dress clothes.

"I've got a little bit of business to take care of today." With this news, the look on her face is one of worry. "I want you to make yourself at home, Julianna. What's mine is yours. I promise I won't be gone but for half the day."

"What if I need you? What if something happens? How am I supposed to get in touch with you?"

I take pause, regarding her sudden separation anxiety, trying to figure out if it's real or not. She's not putting on a show, acting as if she's someone who would be scheming for escape with my news, she's genuinely distressed. "You're perfectly safe here; in fact, you're so safe I don't need to post but one guard at the gate." I throw that little tidbit out there on purpose, blatantly lying just so I can plant that seed in her head, but she only looks more worried with the news.

"Sweetheart, I'm king of the mountain out here. Number one, nobody is going to find us, and number two, nobody would be foolish enough to challenge me, even if they knew where we were.

My eyes drift down to her hands; their movements having caught my attention. She's wringing them nervously, and I can plainly see she's not faking it. I cradle her cheeks, giving her a chaste kiss on the lips.

"If it will make you feel better, I will write down the number to my cellphone, okay?"

She nods emphatically. "Okay."

I regard her for a moment, arching my brow before I turn toward the nightstand and rummage through the drawer to find a notepad and pen.

I write my number down and hand it to her, and she takes it with a pout on her face. "It's only half the day, sweetheart. C'mere, let me give you a kiss to get you through." She leans into me, wrapping her arms around my neck, pleading with her angel eyes for me to stay. The look almost makes me cave. I bend down and capture her lips in a sweet kiss, but she's not having it. Her tongue traces the seam of my lips...and oh, fuck, I'm in heaven. I slip my tongue into her mouth and groan, 'cause damn if I don't want to fuck her right now. My dick is already on-board with that idea.

I pull away before our heated kiss gets out of control, and rest my forehead against hers. "As much as I want to stay and have you blackmail me with your hot kisses right now, I can't," I rasp. "The cook has come and gone already. She even made you a huge breakfast so you'd have lots to choose from. The food is in the oven warming drawer waiting for you."

"Nick, please. Don't leave me right now," she pleads, grasping onto my shoulders.

"Baby, look. By the time you shower, eat, and explore around the house, I'll be back. I promise you I won't be gone for long, okay?"

I can see her warring within herself as she thinks it over. "Okay," she says reluctantly.

"Good girl." With one last kiss on her lips, I turn to the nightstand to retrieve a bottle of water and give Julianna her morning medication.

I haven't gone anywhere. I had planned on observing her for a few hours today from my computer room upstairs so I could watch her every move and see what she'd do when I gave her a moment's freedom. One of the good things about being near the mountains is there's no way anyone is ever going to find us. Lance Oakley doesn't even know of this place.

My heart falters when she takes her first step outside past the threshold of the house by herself, and into what she thinks is freedom. She tips her head back, bathing her face against the morning sun-rays as her fingers thread through her long hair. My God, the woman has a natural beauty and she doesn't even recognize it. I watch as she scopes the edges of the property line, which is full of trees. The blood rushing through my veins comes to a screeching halt, stopping the beat of my heart as I wait with baited breath for her next move. I'm not a fool; I have a few men on the perimeter of the property, just in case she decides to bolt.

I slump back in the chair when I see her casually meandering her way to the edge of the pool. She balances on one leg while dipping her toes in the water, testing the temperature.

Once I feel confident she's not going to make a break for it, I begin to work on other matters concerning the facility while I keep an eye on her at the same time. I keep glancing back and forth between computer screens constantly, and I quickly realize I'm not getting much work done. I give up and lean back in my chair, stroking my jaw in thought as I take in the sight of my princess.

She must've sat at the edge of the pool with her feet dangling in the water for about fifteen minutes before she got up and headed back inside. I watch as she slowly wanders through the house alone and unattended.

I imagine she's most likely bored, because I don't see her eyes dancing with curiosity like I have in the past. The solemn look in her eyes and the slow shuffle in her steps tells me she's still struggling mentally.

I shake my head in disdain. *The bastard.* I honestly never knew he was wacked in the head, and he should have never told her that he murdered her entire family. Some things are better left unsaid. I've watched her far too long to know when something is amiss, and something has definitely split and twisted inside her psyche. If I don't see that sparkle back in her eyes soon, I will personally break Lance's neck with my own two hands. Mark my words: he *will* pay for taking a piece of her soul and marring it, whether she bounces back or not. I haven't decided yet how I'm going to handle that situation, but there's plenty of time to figure it out. In the meantime, I'll make sure I'm ten times the family she ever had, or will ever need.

I tap my forefinger on my lips in deep thought. I didn't think it odd when Lance noticed the way I looked at Julianna after I saw her for the first time. He was able to pick up on it immediately, as any parent should. I thought he was going to ream me out and threaten to cut off my dick, but instead, he gave me an offer I couldn't refuse. At the time, I figured if he was willing to give her up the way he did, he didn't deserve her. I lost a shitload of respect for him that day, but obviously, he had two things I wanted very badly.

At the time, Blyss was on the brink of becoming something, and I needed investors. I heard through the grapevine that Lance Oakley was my man, and apparently, he was indeed.

I suppose I was so thick with greed and blinded by lust for her I didn't stop to consider the many facets of his motives. Maybe because I'm just as fucked up in the head as he is, but at least I love her, something he would know nothing about.

I shake myself from my daze, noticing she's settled into the library. It's a room I had made specifically for her, because I know how much she loves to read books. I have a small fortune wrapped up in all the hardbacks.

She begins exploring the multitude of books on the shelves as she runs her fingertips randomly along some of the spines, but she surprises me when she doesn't pick one up out of interest. Soon, she gives up and ventures down the hallway.

When she comes across a closed door, she stops to try the handle. "That's right, sweetheart. It's locked," I say aloud to no one. That's the door to my playground.

I remembered the promise I made to myself, that if I were to ever get her back, I would try to win her over, come at her from a completely different angle, and I refuse to lose my temper again. I don't plan on showing her that room anytime soon, but once she gets acclimated here, and with the continued dosages of Blyss, I have no doubt she will be begging to get into my kink soon enough.

I perch on the edge of my seat, giving her my full attention on the monitor in anticipation when she stops outside my office door. I've already shown her my office, making sure she knows where I might keep important papers and electronics. She saunters slowly into the room, her light golden hair shimmering against the natural sunlight streaming in through the windows. I've only locked but a few drawers, and purposely left the majority of them open to see if she'll rummage through them and snoop. Again, she surprises me and does none of that. She doesn't even give pause to stare at the laptop I left out. She settles herself in my leather chair, sitting behind my desk, looking sweet and innocent.

My heart pounds against my chest when she stares longingly at my office phone. I pull up the computer program that can cut her off from the outside world with the click of a mouse as I wait in suspense as to what she's going to do. She used to be so predictable, but now I'm not so sure. She bites at her thumbnail as she contemplates something in that brain of hers.

She reaches behind herself, slipping her fingers into the pocket of her jean shorts, and pulls out the piece of paper I gave her with my phone number on it. I'm fucking flabbergasted. She slowly reaches for the phone, and then lifts the receiver as she lays the piece of paper flat on the desk in front her. I can't believe what I'm seeing. I'm simply astounded. She's actually going to call me.

When my phone rings in my side belt clip, I jump. I was so lost in what she was doing I didn't anticipate the vibration. An indescribable feeling washes over me from her wanting to call me. I pull the phone from its clip and answer with a husky voice.

"Hey, baby, are you okay?"

A long-winded breath escapes her before she speaks with uncertainty. "Umm, is it okay that I called you? I mean...I know you're busy, but I just wanted to hear your voice."

I close my eyes, not believing my ears. "I'm never too busy for you. How has your morning been?"

"Well, I went exploring through the house some, just like you said I could, but honestly, I'm lonely here without you. I miss you."

"You do, do you?" I ask, just so I can hear her say it again.

"Uh-huh," she says as she twirls a lock of hair around her index finger. "When are you coming home?" she inquires as she leans back in the chair, propping her bare feet on the leather seat. My lips twitch with mirth as I watch her make herself comfortable.

"That depends on how fast I can finish all my work." I pause to regard her as she bites her thumbnail again. "What are you doing right now?"

"I'm sitting in your office. It's the only room that smells like you." She stiffens in the chair, suddenly concerned. "I hope you don't mind that I'm in here."

"No, baby," I reassure her, "I told you before when I left the house this morning. What's mine is yours." She slumps back into the chair and relaxes.

"Why aren't you passing the time with your paints?" I ask curiously. She hasn't touched them since she's been here.

She shrugs her shoulders, and then draws an imaginary line on top of the desk's surface, wearing a frown. "I'm not in the mood right now. I guess I still feel a little out of sorts. I wish you were here."

"Are you ready for me to come home?"

Her eyes widen in hope. "Really?"

"I might be able to work something out." Then I pause to consider a question. "Are you bored, or lonely?"

I watch her bite her lower lip and then slowly release it as she hesitates to answer. "Julianna?"

"I'm horny," she whispers shyly. I lay my head back in my chair and mentally sigh. It's about fucking time.

"Is that right?" I ask in a gravelly voice.

"Yeah," she replies huskily.

"What do you want to do about it?

"I want you to come home and make love to me." My dick swells immediately, and I shift myself behind my zipper.

"Mmm, you don't sound like a woman who's turned on and needy," I tease.

Her pink tongue slips out as she licks her lips and grows

bolder. "I've been dreaming about your thick cock between my legs."

"Just between your legs?"

She reaches to her breast and begins to rub a small circle over her nipple, and I stifle a groan. "Uh-huh, maybe between my lips at first, so I can use my tongue to taste the very tip of your dick. I'd then swirl my tongue over your soft head as you swell, and then I'd lick your slit so I can swallow your pre-cum."

I let out an exhale, hissing through my clenched teeth. I squeeze my hard length in the palm of my hand, trying to relieve the pressure building there, but it doesn't work.

"And then after that?" I rasp.

"By then, my pussy would be soaking wet, and it'd have your name on it," she whispers as she slips her hand into the front of her shorts.

"Oh, woman," I growl, imagining myself sliding into her wet heat. "I'll come home now, only on one condition."

"Oh?"

"Take off your clothes," I softly command.

"What? Now?" She removes her hand from her shorts, suddenly looking mortified, and I grin.

"You heard me. Now be a good girl, and do what I say."

"Okaaay," she whispers, looking around the room. "Hang on a second. Let me shut the office door."

"No," I quickly blurt out, and she freezes with a puzzled look on her face, her eyes big and round.

"But someone could walk by and see me," she softly retorts.

"That's half the fun, isn't it? Wondering if you're going to get caught in the act." I arch a brow, challenging her, watching to see what she'll do. "Do it," I demand.

"Okay," she whispers, and her submission makes me smile.

I grin to myself as I quickly make my way downstairs toward my office. Watching her strip naked for me, and then having her compliantly spread herself out on display for my eyes only was a real treat. As I walk into the office, I shut the door behind me with a soft click. The noise causes her to flinch, but she doesn't move, remembering to obey my commands.

My gaze remains on her beautiful form splayed out across the surface of my desk as I slowly approach her. It's nice to be able to appreciate her up close and personal like this, and the icing on the cake is she instigated this. Her breasts are a perfect handful, and my mouth waters at the sight of her pink nipples jutting out on display. Her long blonde hair has spilled out over the edges of my desk, and a tie of mine I had her pull out of my desk drawer has been tied around her head, covering her eyes.

"I think someone's been a good girl for me today," I purr as I approach.

When I reach her side, I lean down and breathe in her sultry scent. She's wearing the exotic perfume I bought her. I then exhale warm air against her neck, and whisper low and husky in her ear, "Are you wet for me?" She sucks in a sharp breath, and then shivers in reply. She lays across my desk like a masterpiece, a piece of art on display. My dick throbs with impatience as it strains against the confines of my dress pants.

I rest my hands on the edge of the desk, purposely not touching her, wanting her to be filled with carnal need.

I lean over her body and run my tongue around the pinkness surrounding her hard nipples. Oh, God, she tastes like sin. When I capture her nipple in my mouth and suck, she exhales the breath she was holding and arches her back. "Hold still," I gruffly command, and leave her nipple to run my tongue leisurely over her creamy skin. I make a warm, wet, seductive trail down across her flat abdomen, and pause at her belly button to make a slow, sensual swirl, ending it with a kiss. This close, I can smell her arousal, and my nostrils flare with unadulterated lust.

I step back and unhurriedly peel off my clothes, savoring her nervous anticipation. When I've shed my clothes, I stalk her like prey, and climb on the table between her legs. I slide the heels of her feet up to her butt, and then rest my palms against her inner thighs, pushing downward to spread her legs wide open.

I growl at the sight before me, as if I've just unveiled a long awaited treasure. She shaved herself smooth and bare for me this morning, except for a little patch of hair on her mound. Movement catches my eye, and I flick my gaze to her chest. Her breathing has turned labored, her breasts rising and falling with excitement. Her chest is flushed, and her nipples are pink and hard. Damn, she's a beautiful sight.

My eyes cascade over her every feminine curve, and when I glance down at her opening, I can see her wetness seeping from her core. As much as I want to fuck her this very second, I need to taste her first. I want to know what it feels like when she writhes herself against my tongue.

I lean down and press the warmth of my tongue into her opening, and receive the most erotic taste of my life. Her sweet juices flow over my tongue like honey as I lap her up like a hungry lion. She gasps aloud as I suck her into my mouth, eating her out with a furious passion. I graze upward, flattening my tongue against her clit, and then swirl it around her hard nub using firm pressure. Her lower extremities begin to shake, and then she grasps onto the edge of the desk with white knuckles, panting heavily. I insert two fingers, slipping them past her soaked folds while I suck with heavy pressure on her clit. Her hips grind onto my hand as she whimpers.

"I've been waiting forever to taste you like this," I whisper over her hard nub, and then blow a cool breath across her overheated skin. I swirl my tongue back over her clit with a new vengeance while curving my fingers deep inside her wet heat, plunging in and out of her.

Her mouth falls open as she arches her back, throwing those perfect tits in the air. "That's it, baby." I reach up with my free hand to gently squeeze her breast before I firmly roll her nipple between my fingers.

My dick is screaming with need, and I want nothing more than to slam into her tight pussy. Her hips lift as she rides my fingers with urgency, and I know I have her right where I want her. Now, I want to hear her beg me for it.

"Do you want my dick, baby?" I ask, giving her permission to speak.

A whoosh of air leaves her lungs as she frantically breathes, "Oh, God, Nick, you feel so good. Yes...I need you."

"Do you now?" I tease. "How do you want it?"

"Please," she begs, lifting that sexy pussy in the air, searching for my cock. "Hard and fast."

"That's it, baby. Show me what you want," I rasp as I sit up and grab ahold of my dick. I use the tip of my cock to dip into her slick sex, and then I spread her juices back over her clit, rubbing myself back and forth, asking, "Is this what you want?"

Writhing her mound against my dick, she struggles, trying to get me to slip into her wet and waiting entrance. "Yes, Sir. I need your cock inside me now."

Her words have me lunging forward, and I watch myself disappear into the depths of her warm pussy in one quick stroke. She lets out a strangled cry as I bury myself deep into her soul. When I pull out and see my dick lathered in her creamy juices, creating a high sheen, I groan and pound back into her hard and fast.

I grasp the underside of her ass, holding her hips up to meet my cock thrust for thrust. I watch myself disappear into her tight opening over and over again. Her cries spur me on, making me pump faster and harder. Her pussy clenches around my length with an ungodly amount of strength, her silky muscles creating a suction that screws up my rhythm as she sucks me back in.

"Fuck." I stop moving and squeeze her ass, holding her hips

still while I try to regain my composure.

"Nick," she gasps, out of breath. "Don't stop." She squirms her fine little ass as I hold the weight of it in my hands, and I squeeze her flesh harder, willing her to hold still. I watch her lick those plump lips of hers as she pants for air. "Kiss me, Nick, please. I want to feel your hard body on top of mine."

"Hold still, babe," I choke out. "I'm not going to last if you keep that up. Give me a sec."

I close my eyes and throw my head back, trying to focus on my breathing. Once I'm back in control of myself, I let go of her hips, giving in to her request. Gripping the edges of the desk on either side of her, I lay myself over her body.

I begin to pump and roll my hips into her while taking her mouth in a passionate kiss.

"Oh, God...yes!" she gasps. "Please, don't stop."

I make sure to grind my pelvis over her clit each time I power into her, stretching and filling her with my fullness. It's been too long; I'm not going to make it. The familiar tingling grabs hold low in my groin, and I pray to God she's close.

"Come for me, baby," I demand, and in a few more strokes, I feel her legs begin to quake and her kisses grow sloppy. "That's it; let go."

She breaks away from my lips and throws her head back, screaming out her release. I grit my teeth and growl as I come deep inside her at the same time, her pussy milking every last drop from me.

"Fuck." I work to catch my breath, keeping my eyes closed as I savor the last of my spasms. Damn, this feels so good. A fine sheen of sweat coats my body, my heartbeat still fighting to return to normal. I look down and shake my head, wondering how long I have to do this. I frown at the mess I've made. Weeks' worth of pent up semen coats my fingers and cock. I glance to the monitor screen and find Julianna in the library, snuggled underneath a blanket taking an afternoon nap. I'm sick of just fantasizing about her initiating the first move. I don't know how much longer I can keep from fucking her.

CHAPTER 20

~Jules~

A few days ago, I became an empty vessel, hungry, looking for an emotion to devour. I can tell I'm on the fast track to being the world's number one, Grade-A, fucked-up psychopath. Since my consciousness has been obliterated, I find myself having morphed into a dark, twisted, and disturbed soul. I'm ensconced in darkness, becoming one with it. As hard as it was to kill Nick's man in cold blood, I know beyond a shadow of a doubt I have the strength and will to do it again.

I've been taking Blyss twice a day without fail. Nick sees to that personally, and in all actuality, I've come to embrace it. I believe this drug has become a blessing in disguise. Within a few short days, it has allowed me to swallow the bitter pill of my circumstances, and give me the strength I need to endure them. It's futile to fight against the drugs anymore; everything in my life previous to Blyss has been in vain anyway. Amazingly, Jared was right. It does have a lot of feel-good properties to it, allowing me to push past the pain and tortured soul I'm living with, and actually smile some.

Nick looks at me skeptically for a moment, staying silent as he tries to read me. "What are you grinning at, sweetheart?

I peer up at him, batting my eyelashes, and the corners of my lips lift into a small grin. "Just the fact that this isn't necessary. Don't you already know you have my devotion?" I question in a soft tone. "There's no place I would rather be than here with you."

He arches a brow, and hands me the bottled water along with my morning dose of pills anyway. I take them and comply with indifference, even though I am thankful for them. I wouldn't have been able to bounce back as quickly as I have without these drugs, but I would never tell him that. Finished, I set the water bottle down, and then Nick leans forward, his hands coming to rest on either side of the armchair, caging me in.

"And why would that be, Princess?" he challenges.

I lose all playfulness as a quiet somberness washes over me, and I frown. "When my dad betrayed me the way he did, it cut me deep. Real deep. I admit at first I was disoriented, scared, and confused when I woke up in your arms. Then to top it off, I was traveling to another unknown destination." My stomach twists at the memory. "The way you took care of me that first night here, I quickly came to realize that you have been the only one who doesn't want to hurt me." My forehead wrinkles as I try to convey my thoughts into words. "All you have ever wanted is to just love me, whereas everyone else has done nothing but feed me lies, and then betray me. You've shown me love at every turn by watching over me for years, protecting and caring for me in ways I can't even begin to comprehend...all before I even knew you existed." His eyes glisten as I continue expressing my gratitude for him. "You've had my back since day one, and I'm so sorry I ever doubted you."

He captures my lips in a searing kiss, and then gently slips his tongue past my lips. Butterflies take flight low in my belly as I mimic his movements, twirling my tongue over his in an intoxicating kiss. I whimper when he pulls away, his brown eyes softening on mine as he regards me. "I believe you," he whispers.

"I deserved everything you gave me that night, you know," I confess softly. Nick is taken by surprise as he stares at me in stunned disbelief. "I'm sorry about what I said."

"I almost don't know where to begin with this conversation," he says, stupefied.

"How about at the beginning," I encourage.

"Yeah," he says, looking away from me, wearing a somber expression. "The beginning...or rather, when I thought it was the end." His eyes flick back to mine, full of compassion and remorse as he holds my gaze. "You know...I made myself a promise that night, Julianna." He squats down in front of me, meeting me eye-to-eye as he wraps his arms around my waist, pulling me into him. "I'm sorry as well. I lost control of my temper, and all I could see was red. I never meant for it to go that far...hurting you the way I did." His eyes silently plead with mine, seeking forgiveness as we both digest the other's apology.

"I forgive you, Nick."

"When I lost you, I swore if I ever got you back, I'd put away those items."

"Is that why you have a locked door downstairs? Is that your special room?" His lips thin, and then he nods in a wordless confession. He looks so anguished, and then his nostrils flare with determination, his voice holding a weighty pledge. "I will never strike you out of anger ever again. I promise you."

I lean forward, pressing my lips to his in an offering of truce. "I believe you," I whisper his own words back to him. A sweet smile then plays on my lips as I place my hands against his scruffy cheeks, changing the subject. "I think I like your scruff," I announce. "It adds something to your sexiness."

His lips twitch with mirth as he raises both eyebrows. "My sexiness?"

"Mm-hmmm," I purr, giving him a chaste kiss. "Take me to your room, Nick. Make me yours." Some fucked-up part of me wants this, and I'm sure the Blyss has something to do with it, but the drug has nothing on my desire to feel physical pain over anything else.

"God, I hope you know what you're saying," he breathes in stunned disbelief. "Where's this coming from, Julianna?"

"I think everyone deserves second chances, don't you? I know you won't hurt me. I trust you."

My heart thunders in my chest, beating triple-time as I'm splayed naked and vulnerable, my wrists and ankles tied to a bed. Nick remains fully dressed as he paces the floor back and forth with an intensity that has me on edge. *He promised to never hurt you, Jules*, I remind myself, but then I argue back, *He promised not to hurt you out of anger. All other bets are off.* I swallow my panic, forcing myself to breathe in a shallow pattern to remain calm. *You asked for this, genius.*

"I'm not going to hold you accountable as much as I am Travis, because I know you had been drugged the entire time he had you," he begins, "but you are still going to be held liable." My eyes bolt open wide and my pulse spikes. He stops pacing to regard me, pegging me with a heated stare as his lips lift in a knowing grin. "What I am going to hold you liable for, my dear, is that for every orgasm he gave you, I plan to replace it with my own, tenfold. I am going to erase away any trace of his DNA from your body, both mentally and physically.

Confused, I have no idea what this man is about to do to me. My mouth goes dry as I nervously glance about, darting my eyes from one wall to the next, where empty hooks and barren display cases decorate the room. Even though I don't see a whip, I know he's got them. I just pray to God my punishment doesn't include that. A cold shiver runs through me, and I visibly quiver.

Nick leans in, hovering over my spread-eagled body, his eyes narrowing on mine. "Are you scared, sweetheart?" he taunts with a hint of arrogance.

I dig deep down, pulling out some false courage I don't have as I force my vocal cords to stay steady and calm. "I trust you, Nick." It's all I can muster without my voice wanting to waver.

Satisfied with my answer, a small smirk tugs on the corner of his lips, and then he steps away. A dominant display of authority and control is evident in every movement he makes, as his expression gives nothing away.

"Good." He leans down alongside me and hoists a bag of tricks he apparently had stashed beside the bed. I hold my breath when he pulls out a large, white device that looks like an oversized microphone, and then I swallow hard when I notice it has a long cord with a dial on it. He leans in behind the bed to plug it in. Oh, geez. I pray he doesn't want to put that mammoth of a marshmallow inside of me, and then turn it on. I'll die; I just know it.

As he continues setting up in silence, he steals a glance at me every now and then, and judging by the unnerved look on my face, he must find humor in it, because he fights to keep the corners of his mouth in a straight line.

"Did you know," he says, interrupting my thoughts, "that having at least three orgasms a week can help reduce the risk of a heart attack or stroke by about fifty percent?"

I can't help but let a little nervous laughter bubble to the surface. "Interesting trivia you've got there. I wonder if science has done a study on having sexual escapades so freaky and scary that they increase your risk of a heart attack by a hundred percent."

He throws his head back and laughs a deep, throaty laugh, and I stifle a smile. I think this is the first time I've ever seen him laugh, and I mean *really* laugh. He wipes the corner of his eye as his mirth dies down, shaking his head at me in amusement before he leans down, chuckling over my lips. He wears a broad smile as he gives me a light-hearted kiss, and I immediately relax.

"You are so fucking adorable." He grins, his chocolate eyes twinkling and his mood no longer intimidating.

"Are you ready for your sweet torture, Julianna?"

Believe it or not, the little comedic relief has me ready for whatever it is he wants to dole out. I lift my head to steal a quick kiss from his lips.

"Yes, Sir."

Ten thousand volts of electrifying sexual energy zings through my body as their vibrations sing a chorus of ethereal voices to my soul. In simple terms, I'm in vibrator overload. It's an exhilarating thrill, and I'm on the edge of another explosive orgasm.

He wasn't lying when he said I was going to pay tenfold. I've had so many orgasms I've lost count. After I came down from the last orgasm—which felt like my twentieth, by the way—I wondered if one could die from too many.

"Ohhh," I wail, crying out in what could only be the most superlative torture ever known to a woman.

He plunges the five-star vibrator from paradise in and out of my pussy at breakneck speed as he punishes my clit with the big white vibrator, which is to die for. I'm about to cry out with yet another over-the-top orgasmic release, when Nick removes the magic wand from my clit. I pant heavily in quick, successive breaths, lifting my head to look at him with incredulous disbelief.

"Who owns your orgasms?" he asks in an authoritative, stern voice.

I drop my head back on the bed and close my eyes. I'm drenched in sweat as I breathe out for the hundredth time on a heavy whisper, "You do, Nick. You own my orgasms."

"That's right, baby, and I don't suspect you'll forget that anytime soon, will you?"

"Never. I will never forget who owns me." I'm actually glad for the reprieve; I'm able to catch my breath. This must be what it feels like in between contractions during labor. My body is spent, and it falls listless and floaty the second all of the intense stimulation ceases.

Keeping my eyes closed, I'm too exhausted to open them. I'm so tired that the short sixty-second reprieve he gives me feels like a ten-minute break.

He clicks the vibrator back on again, the familiar buzzing sound I hate yet love echoing throughout the room. *Oh, God, here we go again.* I'm so overly sensitive I scream on contact. I'm absurdly wet, not needing any more lube as he slides the phallic-looking vibrator past my swollen folds, stretching and filling me with exquisite sensations. He begins pumping in a rhythm that makes me move my hips in tandem as I seek to gain more of everything he's doing to me. Surrendering myself to the wild indulgence, I still can't seem to get enough, even though I've definitely had enough. My sexual appetite is unquenchable. He's been relentless with his instruments of penance, fucking me with them for what feels like hours.

My breathing picks up again, and I feel beads of sweat rolling off my forehead as he stays on task. In a delirium, my back arches off the bed as he holds the vibrating device directly on my clit, pressing it there without mercy.

My voice hoarse by now, my screams become raspy as I voice my pleasure. "Oh...God...Nick...please don't stop... please," I cry out, and he moves the vibrator away from my clit.

"How bad do you want it, Princess? Are you about to explode for me?"

"Nick!" I wail. "Please!" I'm desperate and he knows it. He chuckles over me, enjoying this torturous display.

"Oh, God..." I moan in frustration.

His gaze penetrates mine, burning a hole of molten passion through me as he declares, "God's not the one who is going to make you come; I am. I want to hear you scream out *my* name."

"Nick," I breathe out his name as if my life depends on it while pleading silently with panicked eyes. He rewards me by moving the vibrator back over my sensitive nub. With the force of a lightning bolt, electrical shockwaves shoot through my body, making my toes curl.

I do as Nick says and scream out his name. Another orgasm ripping through me only to leave me breathless and weak. My arms and legs are tired from pulling on the restraints.

I roll my head to the side and see through half-lidded eyes that Nick has decided to take another break. Thank God. I watch as he reaches for the decanter of liquor and slowly unscrews the lid. As he pours himself a small glass, I check out his perfect ass in his pinstripe pleated dress pants from behind. His broad shoulders are wrapped in fine fabric, and his cuffs are rolled at the sleeves. He's so damn enigmatic, and how he can go this long without stripping bare and getting down to business is beyond my comprehension.

When he's finished pouring his glass, he turns around, and my heart pounds at the sight of his beauty. He leans against the bar as he takes a sip of his drink, and as he does, my gaze travels down from his broad shoulders to the sexy bulge straining against his neatly pressed pants. I want to touch it. I want to feel the weight of his balls in the palms of my hands. You would think I would be sated with all these orgasms, but I'm not. Nothing can replace the feel of a man's warm touch, a man's hot kiss, or a man's hard dick.

Nick catches me staring at him out of the corner of his eye, and his mouth quirks up in a half-smirk as he purposely adjusts himself. God, he's so damn sexy I can't stand it. I lick my lips slowly with a sultry dance as desire runs back through me. I want those lips on every inch of my skin. The liquor must go down rough, because he makes a noise at the back of his throat as if it burns him.

"God, that's so sexy." I suppose everything is sexy to me at this moment.

His rich baritone voice caresses over me. "What is so... sexy?"

"When you do that. Take a stiff drink that only a man can swallow, and then make that rough growl at the back of your throat."

"Is it now?" He arches a brow as he takes another sip, staring at me with an intense heat.

"Yes." I pause briefly, letting my eyes roam over his muscular build, and as I bring my gaze back up to his striking facial features, butterflies take flight.

He swirls his drink in his glass before taking another sip, and then cants his head to the side in question. "What are you thinking about?"

"I'm thinking I love you," I whisper sincerely.

Nick barks out a quick laugh, and then shakes his head as he grins. "All the woman say that by the tenth orgasm. It's mostly due to the oxytocin triggering a prodigious amount of other feel-good hormones. It happens every time."

My smile fades, and I grow solemn. "No, Nick. I mean it. I think I'm falling in love with you."

His face turns hard and serious as he puts down his glass of liquor and is immediately at my side, searching my eyes. "Don't fuck with me," he sternly warns.

"I'm not." I lick my dry lips, trying to give them moisture, but it's a lost cause. "I promise I feel this."

He leans in close, scrutinizing my eyes. I can tell he wants so badly to believe my confession, so I continue, "These past few days have been hard, but I couldn't have gotten through them without you. My feelings are real, Nick."

His breathing picks up and the muscles in his jaw clench. "Please make love to me," I plead. "I need to feel *you*. I need *you* to be the one, not these plastic devices."

I watch as he steps back, remaining silent, and then he slowly begins to unbutton his dress shirt. His eyes have turned half-mast and sultry, and they scream inaudible promises only he can deliver. "Please...I need to touch you and wrap my legs around you."

He removes everything except for his boxers, and then he unties me from my binds. He rubs my fatigued arms and legs, massaging them for a few minutes, bringing back the much-needed circulation before he lays down beside me.

Resting on his elbow, he leans forward to touch me in an oh-so-tender, velvety smooth stroke as his fingertips draw an invisible line from my neck to the swells of my breasts. My heart skips a beat, and my breathing quickens. He stays quiet for a few minutes, lost in contemplative thought as he trails his fingers over my skin. I'm burning up. I need the physical contact.

"Please make love to me, Nick. Make it slow, make it passionate, and make it last," I breathe in a husky whisper. "Make me yours."

His eyes flick to mine, pulling him from his thoughts as his hand freezes underneath the swell of my breast. "Tell me again."

I lift my head to seductively run my tongue along the ridges of his neck, and then whisper over his ear, "I'm falling in love with you." I suck along his strong muscles that flex under my ministrations, and grin when he lets out a low growl. Nick slips on top of me, laying the weight of his body over mine. His hands cradle either side of my head, and as if I'm a dream come true, he leans down and softly presses his lips against mine in what could only be a reverent, loving kiss.

His strong leg nudges the inside of my thigh, spreading my legs far apart, making room for his erection. I close my eyes and embrace the feel of his thickness at my opening as our tongues tangle with passion.

When he pulls away from the kiss, I open my eyes to his, and I'm faced with ones full of passion and desire as he stares down at me. "This is how I wanted our first time to be," he softly confesses.

I smile, cradling his cheek within my hands. "Let's just start fresh, pretend this is our first."

A heavy breath leaves his lungs, and he reassures me, "I'm going to make you feel every ounce of my love. Soft and sweet, the way it should've been the first time."

He moves his hips, grinding his erection into me. I lose my breath, and maybe I was wrong about him going slow. I need his boxers off now. I lift my hips, needing his hardness inside of me as he swirls his tongue around mine. I urge him on, grinding my bare pussy against the hard length in his boxers. "You don't fight fair," he groans, softly nipping at my lower lip.

"I love you, Julianna. I swear to you I will always love, cherish, and protect you."

I run my fingers along the waistband of his boxers, and then slip my hand inside. "Ohh..." I moan, coming into contact with the tip of his cock, and when my fingers wrap around the warmth of his thick skin, I shiver with need.

I run my thumb along the opening of his slit, the wetness of his pre-cum already having bathed the tip. He's so wet I wonder if he had come at some point during my punishment. My thumb creates a pattern as I rub his crown in gentle circles, and his eyes involuntarily close.

"Fuck," he draws out on a winded breath, "you totally undo me." When he opens his eyes, I can see them swirling with emotion. My mouth goes dry the second he peels off his boxers, and his cock springs free. It's the first time I've seen him up close and personal in all his hard, naked glory. He's beautiful, and I can't wait for him to fill me with it. My core clenches with anticipation of being stretched and fucked...fucked hard.

A deep, husky voice pulls me from my trance. "What's going through that beautiful head of yours?"

I flick my eyes from his straining erection and look up at his beautiful face, my lips curving up in a devious grin. "I want you inside my mouth. I need to taste you." I lick my lips seductively as I bend forward to do just that.

He growls low and deep, his hand grasping my shoulder to stop me, and then he pushes me back down on the bed. His eyes are filled with an animal hunger as he shakes his head. "I've been watching you orgasm for the past two hours. I already won't last but a minute this go 'round."

When he lays his bodyweight on top of mine, I moan aloud. The feel of his sultry body and taut muscles touching my oversensitive skin warms me. I wrap my arms around his neck, pulling him into me for the best kiss of his life.

CHAPTER 21

A huge crash sounds out amidst our quiet interlude. The sound of wood splinters like lightning striking a tree, and then crashes to the ground with a loud boom. Nick jolts back, and what I see next has my heart stopping mid-beat as Travis and his men come barreling through the door. Bright lights flip on, and in my peripheral vision, there must be at least five men in all, dressed in black with firearms at the ready.

"Freeze!" someone yells out.

Before Nick or I can process a second's worth of the chaos, his body is ripped off mine. It's Travis, and he's a six-foot-five tiger out of control. His nostrils flare in anger, his expression murderous. His entire body hums with incredible fury, and I watch in slow motion as he pulls his fist back, and then pummels the shit out of Nick.

"Motherfucker! Did you really think you could get away with this?" Travis bellows as his fist comes down again and again, pounding on Nick's nose with a sickening crack. My eyes squeeze shut, and I have to look away from the gut-wrenching scene. "Fuck off, Quinn," Travis roars. I flick my eyes back to the horrendous sight to see Quinn holding Travis back in an arm-lock.

Chase steps in, grabbing Nick's pants up off the floor. "Get some clothes on," Chase says with disgust as he throws Nick's pants at him. Nick catches them with one hand as his other hand presses against his bleeding nose.

"Let me go, Quinn," Travis sneers contemptuously. He yanks at both his arms, his chest heaving with breaths of a charging bull, trying to free himself.

"I don't think so, Trav—"

"I'm done with the asshole...for now," he explains, cutting Quinn off.

Travis turns his head, and his eyes flick to mine with an intense glare that has me holding my breath. The thumping of my heartbeat thuds and pulsates in my ears. I swallow hard with the realization that I'm suddenly naked in front of a roomful of men.

Chase suddenly appears in front of me with a lightweight blanket, and quickly shakes it out in one motion as he lays it over top of me.

"I said let me the fuck go, Quinn!" Travis thunders out through gritted teeth. All the guys are dressed the same. All of them are wearing black pants and black jackets despite the late August heat outside. Travis' glare eats through me, and I have to turn away from it as I wrap myself in the blanket and curl into a ball.

"You got your shit together?" Quinn asks in a rough voice.

"I'm good. I'm done with the motherfucker for the time

being," Travis barks out.

I watch out of the corner of my eye as Quinn releases him. His chest heaving with barely contained anger as he visibly tries to calm himself down. Travis shakes his arms loose as he hones his narrowed eyes back on Nick, who now has his pants on. Another broad and ominous looking man I haven't seen before has a hold on Nick.

Nick's nose is bleeding profusely, but he seems unaffected by it as he stands up straight, vibrating with unmitigated hate. Spitting blood out of his mouth and onto the floor at Travis' feet, he hisses, "What's the matter, Travis? Did you hear her calling out my name in ecstasy?" Nick taunts. "I do have to tell you that you're wrong about one thing. Her pussy does taste sweet, but it's even better wrapped around my dick." He then lets out a snicker. "My cum has just filled her to the brim. Her pussy has runneth over."

Travis lunges for Nick again, but Quinn is quick to pull him back as he struggles to get loose. Travis' veins are bulging out of his neck, and he's lost his self-control. There's enough testosterone in this room to fuel a nuclear submarine.

Trembling, I clasp the blanket tighter around my naked body and I scramble from the bed, but my legs get tangled up in the blanket, making me stumble and fall to the floor. I scoot back and huddle myself against the wall.

He's ruining my plans. All of them are ruining my plans. They need to go away! Blood rushes through my veins with anger now as reality begins to catch up with me. My plans are slipping through my fingers. They had no right to barge in here like this. The glory and the revenge were mine, not his. Rage fills me. I feel like a highly prized animal, one that these men keep playing tug of war with. They act as if they each have the right to own me.

I lower my head, withdrawing into myself as my blonde hair spills over my eyes, creating a veil. A set of heavy, dark boots come into view, and I know it's Travis. He squats down to get on my level, resting his elbows on his knees as his voice approaches me with extreme caution.

"Jules, it's me. You're going to be okay now," he assures me.

Travis leans in a little closer, his very presence making me lose my breath. The air grows stale in my lungs, and I can't breathe. He holds out his hand in a gesture for me to take the lifeline. My chest constricts with pain. I have no life. There is no rescuing me from my hell.

I shake my head back and forth, whispering a despondent, "No, go away."

"Jules, it's me," Travis pleads.

I lift my chin in defiance, narrowing my eyes on him, sounding harsh this time, "Go away, Travis. Leave us be."

His stone wall has crumbled, leaving him exposed as a look of distress and pain flash across his eyes. I've shocked him.

He shakes his head, refusing to believe me. "You don't mean that, sweetheart," he whispers, and then repeats, "You don't mean that."

"Leave Nick and me alone." The anger in my tone cannot be mistaken.

Travis' eyebrows narrow, and he stands and stumbles back a step as if I've slapped him. A large man dressed in the same black outfit as everyone else squeezes Travis' shoulder. "Let me handle her."

I hear a soft chuckle coming from the other side of the room, and I know it is Nick. His laughter becomes sinister as he proceeds to arrogantly tell Travis, "Don't you see, Travis? She wants me. She's always wanted me." Then his voice rises in anger as he bellows, "She chose me!"

Quinn's deep voice cuts through the chaos. "Take him out of here...now."

The last thing I hear Nick say as they escort him out the door is, "Has she told you that she loves you yet, Travis? She told me. Why don't you ask her about it?"

Suddenly, Travis has found his bearings, and his voice. "I'll fucking kill him!" he grits out, and then he makes a move for Nick.

"Jackson, stand the fuck down!" someone bellows from the doorway, his words slicing through the air with finality.

"You fucking went rogue, didn't you?" The man punches the wall beside him with his fist, the sound of drywall crackling from the force. Anger doesn't even begin to describe what this man is feeling. "I fucking knew it!" His face twists in fury.

Travis turns around and squares off, confronting the burly man with hands balled into fists. "I answer to no one. You knew that when you hired me, and you didn't seem to mind that when my life was hanging in the balance every day."

Quinn pushes the stranger aside and squats down in front of me. Travis stalks off toward the man standing by the door, and their conversation dissipates in the background as soon as Quinn reaches out to me. His rich blue eyes pierce mine as if he's trying to hypnotize me. "Let me help you," he softly whispers.

I stare blankly into his eyes. *There is no help for me now.*

I close my eyes and shut the world out, letting my hair spill back over my face. I start to rhythmically rock myself back and forth.

So many people are talking and arguing, and it's too much auditory stimulation. It all blends together, and I grab at my tousled hair and tug at the roots. I've slipped deep inside my own head, and into a crazy state of mind. I'm drowning in the darkness, and there is no climbing my way back out of this black hole.

Quinn tries to whisper something to someone, but his deep voice carries, "She's going to need some help, Travis. I'm talking serious help."

Travis' voice bellows throughout the room, silencing everyone, "The fuck she's getting any help other than mine. She's going with me."

Travis squats down in front of me again, trying to disengage my fingers from my hair, but it's no use. He uses his fingers to lock around my chin, tilting my head back, forcing me to meet his gaze. I can tell he's trying desperately to bring me back from the dead, but it's too late. I'm ruined, scarred for anything remotely normal. I'm a hazard to anyone who comes within a foot of me. I close my eyes tightly, wishing them all to go away, wishing I was simply dead.

"Jules," he whispers to me, "no one is going to hurt you anymore." What he fails to realize is he has just hurt me ten times more than my father or Nick ever could. With my plan of revenge plucked from my grasp, I have no other reason to live.

It's game over.

"Travis, she's already checked out; just look at her. She's rocking back and forth nonstop. How can you think she doesn't need help, man?"

"I don't give a fuck. She needs *me*, not doctors." Travis turns his head to address his men, or the one supposedly in charge, using a sharp tone. "I've brought the crime syndicate of the century to its fucking knees. The very least you can do is let me handle this."

"You went and made this personal, Jackson, didn't you?"

Travis doesn't answer back, and the entire room is silent with tension. "Dammit, Travis, you don't know how many strings I'll have to pull for this." Travis turns back toward me, trying to lock his gaze with mine, but he doesn't have the effect on me like he used to. The man behind him lets out a huge sigh. "Fine, I'll give you a week with her, but you are to report back to me daily. Am I clear? If she gets worse, and I mean in the slightest, I'm coming for her," he threatens.

"Got it." Travis' voice is low and rough, and I can't help but think I'm being bargained for yet again. As I pull harder at the roots of my hair, Travis pleads with me on a choked whisper, "Shit, Jules, stop...you're killin' me."

He drops down on his knees and pulls me into an embrace, drawing my lifeless body against his broad chest. His arms squeeze me tight, but I don't feel him. I'm numb.

"All right, men, show time is over. Let's get this wrapped up." Quinn claps his hands loudly, and I hear multiple heavy footsteps moving about on the hardwood floor.

Travis scoops me up into his arms and orders out,

"Someone find me something for her to wear. I'm not having her traveling in a damn blanket." Traveling to another unknown destination again, I see. Whatever Travis' plans are, they will be in vain. I'm hollow inside. Desolate. There is nothing left for me to live for. I curl up inside myself, denying my surroundings as I shake with violent tremors. I'm nonexistent.

CHAPTER 22

~Travis~

My adrenaline was running so high it was all I could do to wait for the signal for the guys and me to bust through the door together as a team. With my heart hammering in my chest, I somehow knew what was going on behind those closed doors. A large part of me didn't want to open them, because I knew it would be an image that would take years to work out of my mind. I counted to ten, focusing on each breath, preparing myself against what lay on the other side of those walls. I held my hand up and gave the three second countdown to my men, who knew the drill.

The second I busted down the door and saw Nick's naked ass as he was dick-deep in my girl, all I could see was fire engine red. I do not see myself getting over that scene anytime soon; the very memory twists in my gut to the point I want to vomit. Someone may as well be driving a hundred ice picks into my heart right now. I was seriously planning on killing the motherfucker until Quinn pulled me off him. I couldn't hear or see anything except for wanting this man's blood on my hands.

Only God knows where Julianna's mental status lies right now. She's been pushed over the edge one too many times. Judging from her tremors and blank stares, she's not in a good place. Her despondency has me more than concerned. She probably does belong in a psych ward right now, but I will be damned if she winds up in one. I blame myself for not having heard her escape in the night. She should have never been able to crack the window without me knowing about it.

I hold her in my lap, my arms wrapped tightly around her as I rock her listless body soothingly. Stryker is driving us back to the cabin. I plan on rehabilitating her myself. I don't know what the fuck to give her or what the hell she needs, but I will die trying to figure it out. I refuse to leave Jules to the professionals, the ones who don't understand. Just because they hold a degree, doesn't mean they are the ones who can always heal. They weren't there, and they sure as fuck didn't help Clarissa. They say they can relate as they relentlessly poke and prod into the victims' psyche, asking inane questions, which only serve to set them back. They would probably condemn Jules to a life of prescription pills and doctors.

I was the one who was there, and I lived with her turmoil every damn day. There is no one better or more qualified to handle her than me. I will not let her leave the confines of the cabin until she faces her demons head on, because dammit, I have a fear I got to her too late, just like Clarissa. Two days of torture is all it took for Clarissa, and I pray to God those few days with Nick didn't destroy Jules.

I thought I was going to have a fucking heart attack before

we got to her father's house. I remembered going numb on the inside when I heard through the transmitted receiver what her father had confessed to. Thankfully, Quinn had their conversations recording onto his laptop, because I was stunned. I knew something wasn't right with her father, but holy shit. There are simply no words.

When her father took her medallion, Quinn couldn't scramble fast enough to get systems in place to sync his software with her hip tracker. Yes, when Stryker removed her GPS tracker, we put one of our own in. Quinn was able to get his hands on one. How the fuck he did that in a matter of a couple hours was a mystery to me. Since he's the guru of all this shit, it seems as if he has contacts in every corner and facet of the world.

Unfortunately, we didn't bank on this happening. It's unusual for us, but yes, we were unprepared. It took hours to get the new software downloaded and installed. Then he had to work through the system bugs to get it working. By the time it was operational, she was gone, off the fucking radar.

Needless to say, when we got to her father's house and he didn't know where Nick could've taken her, he was worthless to me. Thank God for Chase getting shit lined up ahead of time with the authorities, because if they weren't there, I would have killed the bastard with my own two hands. As it was, my own men had to hold me back, authorities and legalities be damned.

I could now see Nick's frustration with the new tracking technology. There were too many false positives, and if they wound up going somewhere out of range like the mountains, we were screwed. Most definitely we wound up being fucked, because that's exactly where they took off. Every hour that ticked by, all I could think about was history repeating itself. I fucking couldn't sleep, and I was a hateful son of a bitch to deal with. Once Quinn pinned down her coordinates, we were able to call in for backup. I wanted a fucking army charging in, and thank goodness that's almost what I got. I feel like I've failed the most important mission of all, and that was keeping Jules safe.

"Trav, let me give her a sedative," Stryker says, glancing at me from the driver's seat.

"No, she will just feel like I'm betraying her all over again, using drugs on her. I can help her through this."

"Shit, Travis, she's shaking like a leaf. That's not good, dude. She needs something to take the edge off. I don't want to knock her out either, but maybe a Xanax or something?"

I contemplate Stryker's words as I cradle her head to my chest. Since my adrenaline rush is now dissipating, I'm starting to notice small details about her, such as her wrists. They're chafed and red. I clench my jaw, trying to suppress the rising anger. The fucker tied her up again. Maybe she does need something to help her with the initial shock.

"Jules, sweetheart, I don't want to give you anything unless you want to take it. I'm not gonna drug you," I softly say while stroking her hair. "Would it make you feel better to have a little something to calm your nerves? Stryker's probably right, you know. You're shaking like a leaf."

I imagine she's dehydrated too, but she doesn't answer me. I look into the rearview mirror, and meet Stryker's gaze. He looks as if he wants to say something, but he keeps silent. She's probably not in the right mental state to know what she needs. "All right, Stryke." I let out a sigh. "Why don't you pull out your bag of tricks? I'll see if she'll willingly swallow a pill for me, but if she doesn't, I'm not gonna force it."

"You got it. Give me a sec to pull over and I'll get her something."

Holy shit, what a long day. I step out of the vehicle and arch my back, stretching out. We spent seven hours on the road, and after the morning we had, both Stryker and I look like hell. Jules finally did take some medicine to calm her nerves, which made her sleepy, so she slept half the way. When we stopped for dinner and fuel, I could barely get her to eat. Stryker assured me this was normal, and the most important thing was to push the fluids, so I did.

It's about eight o'clock, with a little bit of daylight left. I turn around and look at Jules. She's laying down on the back seat staring blankly at the ceiling. I rub my forehead, the tension mounting.

Stryker comes up behind me and slaps my back. "Buddy, it's late, and by the looks of her, she ain't walkin' in. Let me go unlock everything so you can carry her in."

"Yeah, okay," I agree in a tired voice. Once Stryker is inside and flips on a few lights, I give her a light kiss on the top of her head and heave her into my arms. I damn near break my back getting Jules out of the car. She's dead weight.

Just before we hit the first step of the cabin's front porch, she starts to push against my chest, making my step falter. "Jules, what are you doing?" I ask, my brows knitting together.

She starts to come alive in that moment, like a light switch has just flicked on in her head, and her motor skills kick in.

Highly distraught, she puts up a powerful struggle, fighting to get loose. I wind up losing my grip, and she falls to the ground. She starts screaming, and I stand here looking down at her in bewilderment. "What the fuck is going on?"

"No...no...no...no," she screams profusely, shaking her head. I bend down to try and pick her back up, and she goes ballistic, uncontrollably thrashing around on the ground. Stryker leaps off the porch and skids to his knees beside us, grabbing her face in his hands.

"Jules, it's okay. The house is clean," Stryker says in an urgent voice. "The house is spotless; you would never know."

Then it dawns on me. This is where she took down one of Nick's men. Why the fuck didn't I think about this? Stryker sees the look in my eyes, and tries to reassure me, "Travis, we both fucked this up. We're men. Men who can kill, and move on. Neither one of us thought this through."

Desperate, shrill cries fill the silence of the night air. "Get her some meds, Stryker," I order. I can't take her being this distraught. "Jules, we're not going in, okay?" I take her into my arms and hold onto her tightly. She's shaking all over. "You don't ever have to go in there, okay?" That seems to be the magic words, because she starts nodding her head instead of shaking it back and forth. "Okay, baby. It's okay. I've got you."

Stryker comes back with another pill and a bottled water. When he tries to slip a pill into her mouth, she gets combative and knocks the water and pill out of his hands, sending them flying. "Well, alrighty then. Looks like we're not thirsty," Stryker says cooly, letting the stress roll off him.

She starts that rocking shit again, and I don't know what to do other than start rocking with her. "How about I take her to the bunker?"

"How do you plan on that? You can't carry her like this," Stryker rationalizes.

"If you'd get the ATV out, I can take the back route."

Stryker pauses for a second as he thinks about my suggestion. "All right, we'll try it. If that doesn't work, we can always pitch a tent."

I shoot him a half grin, thankful for his little bit of humor to ease the tension.

I sit outside holding Jules for the next few minutes while Stryker makes quick work of pulling out the ATV. "Hey, baby," I whisper. "We're gonna go for a little ride. Need you to hang on tight for me, okay?" I try to keep whispering reassurances to her. I don't know if they are sinking in or not, but she seems to calm down slightly.

I'm thankful once we're on the ATV and she wraps her arms around me. I wasn't sure if she was going to be listless deadweight or not; otherwise, I would be helping Stryker pitch that tent. We make it to the bunker with a little daylight to spare, and I cut the engine. I slip off the ATV, taking Jules by the hands, and she dismounts for me.

"Do you want me to carry you, or do you want to walk?" I ask softly. She stares at me blankly and takes a step toward the bunker on her own. I consider that an improvement. I unlock the bunker and take her by the hand, guiding her inside. She walks into the little living room and just stands there, staring at nothing. *Shit.*

I decide at this point I'm not taking any chances. She's not going to escape me this time. I reset the alarm to lock us in using a different code. If I get some sleep tonight, it will be a miracle. When I turn around, I'm met with a hateful glare. My brows rise. *What the hell did I do now?* This is certainly a different emotion than what I've been given all day.

I take a step forward in her direction and she snaps.

"Is it your turn again to take me hostage? Locking me behind a steel door now, Travis? What's in it for you this time? Hmm?" Intense sarcasm drips from her voice, and then she gets animated. "What?" she questions. "You want a piece of this too?" she asks, pointing her finger inward at her body while making wide, continuous circles over her torso, referring to her person.

"Did you get your little toy taken from you? Aww...the poor baby. You want it back?" she mocks as if she's talking down to a kid, and then she turns into Jekyll, unleashing her fury on me.

"You want to fuck this? Tell me, Travis. What are your *fetishes*?" she air quotes with her fingers. "You tried to train me for Nick, but I don't believe you've trained me for your very own proclivities. Do you have some toys floating around here that you want to give a whirl? Tell me...how can I please *you*, Sir, Master...which do you prefer?"

Lunacy has gotten ahold of her. I really just want to bust out laughing at her absurdities. I bite my cheek with force, trying to keep my own sanity in check. It's been a long fucking day. I have never seen a more pissed-off Jules, but anger is good; it means she's letting it out. I'll take anything over her being a zombie, withdrawing into the abyss of nothingness. This? This I can handle.

"You can hate me all you want. I'm not going to let you go," I simply state. "We've got a lot of shit to work out, and in the end, if you still want to walk away, so be it."

"I want to walk away now," she snarls. "Open that Godforsaken door now, Travis."

"No, I don't think so." Amazingly, I feel calm. "When I feel you've healed enough, then I'll let you be, but not until then."

"You are nothing but one big lie! Everything you say, you do the opposite." Then she stands to her full height, and in the calmest manner she can muster, she requests again, "Open that door now, please."

CHAPTER 23

~Jules~

"I'm sorry," he replies, politely mocking my tone, "but that's just not going to happen. I have a chance to save you, and that's what I'm going to do."

My eyes turn wide, stricken with incredulous disbelief. "Is that what I am to you? A charity case?" My voice then screeches incrementally higher. "*A fucking charity case?!* I don't need your fucking sympathy or your charity. You can shove that shit back up your ass."

I make a break for the door, trying to punch in the numbers that I had memorized, but they don't work. "Dammit!" I scream, pounding on the keypad. I'm so sick of being locked up. When I first stepped foot inside this bunker, I was starting to calm down. That was, until I heard the sound of Travis entering numbers into the keypad, locking us in.

"Open this damn door now!" I hiss through gritted teeth.

He grabs me by the shoulders and spins me around. I'm so furious I raise my hand to haul off and slap him, but he's too quick. He catches my wrist just before my hand meets his face. I struggle against his strong grip, his fingers painfully digging into my skin. Before I can strike him with my other fist, he captures that one too. I can't break free. I have so much rage radiating off me my upper lip twitches. He breathes in my face like a charging bull. Yeah, he's pissed off something wicked, but his anger doesn't faze me in the least.

"Let me go," I hiss. He ignores me and pushes the weight of his body against mine, forcing my back to slam against the steel door, taking my breath away. He forcefully places my hands above my head, his eyes fierce with determination.

"That's not what I meant and you know it," he barks in my face. "You are anything *but* a charity case to me." I struggle again, not wanting to hear anything he has to say.

We're in a standoff, each of us challenging the other with a set of narrowed eyes. The tension is just as thick and solid as the steel door I'm pressed against.

"Did you mean it?" he growls with a sneer.

"Did I mean what?" I spit back.

"You said you loved him. Did you mean it?"

I stop struggling for a second, astounded by his stupidity. "Oh, my God! Is that what this is all about?!" I shout. "God forbid your ego be bruised. How fucking dare you? You have no idea what I've been through." I struggle again with all my might, trying to break free. "You know what? This conversation is over. In fact...newsflash, Travis: we are over, so stop trying to rescue me." I use my chest to push hard against his, willing the force of my adrenaline-fueled anger to push him away, but my attempts are futile. Frustrated, I shove at him again as I yell,

"Fuck you, Travis Jackson!"

"Stop it!" His voice roars in my ears. "You're going to listen to what I have to say. Right now, you don't have the ability to discern what it is you need."

I arch an eyebrow; incredibly pissed off doesn't even cover the tip of the iceberg. The man is too audacious. "Oh, and you do? Maybe you need to dole out a little more Blyss, and then suddenly I'll see the light, right? Isn't that how this works, oh great purveyor of Blyss," I spew in his face. "I'm surprised you didn't take me back to the facility so you could start over from scratch."

That might have been the wrong thing to say, because if smoke could come out of his ears, I have a feeling it would. Having to confront this man's rage, I can see where anyone in their right mind would be shaking in their shoes, except I'm not in my right mind, and I'm no longer intimidated by him. I don't even flinch when he lets go of me to pound his fists into the steel door, missing my head by inches.

My eyes narrow with venomous temper, daring him with my eyes to strike me. My voice turns low and deep, "You don't scare me. You want to hit me, big man? Huh? Take your best shot, motherfucker." I shove at his chest, egging him on. "You think you can force your bullshit on me, thinking you can mold my mind to your will. Well, if you think you can manipulate me by distorting my reality again with drugs and your useless charm, you've got another thing coming, you asshole."

His breathing escalates to the point I think he's going to blow, but I don't care. "I'm not the same person anymore, Travis. If you could see into my soul, you'd run the other way.

It's ugly, very fucking ugly. The damage has been done, and there is no coming back from that." The backs of my eyes begin to sting. I feel tears beginning to form, but I force them back down. "I had plans, damn you! I had plans of vengeance, and you stripped me of it."

He leans in until we're nose-to-nose as he speaks in a low, ominous tone, "You think you're the only one in this life who's suffered, or had bad shit happen to them? It's the devil's world, baby. Bad things happen to good people. Living for revenge will destroy your soul. Trust me; I know it firsthand. It will eat you alive, and then when you finally do get to deliver retribution, guess what? You're still left feeling the same miserable emotions on the inside. You're still consumed with immense hate, anger, and bitterness. It's a downward spiral, and it makes you miserable for the rest of your life. You have to push that negative shit behind you and move on. You can age ungracefully, or you can fight, and the Jules I know isn't a quitter."

"I'm not your little soldier, you arrogant pig. You don't have the right to talk to me about bad shit. When your world gets shattered to hell like mine, then maybe we can talk," I spit back. "You don't know shit."

Immediately, I'm airborne and thrown over his shoulder. I scream out in both surprise and resentment. "Let me go!" I pound my fists into his back with all my might.

"My world has been shattered more times than I care to count. So looks like you owe me that talk."

Upside-down, my heart pounds in my throat, wondering what he's going to do with me. When we reach the bedroom, he unceremoniously tosses me onto the bed. Before my body has a chance to spring back from the mattress, his body weight lands on top of mine, pinning me down. He grabs my wrists again, and holds my arms out to the sides while he straddles my hips. I struggle in his hold, vexed that he's so much stronger than me.

"I am so sick of you manhandling me, trapping me, drugging me, lying to me, and kidnapping me!" I yell, thrashing my body left and right. "Damn you!" I can't break free, so I do the next best thing I know. I give up the fight and let my muscles go slack. I mentally shut myself down, allowing my eyes to glaze over, displaying a blank and empty Jules.

"Oh no you don't, missy," he barks out. "I know this game. You're not going to shut down. You're going to hear me out."

Since I'm no longer fighting him, he lets go of my wrists and cradles my face in his hands, searing my soul with those stark eyes of his. "You can hate me, Julianna. I can accept that. Hell, I even deserve that, but what I can't accept is you checking out on life."

"I have no life, so there's nothing to check out of," I respond with an emotionless voice. "My heart and soul are already gone. It's black."

"The hell it is. Your life is just beginning." His eyes flick over mine as he leans in close. "I'm not the enemy here, sweetheart, and you're not my captive. If you want to leave, you can leave, but only after I know your head is on straight."

"Good to know," I deadpan.

He lets out an exasperated sigh. "Look, the guys and I are independent contractors. We work undercover for whatever job

297

we're needed for. We've worked in all realms and situations, but it's always been my life mission to bring down as many slave trade markets as possible."

I scoff, deriding him. "Some life mission. Having all those horny women to choose from... gee, I'm sure it was tough work."

"Don't even go there," he warns, his voice turning to stone. "It fucking gutted me to go into work every day and see that shit going down. You are the only one I had ever let touch me the way you did," he grits out between clenched teeth. "I would go to work every damn day reliving the nightmares of my own, and baby, let me tell you, I've had my fair share of them."

"Do you even realize what you're saying, Travis? You were still a part of that game. You helped steal innocent women, drugged them, and did sadistic and vile things to them. You're just as sick and twisted as the rest of them. You didn't prevent the horror of what those women had to go through; you enabled it."

"What you fail to understand is that their days were numbered with or without me, just like yours were. They were going to be captured whether I was part of it or not, and if that was the case, the least I could do was try to bring the bastards down. My goal was to integrate myself into the business and do just that. Trust me, sweetheart; I think every one of those men should be castrated with an ax on a chopping block for abusing women like that."

I'm temporarily stupefied. He's got my full attention now, and he's taking full advantage of it. "So, yes, Juliana, I was very much a part of that debauchery, and damn proud of it. Even though I couldn't help all of the women, I felt like the few I could help, I served justice." His eyes drift off for a second, as if he's reliving a some torment. "It's horrifying some of the shit I've seen over the years." Then his eyes narrow on mine, his voice low and full of derision. "Compared to those women, you were living in the Taj fucking Mahal. What you had was a fairytale, Princess."

"Yes, it was one big party, Travis, especially when you kept drugging me with Blyss after you took me from the facility," I hiss. "Why was that? Did you need to ensure that you'd get some?"

"That's a low blow, Jules," he spews, grating out his words between clenched teeth. "I was nothing short of a gentleman, and you know it. Yes, I did drug you, and don't think for a second I wasn't at war with myself over it. Jared had told me you had quit taking Blyss, but I didn't know for how long. Shit, Jules, cut me a break." His jaw muscles flex under the tension, and his voice turns cold. "The way I stormed into the facility to rescue you, I didn't really have the time to have a coffee and consult with Jared now, did I? Of course, you wouldn't know I had Grant incrementally reduce your dosage so we could get you off that shit in the safest way possible." He pauses to catch his breath, closing his eyes briefly, and then softens his tone, "I thought it was better to be safe than sorry. Whether it was right or wrong, I don't know. I only did what I thought was best for you."

I have nothing to say. He keeps coming back at me with valid answers for everything. He lets go of my cheeks and lays his body over mine, resting his elbows on either side of me. He nuzzles into the side of my neck, and kisses me there slow and tender. Shivers race through my body. Damn him for always being able to manipulate me with a simple touch, a sweet kiss, or a seductive look. Of course, it doesn't help that I'm still drugged. His anger is dispelled, his touch soft and gentle as his lips move to my ear, whispering, "From the moment I first laid eyes on you...when I took care of you that first night...I felt something I hadn't felt in years. I don't know; I can't explain it."

"Don't. I don't want to hear this," I croak. He's trying to make me feel, and I don't want to.

He lifts his head, and gazes into my eyes. "You need to hear me out. Don't you see, Jules? You are saving me too. We're each other's lifeline in this crazy life. We have this unspeakable and inseparable bond that people can only dream of, and I think you felt it too the first time your eyes met mine."

"Travis..." I start off, but he places two fingers over my lips, shushing me.

"I don't want to go through this life alone anymore, baby. I want someone to grow old with, and I want that someone to be you. I need you. I will break if I don't have you."

"You don't know what went down, Travis. I'm already so broken."

"I know what went down, and I may not have been with you physically at your dad's house, but I was there, Jules. I was there every step of the way, and I heard every gut-wrenching detail of what your father told you."

My brows pinch together in confusion. "What are you saying?"

He sits up to straddle my waist while reaching into his front pocket. A silver chain shimmers against his tanned, calloused hands. I flick my eyes to his in question. "What's in your hand, Travis?"

"I've been saving this for you. I've been waiting for the perfect time to give this back."

He opens his hand, and there lays my medallion. "How..." I can't speak. He reaches out and places my family heirloom in my hand.

"I knew how important this was to you. I kept it safe since the day I took it from you in the facility. I didn't want you to have it back until I knew you were out of harm's way once and for all."

Tears sting the back of my eyes as I clutch the necklace in my hand, bringing it to my chest. "How? When?" I choke, my questions getting jumbled up in my head.

"I gave you a decoy, a perfect replica," he explains as he tenderly strokes my cheek. "I had a voice transmitter and tracker implanted in it the first second I got. Somehow, my subconscious knew I was going to break you out of there before I even knew it myself. In case you got recaptured, I would've been able to find you and come rescue you."

"How did you find me, Travis? Because I didn't have this medallion on at Nick's house."

"Stryker implanted a new tracker in your hip." He pauses, his eyes becoming glassy, and his voice wavers. "The thought of losing you..." He swallows hard and shakes his head.

"You had this planned all along? From the beginning?" I whisper disbelievingly.

"From the moment you wanted me to take your virginity, I

knew...I knew I had to have you, but I warred with myself. I spent a lot of time in denial." I watch with curiosity as he reaches behind his neck and pulls his t-shirt up and over his head. The moment I see his bare chest, my eyes squint as understanding dawns.

"Oh, my God," I gasp.

"The minute I got this tattoo...I knew what I was giving up," he softly begins. "I gave up my heart. It's yours, Jules." My eyes flick back and forth, from his eyes to his tattoo.

"It's beautiful," I whisper, mesmerized by its beauty. I can't believe he did this for me. It's an intricate design of celtic love knots with a modern twist, representing all the things my necklace stands for. Thick lines spiral outward, and they end with thin points. It's sexy, manly, and hot as hell. "You really marked your body for me?" Feeling an overwhelming desire to trace the pattern with my fingertips, I reach out with my shaky hand to touch the design.

His hand comes to rest over mine on his chest as he holds my gaze. "I wanted to replicate the part of your medallion that meant eternal love, because that's what I have for you, Julianna. It's an undying love."

A trail of tears slips from the corners of my eyes. "That's why you wouldn't take off your shirt when we made love. You weren't ready to show it to me yet." As I realize this, he gives me a soft smile in response. "I love you," I croakily whisper with the last ounce of love I have left in my soul. "I've loved you for so long, Travis." I catch my breath, determined to finish. "But you never told me how you felt. That hurt. It left me confused more times than I can count."

"Oh, baby, I wanted to tell you those words for so damn long." He draws in a shaky breath, and then pauses to get a grip on his emotions. "I love you, Jules. Say you won't give in. Tell me we can work this out."

"I don't know what to say." I didn't see any of this coming. I had no idea he had planned out all these things in finite detail from the beginning.

"Did you ever stop to think your life was destined to be on this collision course? It was going to crash regardless of us meeting or not. Don't you find it interesting that we had an immediate connection despite the circumstances of how we met? We're meant to be together, Jules," he softly pleads. "Call it fate; call it divine guidance; call it luck for all I care, but the bottom line is our souls were born to be connected."

He lays back down over me, his elbows propped on either side of me, and I wrap my arms around him. The warmth of his bare skin beneath my fingertips is one I've missed severely. I run my hands up and down the length of his back, enjoying the feel of each ripped muscle. I feel at home in my soul when I'm with him. He's right; he is very much a part of me.

"I love you, Travis." He wipes away a silent tear with the pad of his thumb as he stares lovingly into my eyes. "I don't know what's left in my heart to give, but whatever is there, it's yours."

"I'll scrape the bottom of the barrel to get it if I have to."

I briefly close my lids, savoring his soft touch on my skin. "I didn't have sex with Nick," I blurt out, and he immediately pulls back, his eyes wide with surprise. "We were about to...before you busted in, that is."

He blinks his eyes several times in disbelief. "But he had

you for several days."

"He was playing a reverse psychology game. He was waiting for me to make the first move." He closes his eyes tightly, and then releases a deep sigh of relief. I run my fingers through his thick hair and pull his lips to mine.

"I gave into his game," I whisper over his lips.

"I can't blame you for that, sweetheart. You had drugs running through your system, and to top it off, I know you felt you were hung out to dry."

I turn my head away from him, staring off at nothing, wearing a frown. "I'm not in a good place, Travis. I don't think I will ever be the same." My lips tremble and my breath hitches as I try to hold back the tears. "The emotional ups and downs have screwed with me beyond repair. I'm a mental wreck."

"That's not true. You're stronger than you think you are, Jules." I shake my head, disagreeing with him. He steers my chin back, forcing me to face him. "We've been through too much shit together not to be able to move past this. We'll take the cards we've been dealt and we'll move on…together."

"Don't you see?" My voice raises, and my hands begin to shake. "I was going to kill them, Travis." My eyes silently spill over with a heavy heart. "I was planning a sick revenge, and I was actually going to savor it. Hell, I was so deep inside of myself I was believing my own lies. I even told Nick I loved him." My breath hitches as I realize just how messed up I am. "It makes me no better than my own father."

"Shh…" He wraps his arms around me, resting his cheek against mine, whispering in my ear, "I would've done the same thing. Nothing's wrong with you for wanting revenge, and you are nothing like your father."

"He robbed me of my own mother. I mean...who does that, Travis? Who can kill their own wife and parents without blinking an eye, and then..." My throat tightens. I'm too choked up to finish my sentence.

"I don't have those answers, Jules. I don't know what makes people do the things they do," he softly whispers, trying to console me.

"I don't know myself anymore. How can I give you something, when I don't even know if I'm capable of giving it?"

"You're in there, baby. Trust me; you're in there." He kisses my cheeks, wiping away my tears. "I've got you. I'll always have you. There was never a time when I didn't have you." I wrap my arms around him like a lifeline, pulling him into me as hard as I can while I sob into the crook of his neck. "I love you so damn much," he whispers over and over again like a prayer.

I don't know how much time has passed as he holds me while I fall apart into tiny little pieces. "I'm so tired of hurting," I softly sob.

"I know, baby. I know."

When I've expelled the last set of tears, he pulls back and gently wipes my face with his t-shirt. He regards me with tender eyes, and a gentle voice, "I bet you didn't know you can have happiness amidst the sorrow. You know why? Because you still have hope."

"No. No, I don't," I argue, my voice coming out raspy.

"Yes, you do. As long as you have God, and hopefully me, by your side, you'll have hope."

My brows pinch together, and a small laugh escapes him,

his lips curving into a grin. "I know what you're thinking. You're right; I don't do religion. Religion is the devil's ace trump. There was a time when I did hit rock bottom, and when I did, He was the one who picked me up. He restored my confidence and determination, pulling me through my darkest hour." We both grow silent as I study this complex man. Just when I think I have him figured out, he surprises me, and I find myself thinking of what Travis' darkest hour could've been. He's such a strong man, both mentally and physically. To be brought down to his knees...it's hard to visualize him in a time of despair.

"What was your darkest hour, Travis?"

His gaze suddenly turns intense, and I think maybe I've overstepped my bounds. "My first love was kidnapped, just like you. By the time I was able to rescue her, it was too late. They stole her soul. She gave up on life, wound up committing suicide a few weeks later." I'm stunned speechless. "It took me years to work through that shit. I couldn't stop blaming myself."

I stroke the side of his face, trying to give him some comfort. My eyes turning sorrowful, I can't imagine the horrors that girl went through.

"My faith is personal. I keep it to myself, but I do want to share it with you. I promise you'll find that your life will never be empty again. I will make damn sure of that." He closes the distance with a sweet, reverent kiss.

"I don't know how to move on," I choke out.

"Sometimes, it's a minute-by-minute process, and some days, you'll have setbacks, but I'll be with you every step of the way. I promise."

"I'm scared," I whisper.

"You wouldn't be human if you weren't."

"You promise to never leave me?"

"I promise, sweetheart."

"No more lies?" I plead.

His lips twitch, and his eyes suddenly dance with mischievousness. "No more lies. Maybe some surprises every now and then, but no more lies."

He rolls off me and pulls me into his strong embrace. I lay my cheek over his new tattoo and close my eyes, soaking up his love like a dry sponge. As I do, Quinn's words come to mind. *Travis is the type of guy who's more about letting his actions speak louder than words, you know?* His tattoo was his way of telling me he will love me forever. *He's got a few skeletons in his closet, and he has a hard time opening that door of vulnerability.* But he opened his heart to me anyway, risking more than his heart. He risked his life each time without hesitation.

I turn my head and press my lips into the warmth of his chiseled chest, kissing every inch of his tattoo. "I love you so much, Travis Jackson," I murmur between kisses.

He kisses the top of my head and breathes me in. "We will make it, sweetheart; mark my words," he says with determination, and somehow I believe him.

EPILOGUE

I glance over at Jake, and he has a tear in his eye, but he holds his composure. I'm glad he was the one to give me away. He hands the ring to Travis, who takes it, and then turns back to me, taking my breath away. I give him a shaky smile as he gently takes my hand. I don't know why I'm so jittery. This entire moment is so beautiful and surreal. His eyes dance over mine with such happiness, allowing calmness to settle over me.

His rich baritone voice is loud, carrying through the small church as he speaks, "In giving you this ring, I join my life with yours, and pledge my everlasting, eternal love." His words are short and sweet, but every bit as powerful. Tears of joy fill my eyes.

With the final promises we have made to each other, the pastor tells Travis he can kiss the bride. I can't explain how whole I feel in that moment in time. He lifts my veil as he tilts his head to the side, and then leans in for a kiss. I cup his cheeks with my hands, savoring the tender feel of his lips. I want to remember this day for the rest of my life.

I'm on cloud nine and can barely hear the pastor pronouncing us man and wife. Travis breaks away and warmly smiles at me. He gives me a wink, and then holds his elbow out for me to slip my arm through.

"I present to you Mr. and Mrs. Travis Jackson," the pastor announces. Travis leads the way as we walk down the aisle together, and I'm smiling from ear to ear.

"Hey! Why did you turn it off?" I playfully scold Travis as he places the remote on the nightstand. "That was at my favorite part."

"I'm fast-forwarding to get to the honeymoon," he says, giving me a smirk over his shoulder.

"You've had your honeymoon," I retort, raising a brow.

He slips underneath the warm covers, finds me, and pulls me into his body. A smile plays on his lips. "I still can't believe you played that Def Leppard song as we walked down the aisle together."

"What? What's wrong with the instrumental of *Hysteria*?"

He shakes his head at me in mock disapproval, his eyes full of playfulness. "Nothing. It's just so non-traditional."

"Since when have we ever done anything traditional?"

"True that, and I wouldn't have you any other way," he says as his hand skirts over my ribs. I squeal out in protest, "Travis Jackson! You stop."

He starts to chuckle and rolls over the top of me, ignoring me. "Shh...quiet," he admonishes as his elbows come to rest on either side of my shoulders. "You're gonna wake up the house."

"Trav, you are up to no good," I whisper-yell, and make a

halfhearted attempt to shove him off me, but he doesn't budge. "Get off me. You're squishing me." He nips and kisses his way up the length of my neck, sending shivers down my spine.

When his lips caress mine, I let out a helpless whimper. "You really should stop." The way I say the word stop means *don't stop*, and he knows it. "You like placing me in these predicaments, don't you?"

He grins over my lips, and then says in a low, husky voice, "You like my pre-dick-aments."

I roll my eyes at his corny joke, and moan when he rests his hard cock between my legs. Yes...yes, I do like his pre-dick-aments. I easily give in and wrap my arms around his waist, pulling him into me. "These predicaments always have consequences, though."

"Mmm," he whispers. "The more consequences, the better." God, I love this man. Today is our five-year wedding anniversary. Every year, he plays our wedding ceremony on our big screen TV in our bedroom, and every time after that, he makes wild, passionate love to me.

My hands drift to his boxers, and I slip my fingers underneath his waistband.

"Uh-uh, I have different plans," he says as he sits up, grabbing each of my wrists, and then peels off my shirt. When he's done, he places my hands above my head, and locks them in place with one hand.

I watch as he reaches over and opens his nightstand drawer to get something. My brows furrow in question. When I see that he has a large strip of fabric, I immediately go on red alert and tense. Memories of Nick slam into me without warning, waylaying any growing passion we had building between us. I never know when these flashbacks are going to strike. They always hit without warning.

I shake my head incessantly. "Travis, no." Panic lines my voice.

"Shh, sweetheart. Do you trust me?" I take a deep breath and let it out slowly.

"I do." I trust this man with every last cell in my body. His eyes bore into mine with nothing but love and tenderness, and I relax my tensed muscles immediately.

A Cheshire grin then spreads across his lips. "The only implement I plan using on you this morning is attached to me, so relax."

A small laugh escapes me. I love his humor, and just like that, my anxiety is gone. It's taken quite a few years to be able to work through all the bad. It was especially difficult when I had to stand trial against my father and Nick, but Travis and the guys were there beside me every step of the way. My father was sentenced to a looney bin for life. Nick's sentence should've been forever, but it's not. With his contacts, he could be out in another decade or less, but Travis has forbid me to worry about it. He has his own set of men with eyes and ears watching our back. I shudder to think what the world would've been like had Blyss been able to breech the walls of the facility.

"You know I would never hurt you," he reassures me, cutting into my thoughts. He lays his broad, muscular chest over mine and gives me a scorching kiss before he pulls away, leaving me breathless, wanton, and fully focused on him.

Fire burns in his eyes as he takes the fabric and ties my

wrists to the bed-frame above my head. When he's done, I think we're going to get down to business, but he doesn't. He holds up a black piece of fabric before me, and dangles it in front of my face.

I shake my head profusely. "I've let you tie me up, Travis. That's enough."

"Uh-uh, I don't think so." He tilts his head to the side with a raised brow, realizing something. "Did you just tell me no, Julianna?" he asks in an arrogant tone.

I swallow hard. He's dead serious, and he's only ever called me by my given name when he means business. Damn, he's so good at playing this poker game. "I asked you a question," he reminds me when I don't answer.

A defiant grin spreads across my lips. "Why, yes, Travis. I believe that's what I said."

His facial expressions give nothing away as he leans down and whispers over my lips, "You do realize you used to be my captive."

I burst out with laughter, and he can't hold his stonewall expression any longer. A beautiful smile spreads across his lips. "What's so funny, baby? You are in no position to gibe me," he warns. Oh, shit, he's right. He can do anything he wants, and I'd be helpless.

I immediately cut off my giggles and narrow my eyes. "Two can play at this game, Travis. Did you forget we're not alone?"

"Are you saying you'd like me to use a gag?"

"You wouldn't!" I whisper-hiss.

"Oh, baby…I think it'd be sexy as hell." And his poker face is back. I can't tell if he means it or not. Quickly, he straddles my waist, therefore making my legs useless, trapped underneath his bodyweight. His deep, rich voice looms overhead in a stern tone, "You keep fighting me, and you'll find quickly enough that I have more ties. I'll tie your legs apart, and do it in such a way you'll be sorry."

"You wouldn't..." I repeat incredulously. I open my mouth to say something else, but he stops me.

"Ah-ah-ah, watch your mouth. You have a simple choice really. Do want to feel good, or do you prefer to suffer?" His voice and facial features are dead serious. He's not playing around, and I quit struggling, my eyes growing wide.

He calmly whispers as if I'm a frightened filly, "That's my girl. Settle down now." He then places the fabric over my eyes and ties the blindfold snuggly around my head. Everything turns pitch black. My heart rate increases exponentially.

"Travis?" I nervously whisper.

A set of fingers rests over my lips, shushing me. "Shh, I want you to just give in to this. Let me take you away."

Travis stays silent as delicious thoughts begin to race through my head. He palms my breasts, and in turn, my breathing turns ragged. His touch causes a wave of goose bumps to erupt down my arms.

Beginning between my breasts, he skims the backs of his fingers along the length of my body, leaving a heated trail of erotic desire in its wake. He stops just above my pubic bone, and then his touch is gone. I hear the low-pitched sound of the box springs squeak in relief when his weight shifts to get off the bed, and then he disappears.

I listen intently for a sound, but Travis is too stealthy. I have no clue what he's doing, but I can feel the sexual energy bouncing off the walls in the room. The longer I lay in the quiet, the more the suspense kills me. My voice comes out small and meek, "Travis?"

"Shh...no talking." His tone brooks no argument. He's eerily quiet, so quiet I can hear the hum of the fan above us. Suddenly, a cool vice clamps down on one of my nipples, and I gasp aloud in both pain and surprise.

"Travis!" I squirm, my upper body wriggling to get away. My breasts are swollen and extra sensitive right now. *Has he gone mad?*

I catch my breath to ream him out, to tell him I'm not interested in playing this game and to let me loose, but his hard voice rumbles over me, "If you move again or utter a single sound, you can be rest assured there will be a punishment, and I can promise you this; you won't like it," he tersely warns. *What the hell?*

My heart thunders in my chest, and my chest heaves as I gasp for breath. I know he wouldn't ever hurt me, but his tone has me frozen, and I'm not sure what my next course of action should be. He's never really done this before. Yes, we've gotten kinky before, but the nipple clamps are a first.

"Good girl," he soothes, "but I won't warn you again. Let's try this once more, shall we?" I purse my lips, not daring to utter a sound. I inhale a sharp breath when he pinches the hell out of my other nipple with his metal device. The pain has me clenching my teeth together.

"Trust me, you'll adjust to the feeling, and when *I decide* to let you come, they'll make your pussy sing soprano when you climax."

After a few seconds, I feel an odd sensation that travels from my breasts, straight down to my throbbing core. Wetness begins to pool at my opening. His dirty words, combined with the blindfold, restraints, and the nipple clamps are a complete turn on. Who would've thought?

My heart speeds in anticipation as the bed suddenly dips back down, the weight of his body settling over mine. He doesn't straddle me in the normal way, and as he traps me in with his knees, I become fully aware of his position over me. His strong, muscled thighs press against the sides of my upper torso as something soft brushes over my lips. He wants me to give him head.

"Open," he commands. I squeeze my legs tightly together, trying to relieve the pressure.

With the desire to obey and taste his essence, I open my mouth and he slips the tip of his soft head past my lips. I close my lips around him, and I can't help but hum my desire. "Mmm." I use my tongue to run a circle around his thick cock just before I suck him in deeper. When I pull back, I run my tongue over his slit several times. I get the distinctive taste of his succulent pre-cum.

I lift up my head to take in his entire length, all the way to the back of my throat, and he hisses. I internally smile to myself as I let his fullness slide in and out of my mouth. I repeat the process of licking the tip of his soft head, and then apply a heavy suction as I take all of him back inside the warmth of my mouth.

"Fuck," he blurts out. Cradling the sides of my face with his hands, he holds my face steady as he takes back the control. He pushes his hips forward, sliding his hardness in and out with smooth, slow, savoring strokes. I love the feeling of him taking charge like this.

I increase the suction as he continues to smoothly glide his length back and forth over my tongue. He pushes the tip of his cock past my comfort zone, and I gag. "Shh," he quietly murmurs, "sorry, I'll be more careful." My eyes water from the intrusion, and I have to catch my breath through my nose and focus on my breathing pattern. As much as I've wanted to, I've never been able to deep throat.

Once I catch my breath, I moan around his thick shaft, and the vibrations make him curse. He tastes so erotically sinful. Pressure builds in my core, and I need his fullness inside of my body now.

Each time he slides himself back out, I quickly roll my tongue around his head before he plunges his cock back inside the warmth of my mouth. His breathing turns erratic, and I know he has to be close. Only a few more strokes like this, and I will own his orgasm. A sense of pride overtakes me, and suddenly I want him to come in my mouth, but at that moment, he decides to promptly pull out. I whimper at the loss, voicing my disappointment. I wanted to undo him.

The bed shifts as he scoots back down between my legs. He hooks his fingers into the sides of my panties, and I take that as my cue to lift my hips. He then slides them off over my legs, and I'm full of anticipation.

He runs his palms over my breasts and down my stomach, and I shiver. I feel the need to writhe under him and tell him to fuck me hard, but I don't dare speak. I want him too badly, and I know if I speak out, he'll force me to wait for my release.

"Mmmm. Just what I thought. You're soaking wet for me. I think sucking my cock turns you on." I want to tell him I wasn't done with his cock.

Both of his hands come to rest on my inner thighs, and then he spreads my legs wide apart and holds them in place. I suck in a quick gasp when the heat of his tongue tenderly grazes over my opening. His tongue then dances around the outer perimeter of my sex, teasing me, and as much as I would love to lift my hips to guide him back to where I want it, I can't. He has a firm grip on me, preventing me from moving.

I tense when his tongue drifts southward, trailing a delicious pattern around my puckered hole. For all that is holy, it feels so sinfully divine, and yet seriously wrong at the same time. He's never done that before. Still, it makes me uncomfortable enough to risk speaking. "Travis, no," I firmly command.

Before I know it, he sinks his teeth into my pussy with a quick, sharp bite. I yelp out in pain, shock, and dismay. "Don't tell me no," he harshly growls, and then he returns to his business just as quickly as he left it. *Well, that was kind of sexy.*

His tongue skirts back around my opening again, and my hands curl around and twist the fabric that my wrists are bound to. His movements are gentle and sweet as he takes his time experimenting around the forbidden area.

He slips his heated tongue into me. "Oh, God." I can't help but voice my erotic pleasure; it's a feeling like no other. I have a fire of intense passion pulsating through my veins, and the need for him to consume me.

As if he's suddenly starved for a steak, he moves back to my sex and begins ravishing me with an animalistic hunger. The way he invades me with firm, strong strokes has my legs shaking uncontrollably. He inserts a finger into my ass while swirling his tongue deep inside my silky walls. My breath hitches, and with the nipple clamps adding to the sensations, I'm seconds away from exploding.

"Travis," I breathe out. He ignores me. His tongue fervently works in and out of me along with his finger. I thrash my head back and forth, panting heavily and praying to God that he never stops. He's driving me absolutely insane with need as he increases the suction. The sensations overtake me, suddenly becoming more stimulation than I can handle, and I scream out, "Travis!"

He whispers intermittently between his feasting, and immediately begins to slow down the pace, "Shh, baby, I know what you need." He stops to blow a cool breath into my overheated pussy, and I groan. I was so close. "The only way you get to come is when my dick is deep inside you," he lewdly states.

The bed shifts as he commands, "Lift your hips for me." I do as he says without question. I so want to feel the euphoria that only Travis can bring me.

I feel him place several pillows underneath my butt, elevating my bottom half. When he's finished, he leans his massive body over mine, his familiar weight comforting me. "Are you ready to get fucked, Jules?" he asks, grazing the bridge of his nose along my neckline. My heart beats at an insane pace, his filthy words turning me on.

"You'd better brace yourself," he murmurs against me, and then his tongue slides along the seam of my lips, and I open to him. The man is on fire, and full of white-hot passion as he delves his tongue in deep.

He lifts his bodyweight off me briefly to position the head of his cock at my opening, and then slams into me with unrestrained force. All of my breath leaves me in that one extraordinary movement as he fills me to the brink.

"Oh, shit, you feel like a piece of heaven," he rasps as he lays his body back over mine, taking my mouth back in a heated kiss.

He doesn't hold back. He begins fucking me, and it's not slow or sweet; it's instinctive, animalistic fucking. At this angle, I feel him extra deep as he relentlessly pounds into me at a vigorous pace. He's out of control, and as his chest rubs against mine with forceful friction, it only serves to stimulate the pain-pleasure my nipples have been receiving. Being bound, blindfolded, and fucked ruthlessly with the use of the nipple clamps has me feeling the familiar tingling sensations of a stellar climax.

"Trav, I'm going to come," I warn.

"Yeah, you are," he breathes heavily, his voice full of pride over his masculine abilities. He then rolls and grinds his pelvis against my clit, and I scream out his name. The intensity of my earth-shattering orgasm has me curling my toes as I go numb from head to toe. He quickly removes the nipple clamps, and I can barely hear myself scream out his name as I'm caught up in a thousand watt electrical current that seems to never end.

I hear him curse, and then his movements become erratic. Two more strokes, and then I feel him pulsating inside my core. He pushes the blindfold off my face as he comes deep inside me, and I'm met with his stark green eyes, which silently speak to my soul. I can feel this magic between us, and it never gets old. It only grows stronger with time.

"I will never be able to get enough of you," he rasps, out of breath. A fine sheen of sweat coats his body. "I love you, woman."

"Travis, I love you." Tears of joy sting the back of my eyes. He's made me so happy, and not a day goes by that I don't give my thanks for him.

Once the vestiges of our orgasms have dissipated, he removes all of the paraphernalia. Lying back down beside me, he pulls me into his arms and draws the covers over us. I snuggle against him and smile with a sated grin.

"Mommy?" a small voice sounds out from the doorway, and I stiffen. We both turn to see Travis' little replica rubbing the sleep from his eyes.

"What's the matter, son?" Travis' deep voice trails over my head.

"I heard Mommy scweam," he says in that cute four-year-old voice. He doesn't have all his syllables and pronunciations down quite yet. He's so damn adorable. "Mommy?" he asks again. "Did you see anotha bug?"

Travis chuckles at Aiden's comment, and I smile, but I give Travis the stink eye. "Yes, it was a huge, huge bug."

"Ooohhhhh," he says with fascination, his eyes growing

round and big. "Did Daddy get 'em?"

I laugh loudly at his cuteness as Travis pipes in to answer, "Yes, son. I got 'em."

Aiden narrows his eyes in thought, studying us for a brief moment before he speaks. "Daddy, get off Mommy. You squishin' the baby."

Travis groans. "Son, why don't you go back to bed?"

"But I not sweepy. I hungwy."

Our quiet time is officially over, and I softly giggle. Travis lets out a defeated sigh. "All right, son. How about pancakes?"

He nods emphatically with excitement as he stands there looking so damn adorable in his Ironman PJ's. "I love pamcakes." He pauses, and then continues, "Are they gutten fwee?"

"Yes, little man. They're gluten-free," Travis says with a grin. He's just as affected by his cuteness as I am. "Go on downstairs and get all the stuff out. I'll be there in a second to help."

"Yesss!" Aiden fist-pumps the air and takes off down the hallway.

Travis turns to me, shaking his head. "At least the boy has impeccable timing, just like his daddy."

I playfully slap at his chest, and he captures my hand, raising a brow. "Do I need to tie you up again, woman?"

I grin ruefully. "There is a fine line between bravery and stupidity, Travis Jackson." He throws his head back and bellows with laughter.

"Fair enough."

When all circumstances and events come to a close, we have the chance to reflect on our efforts and fortitude through which the journey took us. We leave a mark...In ourselves...On ourselves...With others.

~ Zeke Samples

Do you remember the dedication I wrote at the beginning of *Blyss*? You see, I wrote this series to escape the pain and anguish of my father's passing away. My dad was my world, my rock, and I didn't know how to move on without him, so I immersed myself in reading books and soon after, I began writing my own story.

With reflecting on the statement above, and as the final book of The Blyss Trilogy has come to a close, I can honestly reflect back on all my efforts and hard work. Writing has allowed me to push through the heartache and distress as I endured the journey of life with a courage that can only be from God.

It's interesting to me how God always places people in our lives at just the right time when we need them most. Whether it's for a simple piece of advice that speaks to our soul, or providing us with a lasting friendship, it is a gift from above to be cherished. Zeke had spoken those very words above at the completion of this trilogy. It was perfect timing. Those words struck a chord with my very soul. Zeke is a very caring, perceptive, and intelligent individual who exudes integrity, and I have no doubt our paths crossed for a higher purpose.

I pray I have left a positive mark in this little book world and touched a few people's lives for the better. I know I have found some wonderful friendships with others and found that each one suffers with their own pain, whether physical or mental. We've become a support group of sorts, sharing laughs, and holding each other up in times of need with prayer.

I have learned that it is okay to take a certain amount of time to grieve, but at some point, it has to come to an end. What is left after the grieving process are sweet fragrances of memories that will remain in our soul as we remember the happier times. The good memories will always be there, but we need to move on.

As my father would always say to me, *"Saw Wood."*

Not everyone is going to agree with how this story should have ended, and perhaps, just maybe, it's because you didn't want the journey to end. This story wasn't about obtaining revenge in the end.

This story was so much more for me than about the intimacies between a man and a woman. The most important thing I wanted to show at the end of this journey was that Jules was able to heal after experiencing soul crushing destruction to her spirit and psyche.

When all hope crumbled at her feet, and after going through the dark passages of hell, she emerged on the other end with renewed hope. A different hope that allowed her soul to heal.

Unconditional love heals, while revenge, anger, bitterness and hate destroys. It destroys everything in its wake. God in His *mercy* and *grace,* provided Jules a soul mate to help pick up the pieces when she was too broken to piece her life back together. She was able to focus on the victorious path of healing through God and his awesome provisions.

What Jules had to go through to find healing is what all of us must do at some point in our lives. To learn how to have happiness amidst the sorrow, because there is still hope and you are always provided for, you just have to have faith.

I enjoyed creating a balance of action and adventure while finding a way to intersperse a little humor and romance along the way. I promise to bring you more action, adventure, mystery, and romance in the near future.

 AUTHOR NOTES

PLEASE leave a *SPOILER FREE* Review on
Amazon!
One or two sentences is fine with me…Easy Peasy.

*Please stay in touch to find out what suspenseful
adventure awaits next.*

Newsletter:
Www.http://eepurl.com/bgktn9

**If you're interested in getting your hands on upcoming
releases, sneak peek teasers, or information on her
upcoming personal appearances, and sales, you can join her
newsletter listing, and get those details delivered right to
your inbox.**

~~*

Website:
Www.http://JCCliff.com
Facebook:
http://www.facebook.com/BLYSS.TRILOGY
Goodreads:
https://www.goodreads.com/book/show/22928107-blyss
Twitter:
https://twitter.com/Cliff3J
Instagram:
@j.c.cliff

CKNOWLEDGEMENTS

There are many *Perfect Timing People* in my life I would like to thank from the bottom of my heart. Thank you for believing in me, standing behind me with your prayers, support, and friendship.

My husband and children always go without saying. My husband has been my biggest supporter, even though he won't even read the synopsis of any of my books. :-). I love you hard, my soul mate, my best friend. He's my special gift from God, who handed my husband to me on a silver platter.

A special mention to some pretty special people close to my heart: Laurie Szoka, Mary Brown, Kayla Robichaux, Theresa Alberts, Rosie Snowdon, Tanya Drummond, Heather Lane and her impressive movie trailers and teasers, Sommer Stein and her awesome cover design talents, Jamie Zishka, Katherine Mazur, Sandra Hearn, Pauline Digaletos, Dawn Nicole, Costiera, Terra Oenning, Jo Turner, Jess Peterson, Clare Flack, Kiki Amit, AC Bextor, Jennifer Juers ~ Please forgive me if your name is not here. It is not intentional by any means, 'cuz you all know I'm blonde. :-). I adore you all.

Becky Johnson with Hot Tree Editing, I want to thank you for creating and providing a quality service to your clients.

Your skills and professionalism will always keep me coming back.

Everything I have mentioned about my faithful supporters in my acknowledgments from my previous books still stand. I am thankful for the lasting friendships which have transpired over the course of the last seven months.

Regardless of me repeating myself I have to give special mention to these most wonderful people.

To my ever-faithful *right-hand man* beta reader, Theresa Alberts. You've gone above and beyond each and every time without complaint, and you've stuck with me through thick and thin since before the release of *Blyss*. I seriously never want to write a book without your two cents.

Tanya Drummond, you have been with me through thick and thin. We've had a slew of laughs, and I grin just thinking about your quick witted humor. Rosie Snowden, I love our growing friendship, and despite the Atlantic ocean separating us, it's nice to know you are just a "message" away. You both are amazing women and are very dear to my heart.

To my faithful cheerleaders:
Rosie Snowden, Katherine Mazur, Sandra Hearn, Terra Oenning, Heather Lane, Jo Turner, Clare flack…to wake up to scads of Facebook notifications every morning that you've posted about this trilogy to the world, humbles me. Your friendship and support went above and beyond, and when I became tired and burnt out on social media, you guys kept the momentum going. I am forever grateful. All of you are priceless people in which I am blessed to call

friends.

A huge thank you goes out to all of the blogs who have supported me and suffered through all of the horrendous cliffhangers with patience....okay maybe not so much patience. I still have a silly grin on my face from some of the *off the cuff messages* I've received upon them finishing each book, and then dying to have the next installment. To receive a message that only says WTF...still makes me giggle. You've brought me many laughs and a camaraderie in which I will always cherish.

Submit and Devour, For the Love of Books, Sassy Divas, I love Story Time, Ms. ME28, Reading is my Superpower, Book Happiness, Book Lovers Obsession, Crazy a Daisy Book Whore, Kinky Girls Book Obsessions, Elaine and Tami's JB3 Blackbirds, Hooked on Books, Isalovesbooks, Summers Book Blog, Whispered Thoughts, She Hearts Books, Books and the Big Screen, Lustful Literature, My Book Filled Life, Naughty Book Eden, Nice and Naughty Book club, Reading Diva's Blog, Renee Entress's Blog, Undercover Book Reviews, Sassy Moms Say Read Romance, Short and Sassy Book Blurbs, Romance and Fantasy for Cosmopolitan Girls, Who Picked This?, Mommy's Naughty Playground, Teetee's Book Blog, Paperback Junkie Book Review, Bound by Books Book Review, Stephanie's Book Reports, Naughty Nympho's Book Promotions, All Romance Reviews, KinkyGirlsBookObsessions, The Art of Romance.

The Blogger Diaries Trilogy
By K.D. Robichaux

The Blogger Diaries Trilogy is the true story of how I met, fell for, lost, and got a second chance at love with my soul mate. The names of everyone EXCEPT me, Jason, my family, and my best friend have been changed to protect their identities. Full of youthful stupidity, leading to bad decisions and lots of angst, it is a real life story, where inevitably things are messy.

No one can look back at their late teens and early twenties and not think of moments that make them ask, What the hell was I thinking? Every second of this trilogy is true, exactly as it happened.

The first book, 'Wished For You', is a tale of finding 'the one' too early, and then having to let them go.

PLEASE NOTE: This is a true trilogy, meaning the first two books END ON CLIFFHANGERS. But if you take the journey with me, in the end, I promise you a happily ever after you will never forget. I know I won't.

PR♠LOGUE

Kayla's Chick Rant & Book Blog
Blog Post 1/23/2007

I'm a happy person, damn it! I'm happy sober; I'm a happy
drunk, and I smile until my cheeks hurt. I'm so freakin' perky
all the time. I always get invited to everyone's parties; I never
get scrolled over when people are looking through their phones
to see what's going on. Everyone loves for me to be around
because I bring no drama. I'm shameless, and will make a fool
of myself to make everyone laugh. I don't say these things to be
conceited; I say it to show you how unlike me it is when I tell
you...
I cried myself to sleep again last night. I cradled my swollen
belly in my hands and rocked myself back and forth praying in
a whisper, "Please, God, make him love me. I know you put us
here to be together. Just make him realize it. Please!" The last
word came out on a sob. I swear I'm not a horrible person, as I

CHAPTER One

January 7, 2005

I'm in my 2002 Chevy Malibu, with its cherry-patterned seats, steering wheel cover, and CD holder hooked to the visor. My big brother Mark is in the driver's seat while I sit next to him with my turtle's 10 gallon aquarium at my feet and my lovebird's giant-ass, castle-shaped cage in the backseat. The rest of the car is stuffed to the gills with my TV, clothes, and books. Couldn't leave home without every last one of my Sherrilyn Kenyon's, Julie Kenner's, and the rest of my paranormal romances.

I'm a book blogger, you see. I use my AOL profile website as a sort of scrapbook to keep all my reviews and notes about my favorite authors. It's not just for books though. It's kind of like a diary too. That's why I named it Kayla's Chick Rant & Book Blog. My mom thinks I put too much of myself on the internet, but I tell her, "I'm not the only one thinking this stuff. I just may be the only one with the balls to say it aloud." I'm from a small town in North Carolina called Fayetteville. Affectionately nicknamed Fayettenam since it's right next door to Ft. Bragg

Army Base. I'm on 95 South about to jump on I-10 West, moving to Texas for a semester of school.

Mark flew in to Raleigh and is driving me to his house in Houston, where I'm going to see what it's like to "live outside that shithole vortex" as he put it. I love my big brother. He's the oldest out of the three I've got. I'm the baby and the only girl. Our relationship is different from most siblings, I suppose, because he was 17 when I was born. Yep, I was an accident. I was born the year Daddy retired from the Navy. But Momma finally got her girl!

I think Mark feels like it was up to him to get me out of Fayetteville. Everyone there seems to either marry a soldier and live the military life, or work at a dead-end job. There's nothing in Fayetteville, really, except for restaurants and stores. A shit-ton of them, mind you, but still.

I'm moving in with Mark and his wife, Kim. She's seriously the most hilarious chick you could possibly imagine. I couldn't have picked a better woman for my brother. Kim and I share a love of paranormal romances, so we'll call each other up and talk for an hour about what's going on in some of our favorite series. I'm looking forward to having her around. In a couple of days, I'll be registering at Kingwood College to work toward my degree in English. I want to be a writer, but until then, I took it upon myself to pimp out the authors I'm addicted to, spreading their stories so everyone else can enjoy the escape they bring.

It's not a bad deal. As I sit here, wearing my "Authors Are My Rockstars" t-shirt, you can tell I absolutely love what I do, because a lot of my wardrobe is book-themed. I even have a nightshirt that says "I Sleep with a Different Book Boyfriend

Every Night". I get to talk daily with people I adore, like others would their favorite singer. Or even like I used to over Brian Littrell of the Backstreet Boys in the 6th grade. Only it's even better because instead of loving them from afar, knowing you'll never actually get to tell them how much you love them (and marry them in my case with Brian...sigh), I actually hold conversations with them! Any time I want, I can email my favorite author just to see how their day is going, how their next book is coming along, and with a select few, I've really gotten close to, check on how that argument with their hubby worked out. I'll never have to worry about one of my authors not knowing how much I appreciate them...unlike Brian. I was so upset when he got married when I was in the 7th grade that my mom let me stay home from school...true story.

Turtle's cage is taking up the entire floor on my side of the car, so my feet are up on the dashboard, swinging back and forth to the "Disturbed" song playing on the radio. Turtle never got a real name because when I got him in Myrtle Beach, the guy on The Strip told me they only usually live for a couple of months. He was about the size of a fifty-cent coin at the time. Well, five years later and that asshole is still kicking and is about the size of a baseball. Not that I wanted my pet to keel over, but I didn't sign up for this! But when Daddy suggested I just let Turtle free into our lake behind our house, all I could imagine was one of the giant snapping turtles making a midday snack out of the little guy. I just couldn't do it.

So now I get to ride over 1600 miles with nowhere to put my long-ass legs. I'm 5'6, pretty tall for a chick I think, going by the fact I was always one of the tallest girls at my school. All my big brothers are over six-feet tall, one's even 6'5. I have super dark brown hair that hits the middle of my back, and the only green eyes in my family, everyone else has blue. My mom told me that her dad and sister had green eyes, but they both passed away before I was born. I glance over at Mark as he reaches for his fourth Diet Mountain Dew of the day, "Liquid Gold" he calls it. "You know that stuff is just as bad, if not worse than regular Mountain Dew, right?" I ask him.

"Yeah, but it helps me keep my girlish figure, Wench." I don't remember exactly why he started calling me Wench; he's done it since I can remember. But it probably has something to do with all my big brothers bribing me with hide-and-seek to go fetch them drinks and sandwiches while they played video games when I was little.

"You getting tired, Marky? You want me to take over for a while?" I ask.

"Hell no! I didn't fly all the way out to NC to get your ass to just ride all the way back to Texas. You coulda driven yourself if that was the case. Plus, Mom would kill me if I let you drive and something happened. It's up to me to keep the princess safe." He smirks at me. He loves to tease me about being the only girl in the family. "Not to mention, I'm more than a little afraid that your turtle would jump up and bite my legs. You don't look comfortable at all."

"I'm fine. All those years of dance class made me pretty bendy. I'll make sure to walk around next time you stop for gas," I say as I poke him in the ribs when he takes another swig of his Liquid Gold. "You're gonna have to pee soon anyways the way you're sucking those things down."

Wished For You by K.D. Robichaux

Available now

If you're interested in getting your hands on upcoming releases, sneak peek teasers, or information on her upcoming personal appearances, and sales, you can join her on the social media links below.

Facebook:
https://www.facebook.com/AuthorKDRobichaux
Twitter:
@kaylaTheBiblio
Instagram:
Kaylathebibliophile

45385945R00194

Made in the USA
Lexington, KY
25 September 2015